IT COULD BE
SOMEONE
YOU KNOW

PAULETTE ELOZIA RIVAIT

BALBOA.PRESS
A DIVISION OF HAY HOUSE

Balboa Press books may be ordered through booksellers or by contacting:

Balboa Press
A Division of Hay House
1663 Liberty Drive
Bloomington, IN 47403
www.balboapress.com
844-682-1282

Print information available on the last page.

ISBN: 978-1-9822-5329-5 (sc)
ISBN: 978-1-9822-5330-1 (e)

Balboa Press rev. date: 09/04/2020

CHAPTER 1

CHILD TRUTH

On a quiet Saturday morning, a quiet little town along Lake Erie called Kingsville, was beginning to buzz with children playing. Mari could also hear traffic in the distance, rushing along highway 18. She walked away from the open window and walked to the back door, picked up the paper on her stoop and brought it to the kitchen. Unfolding it, she looked at the picture of a young woman, and began reading. She had difficulty swallowing. Apart from petty crimes and the usual mischief, usually perpetrated by children and teens, Kingsville's downtown was attractive and busy. A murder can't have happened here! Not near my home! She looked around at her bright red and white kitchen, her eyes resting on the window that bring in lots of light and air. Sometimes the postman caught site of her there, and waved. Now, knowing that she was visible unsettled her. Her gaze returned to the horrific story she had just read, lingering on the victim's smile, and she sat down at her table to finish reading the article. Her family had been trying to call her for several days and alarmed that they couldn't contact her, they'd phoned the police. This poor young woman had faced such a brutal end. The police had found in her in the living room of her apartment, located on the outskirts of town. Her naked, mutilated body, her throat cut, was grisly to imagine. Also, she'd been hog tied with her left arm, the other gripped a table leg. Massive amounts of blood saturated the carpet. There were no leads. Scared and shocked, she held her forehead in her hand. With a stab of anger, she quickly pulled the paper back and looked closely at the picture. Her name was Kristle, spelled

K-r-i-s-t-e-l. She had light, clear skin, medium length straight blondish hair, parted in the middle, a winning smile, and she was wearing a boat neck, brightly coloured top. She looked so sweet. She thought of how people preferred to look at people who "may have deserved it." Expected them to dress like Cameron Diaz, not Princess Diana. In her estimation, this view was invalid, but there were some who would think that this woman appeared wholesome and innocent, therefore this shouldn't have happened. It just makes no sense, anyway you look at it. Walking away from the table, Mari secured the side door with the double lock, and from her slightly untidy, gritty mud room she peered out into the yard. Deep pink and white petunias soaked up the sun, beginning their shower of colour. White, fragrant hyacinths bent under their weight, and swayed. She thought: Suddenly, they've lost their brilliance. Her thinking shifted to Sonny, her husband: Ah, I wonder if he's heard, or read the story. She walked around the kitchen, checking that she had all the ingredients needed for dinner. She'd decided on pasta with Alfredo sauce, and toss lots of garlicky, buttery shrimp on top. He loves it, and he'll be ravenous. The enjoyment of creating the dish they both love pushed the bad thoughts to a tiny place in her head. Her creation finished and feeling very satisfied with it, she called her sister. Fiona answered. Mari asked, "Have you heard about the murder that happened near here?" "Hah, yes, it's unbelievable. I saw her picture on the first page of today's paper. It's terrible!" her voice rising. They talked further about the murder as though discussing a novel-it seemed so unreal. All through the conversation, she thought that regardless of what was being discussed, something else was amiss. Fiona sounded distracted, and her words were clipped.

"Fiona-you sound terribly sad. What's wrong?"

"Nothing. Just a headache."

Mari continued probing, "What's been happening lately?" her tone reassuring so that she could help lift Fiona from her gloomy mood. Fiona finally said, "My soon to be ex-husband is bent on making things so difficult. We're at odds over every little thing." Continuing to listen patiently, she assured Fiona that someday she'd leave this all behind her. It seemed to work, and on a slightly better note they hung up. Still concerned, she thought about Fiona, her alternately delicate and durable sister, a nice way of saying that Fiona could be hard-nosed and unsympathetic, made worse by eyes that flashed like chips of blue ice. She was fond of saying, after a bombardment from Fiona, "The heavens shook anew."

Soon, she heard the car pull into the driveway. Beyond the front door she watched a very tired looking Sonny shut the car door. Wearily, he walked to the door, eyes cast down. Mari opened the door to greet him he and stepped into the foyer. They stood under the ceiling beams of dark mahogany, the floor covered with cream coloured tile. Sonny smiled and hugged Mari, while detecting a creamy, saucy aroma, "Hi. Wow honey, it sure smells great in here. Are we having shrimp?" She cooed, "Mm-hmm", as she watched him shake off his jacket, hang it up, and deposit his keys on the foyer table. She kissed him and tingled in all the right places, thinking: It's been awhile. Those undercurrents were often alive, and more important than that, she loved him with her whole heart. They had their arguments, but they always tried to work things through, although she admits, she is the one who prods and leads their discussions. She left him to check his mail lying next to his keys, and went back to the kitchen. Mari stared at the bowl of pasta and considered that Sonny might be too tired to eat.

He called out on his way to the bathroom, "Be right with ya', I really need a shower."

"I'll start in on the wine. It's something new. Want to be sure it's good." She heard him chuckle. A short while later, looking refreshed, his dark hair wet and spiked, he emerged from the hallway into the kitchen and poured wine for himself.

"Honey, look at this." Mari showed him the paper. As he read the headline, his expression told her that he hadn't heard or seen anything about what had happened. He read the story with a look of incredulity. "Honey, this is shocking! I wonder if anyone we know were acquainted with her. I mean, it is a small town."

"Don't know. Who would have done such a thing?" Mari murmured.

He peered at her over his long-stemmed glass, "Clearly, it's not someone we know."

Late getting to bed, with the moonlight shining through the slats, they made love enthusiastically. Much later, into the wee hours of the morning, they agreed that it was as good now as in the beginning of their "affair." When she'd met Sonny, she'd been on the rebound of a rebound, if that makes any sense, such a stupid thing to do, but people do indulge, not always entirely conscious of the fact that this is what they're doing. They tell others that they only want a friend to talk to, but really, what they hope for is "comfort food," stuff that isn't complicated and they wanted it to be decadent and entertaining…until that runs its course. When her relationship with Sonny started to reach new heights Mari embellished on all of the above. She told him, "After my fiancé, Pete, said that he wasn't ready for marriage and dumped me, I followed that with a "fling" with Rob, his loose description of what we had." For some reason, she didn't want to tell Sonny the extent of her anger against these men, and she could not admit that she had allowed herself to be so demeaned.

After these relationships ended, she'd figured out that what she wanted was absorption in the fun things she wanted to do, with someone laid-back, but decent. Mari did not want to flood her head and heart with any expectations. After describing her history with Pete and Rob, she blithely told him that she didn't expect anything from him, "I'm taking my time." He remembered thinking: *I'll change her mind.* When she started feeling happy with their relationship, she quipped, "Sonny, you derailed all of that delicious free thinking I had when I met you."

At twenty five years old, Sonny had decided that he wanted to get married, have a few kids, and land scape a big yard for them to play in. Prior to that developing train of thought, he never missed an opportunity to meet a pretty woman-no matter what the motive was. He'd joke to his buddies that he'd known more tangled, chaotic bedrooms than Casanova, and he resolved to search for "the one." To his buddies, he'd announced, "It's time to get serious." Meeting Mari had intensified the change happening within him.

One early, very cold winter Sunday morning, some years ago, her mind empty of anything romantic, Mari decided to take a look at their newly updated market. It was great to see that the parking lot was much larger than it was, and when she entered the interior of the market, she was impressed. The deli was the same, as was the produce area, but the little clothes shop, and the kiosks, exhibiting their wares, like the jewelry she was drawn to, made the whole area appealing. Also, she noticed that they'd added a small restaurant, naming it The Harvest Café. The market and the stores hadn't opened yet, so she went directly to the café, invitingly open because she could smell the coffee brewing. Already the booths and the little tables were occupied; she sat at the fifties style counter with those round stools, usually a little smaller than most butts, but not hers-she grinned. "I'll have eggs, no hash browns, sausages, brown toast and coffee please", she recited glancing at the guy sitting a couple of stools away. He looked up from his sheet of paper at the same time, sipped his coffee, nodded slightly, and returned to his sheaf of papers. Mari remained unflustered, and thought: *Except for that blue shirt, rolled up to his elbows, casual-like, sexy, he looks like he could be in charge. What am I doing? Stop it, she* tittered and amused herself. The next thing you know they were chatting away as though they knew each other, and out of the blue, he asked, "Are you busy for dinner tonight?" Taken aback, she retorted, "No, well, okay, I do have to eat dinner anyway," then fell all over her words trying to apologize for such a dim-witted blunder.

"I am so sorry, that was, hmm, that was ungracious. I would love to…" she stopped talking. He just kept looking at her trying to excuse herself.

Finally, he said, "It's quite okay. Do you have a phone number? I'll call you later this afternoon and we can decide where to go." After breakfast he escorted her to her car, and bid his goodbye. Mari climbed into her car and watched a self-assured, good looking guy swagger to a side street and get into his screaming red sports car. He roared away.

She realized that she'd come to shop. "*What a ninny I am,*" she said under her breath, and gathered her wits. "*I'll probably have to cook dinner for myself. Oh well, we'll see,*" she thought, chuckling. She re-entered the market and bought a nice plump young chicken and some vegetables. She got home shortly, put her groceries away, and spent the rest of the day cleaning and looking online for different roasted chicken and potato recipes. Shortly before she was to begin cooking, she left the house to buy the rosemary she needed to spice up the meal. Returning home to prepare dinner, and just as she was going to slip the chicken into the oven the phone rang. Hello. *Oh* wow, *it's him! He really meant it*! She listened to his deep voice and thought: *Chicken Little, you were just about eaten, but you've been saved.*

"I'll pick you up at 6. That okay?" *God, I don't believe this!* Stammering, she blurted, "Yeah, sure." With no time to lose, she tucked the covered chicken into her fridge.

Hurrying to the bathroom, she emerged herself into a fragrant bath.

After drying herself she smoothed her favourite blackberry vanilla body cream all over her body, carefully stroked her finger nails with a mauve polish, slipped on her pink shift, and placed her slick, little blue jacket by the door. While she waited for him, she flitted from the living room to her bedroom, and back, twice, to make sure that she'd picked out the best outfit, then glancing at the clock, she stumbled to the bathroom to check her teeth and pull on her bangs.

He was on time. Opening the door and looking into his smiling face, she said, "Hello. Please come in." She noticed the attractive line of his dimples and wickedly reflected: *This morning I only ventured out for a few vegetables and I got this nice meat, and so far, I haven't had to pay. We'll see how this goes.*

Telling her he'd made reservations at Spago's in Windsor, they made their way through traffic, idly chatting all the while about themselves, the world, and asking questions about each other. Once seated at the restaurant their conversation became more personal. He told her, "I'm in sales, travel for it, and I love it. I sell paper products to all types of businesses, and according to my boss, not only am I a good salesman, I'm an attentive manager. He means that I regularly follow up on my accounts. You know, keep everybody happy. *What do you do?"* She twirled her spaghetti, dropping some on the white table cloth, "I'm following a career in journalism. I write for the Windsor Star, do interviews, and write articles for Chatelaine and other magazines, and myriads of things actually. I also give my time to the University of Windsor part time as an agent for students working toward their writing careers. All of what I do is diverse and interesting...to me."

Their conversation covered a wide range of familiar and personal topics, like discussing their families, their hobbies, how they exercise, and their desires for the rest of their lives, the latter raised by Sonny, and one that Mari didn't fully participate in. She didn't want to come off as appearing cynical concerning men, or about love and commitment. Sonny was easy to talk to, and while he prodded a bit, he didn't push anything.

Seeing her to her door, he brought her closer and kissed her lightly on the mouth: *Ooh, I like this.* He pulled away before she did. He said: "I'll call you tomorrow night." The next night, while she waited for him to call, she heated a late dinner. Over Chicken Little and vegetables, she pushed her fork around, remembering how laid back he was, how smoothly his voice resonated, and that he was attentive. She deliciously replayed how tenderly he looked at her before kissing her lightly on the mouth. Then he asked for another date. *Wow, and I wasn't even looking! No game playing! Talk about winning me over. Is he too good to be true?* They continued dating and another side to his personality appeared. He could be abrupt and argumentative with people who didn't agree with him, usually having to do with, "The man." This included most organized forces such as the police, the government, those in education, and the politicians who said they represented you on the issues. He blustered, "That is bullshit. They represent themselves!" Apart from his tiresome, relentless intolerance for some things, rants actually, they got along well. He was fun to be around and continued to be very attentive. Oh, there were times she needed to voice her opinions, just so he knew she wasn't playing to him all the time. Still, being non-argumentative, it was he who usually walked away with the last word. Something else though; more troubling than his righteous stance on things, she was wary that he had a certain teasing, flippant attitude with other women. For instance, if he got compliments, he was overly solicitous. He would sometimes engage himself too long, forget to ask her to dance, or get her a drink. She placated herself, reasoning that he had an outgoing, winsome nature. She was not jealous to absurd degrees. She knew that she could never look so insecure or dependent, witnessing the immature, destructive game playing some couples engaged in.

A few years into their marriage, Mrs. Mari Dolan could still feel a dizzying delightfulness wash over her whenever he was nearby? Happily gaining anniversaries, they settled into a familiar, yet high spirited life. They had fun together, occasionally went dancing, hiked in parks and walked their neighbourhood, and worked their garden together. They loved their kids, Haley and Vince. They made good love together. However, when he came off as self-important and patronizing toward friends and relatives, or was overly friendly with the ladies, she used euphemisms to gloss it over. She'd say, "Sonny is very friendly" or "He's so passionate about his views" and

"He's direct."

Love and passion have a way of blurring things.

Because of the senseless murder that had happened in their own back yard, it resurrected long buried memories. Mari re-called how her mother had frightened her as a little girl, by telling her things about boogie men and big monsters. Too she would somberly tell her awful things that to a ten year old were terribly frightening. "During wartime men had pins stuck under their finger nails to make them talk. Sometimes, they would be bound up and they couldn't move their heads. Water slowly dripped onto their foreheads, for hours. It made them crazy." Mari was affected by these stories, more so than her younger sisters, Fiona and April were. Malcolm, the youngest, seemed to have been unaffected, probably due to the fact that he had loving attention showered on him by his older sisters. They protected him.

Shaking fresh linens out for the bed, Mari remembered that as a youngster, she frequently was afraid to go to sleep at night, and when she was outside, it got to the point that all people she didn't know could be after her. Growing Into her early teens though, Mari had come to realize that her fears could work for her. She became watchful and careful. Proud of herself, she would revisit what had happened to her when she was a little tyke in first grade.

Only six, she walked home alone from school every day, hungry for a hot lunch. It was a middle class neighbourhood, some houses built by brick, and many were sided. Porches held tricycles and wagons, and one porch even had a rag doll sitting in a blue wagon. Little Mari used to wonder why it was sitting outside in the cold. She wanted to hug it. Covered head down, part of the russet and green snow suit she wore, she listened to the crunch of her feet on the solid ice-snow, and she didn't notice the car creeping along behind her. When she reached the corner she swung her head back and forth to look for cars before stepping off the curb. Ready to step down, Mari heard the car slip up to the stop sign and she turned her head toward it. The man in the grey car with the slicked back hair, window down, was looking at her. He smiled, "Do you want a ride?" while he peered over her head and back toward the dark, tightly closed up yellow and white house behind her. She was already cold, but suddenly she felt colder. Mari's teeth started to chatter. His eyes darted back into hers. They were black and they weren't smiling. She yelled "No", turned away, stepped off the curb and ran the few blocks home as fast as her chubby little legs could go, slipping and sliding all the way. Finally, she could see her mother standing behind the door of the closed-in porch. Trudging heavily up the front stairs, Mari pointed down the street and recounted the story, finishing her story quicker than her mother could undress her. Mom, stooped to her eye level, stood her boots up to dry with one hand and clasped the other over her mouth, wide-eyed. With more of the same admonitions about strangers, she was fed soup and crackers and hot chocolate. With her apple tucked in her bag, Mari was made to walk back to school alone, fearfully afraid, as any six year old child would be. But yes, she was proud that she had run away as fast as she could.

Angrily, she whipped the sheet across the bed. How negligent that was! When this had happened to her, she didn't think of the little ones at home that her mother had to care for, but over time, she realized that her mother had done the best she could in that situation. So why was she so angry right now? Memories of her unhappy childhood and now this horrible murder made her tremble with anger.

Then, when she was a teen, her mother, an alcoholic, deserted her husband and her children. With no explanation, one rainy day, she picked up and left. Then, in another way, her father abandoned them. He withdrew into himself. Mari shouldered the responsibilities as housekeeper and mother. A few years later their father died, and Mari, just growing into adulthood herself, quickly became responsible for the entire household. Thankfully, relatives on both side helped, some by regularly shopping for groceries, and others came by to help the young family do the necessary things they need to do to run a home.

Her king sized bed made, she checked the folds of the chalky blue duvet, and straightened the pillows once more, then walked around the living room, her favourite room in the house. The mahogany in her foyer spanned into the living room ceiling, and was softened by the furniture they she and Sonny had picked out together. She loved her cream coloured leather couch and her pumpkin coloured arm chair that you could sink into to read or watch television. Sonny was usually drawn to the lazy-boy where he could stretch out and chill. The green, gold, and pumpkin knickknacks and candles cheered and warmed the space. The wide windows were covered with white wooden slats that opened during the day, and locked out prying eyes after dusk. She picked things up, rearranged them, put them in new places, or back where they were. It didn't help. Her thoughts flailed again: *Silent against it all, we grow up, we handle things, with our heads held high and our eyes wide open. We do it with the grace of an adult, not with the grief of a child.* At variance with that serene thought, she slammed the candle holder that she was holding against her other hand. The strength of her feelings surprised her. Mari's conflicted mind went back to the crime and the terrible things Kristel endured. It created startling, fearsome visions of violence: *How she must have suffered. Boogie men are everywhere, no matter where you are in life.* The violence that had almost been committed against her as a child, could have been like the same that killed the young woman in town. He needs to be found.

Setting the candle holder down, her thoughts transferred to the first time her husband seemed to be, at the very least, elusive, if not actually transgressing. They were at the wedding of one of his office buddies. A woman, relatively new to Sonny's office, flirted with him, dancing provocatively against him, for everyone's benefit. Tracking every tipsy, clumsy movement she made, Mari asked Carla, the office receptionist, "Have simple good manners just gone out the window? Who is this dirty dancing, tacky, um, Big Hair?" hoping she came off blasé. Everybody noticed that Sonny lapped it up, even though he pretended to be coolly unaffected by it.

"That's Kate. They hired her a couple of months ago. She spends most of her time in the mirror, admiring her biceps," she comically rolled her eyes.

"Come to think of it, Sonny did mention something about a new assistant they'd hired."

When Sonny grabbed Mari's hand to dance she attempted to talk about her as they made their way toward the dance floor. He retorted, "It's nothing. Kate always acts like that." Further attempts to talk about her yielded nothing. Ordinarily, they could kid each other about things like this. This conversation was definitely strained. Attempting to be casual he came off brusque, "Drop it."

A few days later Mari was on the phone with Carla, and they discussed the wedding. She learned more things about "Tacky Big Hair." She was separated, something that had been long in coming according to "Big Hair." Also, Carla said that she continuously blabbed her most personal affairs at the office, running her husband down at every opportunity. She thought: *It's not like Sonny wouldn't know these things about her, so why didn't he bring her up. He jokes about other people in the office.*

When she got off the phone she looked at herself in the bathroom mirror, and she spoke aloud, "Why is this so important and don't pretend you don't know"; she pointed the hair brush at herself. *Sonny may have lied to me.* She plunked the hair brush into her drawer, and decided to think on it before approaching Sonny to talk. She wanted to figure out how she should broach it. He might tease her that she was being disproportionately jealous. How would she counter that?

While the time they spent over the weekend was good, conflict about the murder forced its way in and kept her awake both nights. And, she couldn't make sense of something else that plagued her. Thoughts about her childhood popped up, especially those her concerning her mother.

Six year old Mari was attracted by the hole in the gnarly, unpainted fence that enclosed the yard, large enough to easily slip through. She played contentedly but she kept glancing at the hole in the fence. There was a puddle there and it looked wet and cool, having rained earlier. Getting off her red tricycle, she skipped over and climbed through the hole and plopped herself in the mud. She looked toward the kitchen door: *Mommy's going to be mad, but I'll try real hard not to get dirty.* She picked up a stick and leaned forward and made squiggly lines. With earnestness, she printed, M-A-R-I. Finished, she lay the stick down and proudly studied her name. Tired out, she lifted her little sun-browned neck a little, and stretched. Her tummy squeezed tight so much it hurt, and her head dropped back down to the pool of water. She tried to move, but she couldn't. An indistinct form loomed close, a reflection in the puddle! She looked at the worn black shoes and the ill-fitting pinstriped suit, slung on the old man. *Where's Mommy? It's the bogey man! He'll take me away! I can run real fast but my bum is stuck here!* Frantically, she wiped her hands off on her shirt and she searched the back door. Not seeing her mother, she squeezed her eyes shut. Opening them, she fluttered at the water with chubby fingers to make him go away, but the last thing she saw was the zigzag, snaky, menacing slither of his pocket watch. Eyes tightly shut and opening, by turns, she listened to his feet drag past her. His frame blocked the sun. It blackened the area behind her eyes as he slowly shuffled past. After a little, but very long time, her shiny, brown ringlets swirled as she turned to find out where he was. Hugging her knees she thought: *He's going away and I'm still here!* *Mommy said the bogey man would take me if I'm bad. Mommy doesn't lie, but sometimes she does, and she says scary things.* Tears clung to her eyes. She stood up and wiped her hands off on her little pink checkered top. *This isn't fun anymore.*

"Did the bogey man scare you?" Mommy said grinning, not looking at her, as she crimped the dough on the pie she was making. Mari hung her little head and walked to her room. She pressed her tear and mud streaked face into the soft, fluffy pillow, clutching her rosy cheeked doll…instead of Mommy.

For some unyielding reason, Mari remained plagued by bad thoughts churning within her, predicated by her upbringing. She never really felt loved or appreciated. As she grew up, her mother depended on her to do things she wouldn't do, like keep the house clean, cook, and help raise her younger siblings. Mari did all that. And, she never seemed to value what she did. Eventually, she got so stressed that she had to leave. But, not without the guilt she carried when she left her two sisters and brother behind to fend for themselves. But, she'd had it. She needed to escape or lose her mind.

She kept working through her thoughts about the time when she was six. When she became an adult, her thoughts changed regarding that muddy day. No danger had been present. He just walked by, and when he did she had turned to look back at him and he had done the same. He smiled at her, then went shuffling away. She re-echoed that her mother often used fear to control them as children. It marked Mari the most because she was the oldest and her mother needed her when she finally deserted them all. It fell on her to completely take over the household responsibilities and to finish raising Fiona, April, and Malcolm. As scared as she was, she'd done her best to do it. Until she had to leave or fall apart.

Now, here I am, not feeling the least bit competent, worrying about my seemingly wayward husband, my depressed sister, corresponding with her fearful thoughts about the murder that had just occurred. Nervously, she fiddled with her hair and picked at her finger nails. It all occupied a twisted place in her head. Saddened, Mari thought: *There's nothing you can do, as a child or as an adult to keep everyone warm and safe.*

She discarded the newspaper, but the picture of the murdered girl ripped around and around, and she couldn't still the anxiety it produced.

CHAPTER 2

ADULT TRUTH

The week skimmed along uneventfully at Sonny and Mari's house, but daily mentions of the murder were voiced. Wherever people went into town, the murder was brought up. Things like, "Did you hear anything?" or "I wonder if the police have anything to work with?"

Sonny went back to work at his sales job and she shopped, buying deep purple pansies that would intensify her garden, but before she went home she decided to pop in on her sister, Fiona, who'd been so constrained and nervous lately. Opening the door for Mari, she groaned, "I'm not feeling well. I was just going to lay down." Mari hugged her and Fiona was heading for her bedroom before Mari even got out the door. She stopped and called out, "Fiona, for heaven's sake, don't forget to lock the door. Please." When she pulled away from the curb, she recalled that a few weeks ago, when Sonny and she got together with Fiona and Warren, she'd felt ill at ease with Warren, her husband, whom most agreed was a macho blow-hard with more chest hair than brains. Well, Mari thought, he could be getting to her.

Tiny in stature with big fawn eyes, Fiona always looked easily broken. As a teenager she was fairly quiet for the most part, except when angered or upset, and then the snappy, judgmental, merciless Fiona reared up. Still did. Her appearance, because of those eyes, seemed to render her vulnerable, yet she could confront issues in a very crass and insensitive manner, expressing exactly what she felt. Mari knew that in her own time, when she needed to talk, she would.

Anyway, she had a lot on her own mind. Recently, she'd decided that she wanted to get a job that would get her involved outside of the household, and would keep her from centering all of her focus on family and Sonny, worrying about them, doing for them. She was looking for a position that revolved around writing, such as managing a column and writing articles for a newspaper. Although, she'd ask herself, if she got the job she wanted, would she be able to continue writing for herself? Her passion was writing poetry and short stories, but she knew that some things would have to give if she wanted to land a good job. She and Haley recently watched, for the second time, the A&E special that profiled Erin Brockovich's work. She wanted, in her own way, to be a powerhouse. To be able to produce a body of work that would bring her recognition, would be a fulfillment of her dreams. After the movie, she'd said, "Thank God for the Erin's of the world, Haley."

Wandering toward the kitchen for a snack Mari glanced in a hallway mirror flinging back a bothersome, caramel hi-light, she muttered, "At this rate I'm never going to be an Erin." Job hunting had become so cumbersome and she hadn't written anything profound, or new even, as of late. Where could she focus her efforts today? She fussed, dawdled, fussed some more and brushed her teeth. After lightly touching on some household chores and managing to round out a poem she'd started some weeks before, she called Haley.

"Hi honey, haven't talked to you all week. What's new?"

"We haven't. Glad you called. Nothin' much. Just trying to train Ducky not to jump up on people. I'm sorry he was so crazy the last time you were here. I should have had kids, not puppies. Kids have got to be easier. Right Mom?"

"Ooh," Mari laughed," don't know about that, but we do share a common disaster. Your brother. Have you heard what Vince is up to now?"

A little afraid, Haley answered, "No what?"

"Your brother is involved with someone, a woman who's part of some way out there theatre group. They do different things, really weird stuff, like that dance troupe we saw one day at the Capri Theatre, you know where the dancers were melting into the floor like blobs of mercury."

"Oh yeah, so innovative. I loved it. So, what's her name? Do you know much about her?" The usual vivaciousness lighting her voice.

"Her name is Sally Spring. Cute eh? And I really don't know much about her, the little he told me. He says she's zany and sweet. And, guess what, he dances with her. They're in rehearsal for some musical."

"Great. And when do we meet Miss Spring?"

"Don't know just yet. I hope he'll be bringing her around soon."

"Well, call me when he does and I'll come over."

"Why don't you call him? A lot easier."

"Mom, that way I get to visit with Dad too. He's always so busy, and even when we go where he's playing he's always visiting with friends, talking to his band buddies about their sets, talking to people, other women. Do you ever get jealous?"

"No Haley, there's no reason to be jealous. I've got to go, I started a poem some weeks ago and before I lose affection for it want to finish it. And, I'm getting a few leads on jobs. I've got to keep at it. Love you. Say hi to Rex and Ducky. You know what just went through my mind. You have a husband named Rex and a dog named Ducky."

"Yeah, okay Mom," she giggled, and added, "I haven't upset you with that question about Dad, have I?"

"Not at all." They ended their conversation by discussing the fact that there wasn't much in the news about the murder investigation. Mari commented, "It seems to be dragging."

"Yeah, it's so scary knowing that a killer roams free. Everybody I run into is really frightened. Hope something develops soon." Mari said, "Yeah, especially for the family. It must be unbearable."

Putting the cell down, she thought about Haley's question: *Oh Haley, you always could see through things so easily. Do I ever get jealous? Not exactly. Doubtful is more the word that describes what I feel.*

A call finally came in about an interesting job at the newspaper! A woman who introduced herself as Anne, said, "I have your resume and it looks like you have the qualifications we want." Enthused, Mari responded, and they set up a time for an interview.

"This coming Tuesday at two sounds perfect. I gather we're meeting in the news room." She felt her voice quaver. Anne responded, "That's right. My office is just to the right of the elevator, fifth floor." Mari hoped she hadn't sounded anxious. She gathered herself and picked up her novel on the table next to her, but she sat it in her lap when the phone rang again. It was Fiona.

"Mari, I'm leaving Warren," Mari heard an intake of breath, and Fiona quickly added, "I can't elaborate. Warren just walked in." Mari said she'd call her soon and they hung up. *Whoa! I was not expecting that!* Even though she was not terribly surprised, the reality of it worried her. *I hope she's alright*! She sat there a few minutes more with the Jane Austen heavy in her lap, and usually enthralled by the author's superb chronicle of the manners and attitudes of the time, she could only look at it absentmindedly. She lay it on the coffee table, and before she knew it, Fiona's call pierced her day with distressing thoughts of her own, something she was ashamed to think about. A few days ago, she had called into action an altogether, hasty, ill-conceived move. Sonny had been home for a while and she waited for him to get into the shower. Finally, hearing the spray she searched her husband's email on his laptop, then his briefcase. Thoughts whirled through her head: *What if I find something? What if he catches me doing this? Why won't he get a job that keeps him at home more? How can I feel this distrustful? I don't want to know. Yes I do. Damn it, he's good and loving with me and the kids. God, I love him and I depend on him for so much. Has my world become that small? And admit it, I don't trust him. He's so flirtatious! Where is my head? Land this job and get a life*!

As these thoughts swirled in her head she felt ashamed, but it didn't stop her. She frantically rummaged through his stuff, then realized that she didn't hear the shower spray anymore. Unduly determined and resolute in nature, she thought: *I just need to know. I need time and occasion.* Hastily, she put everything back as it was and returned to her novel in the living room, looking at it, trying to compress her thoughts so they made sense: *When did he start being secretive and so removed...and so restless?*

He entered the room in his plaid underwear and rubbing the towel over his wet head he asked, "Hon, have you seen my razor? Honey?" She looked at him. "Mari, did you hear me?"

"Yes, and no, haven't seen it."

"Is anything wrong? You seem a little preoccupied."

"Nah, I'm okay. Besides, it's your razor. Fiona called. She's leaving him."

"You mean...?"

"Him! The only one of HIM." He looked at her expectantly, waiting for more. She grasped for words, "She doesn't love him anymore."

Sonny and Warren did not like each other, both strong, they butted heads. Still, Mari disliked Warren more intensely than Sonny did, having known him a lot longer. She was introduced to him years ago when Fiona started dating this controlling, advice-giving, critical, intolerable know-it-all, his good qualities. A frequent thing he liked to say when he began most conversations was, "Let me give you a bit of advice." Mari would inwardly cringe whenever she was in his presence because his tongue was always peppered with this little opener. She recalled a day when she'd been visiting Fiona. He was on his lunch hour and he was telling Mari, who was half-listening, that something in his friend's life had irrevocably gone wrong. He told her, "I told them what to do. They didn't listen. That's their problem." Half listening, she had watched Fiona. It was garbage day and Fiona was preparing bags for the curb. Warren, as he talked and ate, was also watching Fiona. He said, "I've told her a million times to crush the boxes and cartons before she puts them in the bags. It gives you more room. She never listens." Fiona ignored him. Mari found it somewhat illuminating, and disturbing. She dealt with him by ignoring his presence. If this is how she coped, it meant trouble. Fiona's propensity at times for keeping things in was not good. She would flee into depression, serious enough to land her in the hospital.

Fiona called the following day and said, "Hi Mari. You busy? I really need to talk," an undertone of anxiety in her voice. Flavoured coffee was Mari's standard response to trauma, illness, global crisis, her sister's issues…so she said, "Sure, let me fix my coffee and you can talk all you want." She bolted for the kitchen, doctored her mug with a huge dollop of creamy hazelnut and wriggled into her comfy chair.

"Okay."

"Like I told you, I'm leaving him Mari. Our twentieth wedding anniversary is coming up and I can't pretend anymore. I'm going to do it, and quick. I'm doing it! I've done so many things wrong. Do you remember a few years back when I was sick in bed for three days and you thought it must be a bad case of the flu."

"Yes, what was it?" She heard Fiona take a deep breath.

"I'd had an abortion!"

"An abortion. Oh Fiona." Stunned, she waited for Fiona to start speaking again.

"Yes, you know he didn't want kids. Besides, I knew I would be leaving him one day, but I didn't know when or how I was going to do it. How could I bring a baby into a situation like that?" Fiona stopped talking. Mari felt a deep sadness for her.

"This is the hard part. It was not his baby...Mari, are you there?" Trying to rebound from the immensity of these words, Mari faltered, "I'm...I'm speechless. Fiona, how could I have not known any of this?"

"How could I tell YOU that I was a cheat, a liar, that I'd had an abortion, and that the baby wasn't even his? It's funny, when I was going through the affair, I thought it was my due because he treated me so badly. I've lived with that ever since, especially the abortion, but it's got to go. I can't hold anything back anymore. I needed to tell you so badly. Do you hate me?"

Mari heard the anguish in her voice and she levelled her own, "Of course I don't hate you. I love you. What are we, fair-weather friends? We're sisters. What plans have you made? Do you need a place to stay?"

Reassured, Fiona said, "No, I have a small place on the outskirts of town. It's mine at the end of the month."

"Okay, well, you've done something. But the worst isn't over yet Fiona. Telling Warren is going to be rough. What do you plan on saying?"

Resolutely, she responded, "I don't love you. I haven't for a long time. I'm leaving. Just like that. I don't want to draw this out and that is why I'm telling him right after I pack my things. I don't want a lot of things, just my entitlement to half of the house. I just need out."

"It's going to be hard for a while, between when he knows and when you leave. Listen, call me anytime. I love you!"

"I love you too. Bye."

Dazed, Mari took a deep breath and tried to register some of what she'd just heard. The depths of what she had concealed...another man, a pregnancy, an abortion! Not Warren's baby! This was 'Faultless Fiona!' who could be quite judgmental. It can't be. *What crippling moment drove her to such lengths, to such deceit?* Mari was worried because she sounded so desperate and lonely.

She remembered the recent occasion where they'd all been at a couple's home for a barbecue, Tim's and Mia's, who were Fiona's friends. At one point Warren, quite intoxicated, launched into a discussion about one of Mia's friends. The woman he referred to was named Paula. He repeatedly used the phrase, "She's creative and likes penis." And he couldn't refrain from suggesting that he had had sex with the woman-all this in front of Fiona. Uncomfortable and embarrassed, Fiona said, "I should take Warren home." After they left, Tim picked up on the fact that Warren couldn't help but imply that he'd fooled around with the woman.

Mari thought: Could his casual, uncouth behavior that night have been the final straw for Fiona?

Dazed from it all, Mari supposed: *What do you really know about people, who they really are, and what they do when nobody's watching. Do families really know each other? Did the killer's circle of people have any sense of who HE was?*

Did they ask: Could he be capable of murder?

CHAPTER 3

SCARCELY KNOWN

Mari met with her writer's group that evening and it was especially stimulating. They always started the evening reading and critiquing each other's work, and tonight's participators had provided some really good work. Added to that, Mary Ann Mulhern, a local published author of poetry, led the group that evening.

When it was Mari's turn, she read a piece that was loaded with dialogue, and it was suggested that while the dialogue was good, some of it sounded stilted. She and her fellow writers discussed how to effectively use dialogue. Mary Ann further clarified, saying that how a person speaks says a lot about them. Did they speak positively, or was their way of speaking cynical or otherwise off-putting? Did they talk at others or did they engage others? Were they loud or soft? You could surmise that this kind of speaker was shy and reticent, or scared. Did they constantly interject when other people were speaking? Did their words rise up at the end of a phrase?

On the way home she decided to stop at The K House for a glass of wine. It was close to home and she wanted to relax and reflect on the kind of meeting they'd had. The K House was the place to do that. It was an Irish pub, authentic in how they presented themselves. Lots of wood, green walls, and wooden benches lining the wall, made it that way. She loved the atmosphere and musicians played six nights a week. Weekends, Irish bands livened things up, but on week days, like this one, single musicians with a guitar delivered their music such that it didn't deter you from talking or thinking. Mari wanted to be alone to think, and let her mind digest everything she'd heard and learned. And, she wanted to celebrate her coveted job with the newspaper. Noting that traffic was light and that there was a parking spot directly in front of the bar, she pulled the car over. *Good.* She wouldn't have to walk far from where her car was. She felt safe.

"A shiraz please", she said to the bartender as she looked for a seat. Comfortable, and promptly receiving her drink, she savoured a few sips while she listened to the animated group gathered at the bar. There were three men and one woman in the bar, besides the blonde bartender. Two of the men occupied stools on either side of the laughing, expressive woman, a friend, it seemed. The third man seemed a little outside the group and stood awkwardly beside them, cutting into the conversation at various points. The light-hearted banter included the bartender, who kept busy, but still managed to chat with everyone.

Suddenly, the standing man left the group and walked straight toward Mari. Perched on a stool at one of those standing tables, Mari occupied the one nearest the exit door, so she wasn't too concerned. He was probably leaving. Instead, he walked straight to her and placed his glass on the table. She could feel her stomach sink. He announced, "I'm going to the bathroom. I'll be right back." She blinked and looked away. *Some pick up line.*

Up went a cautious hand and she said, "I'm here for a quiet drink, by myself, and then I'm leaving."

He repeated, "I'm here for a quiet drink, by myself, and then I'm leaving." Then he stood there. Mari thought: *He's on something.* She didn't respond and looked away, hoping that if she didn't say anything more, he'd leave. He didn't. She looked back. His eyes pierced hers, and she felt goose bumps on her arms. She shivered. He started talking in a monotone, "I'm a mill right, I love my job, some people hate their work, but I love my job." Mari looked into his emotionless face. It spooked her. "You want company?"

Starting to squirm, she gripped the edges of her stool and took a breath, "Not tonight, thank you." *Why do I have to be so damned polite?*

"Not tonight, thank you. You can't even tell me your name?" The bold, unsmiling face stared into hers. Clearly, he was not going anywhere. She made a move to get up.

Hand up, he said, "I'm leaving."

When she relaxed into her seat and picked up her wine he made no move to go. Normally poised, Mari was getting more and more nervous. *Goddamn!* Frozen, she didn't move. He continued speaking, "The boss talked to me today, 'cause he said I was bothering other people." His voice trailed off, and he was silent for about ten seconds, "Someone said I bothered her," oblivious to her lack of response.

She shifted in her seat and looked past him toward the people, trying to think of something different to do. Clearly, this creep was playing a cat and mouse game with her-and he would wait her out. Her fright quickly melded into a feeling of agitation and her heart beat against her chest like a bird in a small cage. Her eyes darted. Alerted, he sidestepped from the spot he'd taken to position himself where he could block her view of the people at the bar, and where they couldn't see her. Now, surpassing her fright, anger pulled her to her feet.

She picked up her drink. He said, "Don't go. I'm leaving." Determinedly, she walked past him to the bar and picked a stool.

He turned toward her and the group and said amiably, "Have a good night. See you later."

The bartender leaned in and said, "Was he bothering you?" Mari nodded and started to say something. A call rudely thrown past her, by some guy who'd just come in, "Sheri, get me a beer, eh?" sent the bartender running.

Ambling back, and wiping the counter, the bartender went into her spiel to inform her that this was a nice club, and that the crowd that usually went in there was a nice mix, there was entertainment on the weekends, and dancing. With a dismissive wave of her hand she said that this guy was just "some creep" that came in on occasion. Mari wasn't impressed and couldn't suppress her mockery, "He's a nut job." The bartender, unconcerned, walked away.

Mari sat stiffly and tried to stop seeing his eyes. He rarely blinked, and he didn't look away. Sometimes his eyes opened wide, and he would momentarily look down. Then, he would slowly raise them again, and stare into hers. *Was he the murderer? Impossible. He'd be long gone out of town by now.*

She couldn't get over the fact that this creep had kept chatting to give the impression to others that might be watching, that everything at the table was just fine. So brazen, so obtrusive, so sinister. She wondered again if she was looking at the killer. A jolt of fear flashed through her. She released the tension in her shoulders, took some deep breaths, and decided to enjoy what was left of her evening. With the last sip of the really good wine she'd ordered, she slipped off her stool, walked quickly to her car and drove home.

Sonny was in his favourite chair, reading. Mari was still upset when she walked past him to fix tea. He put his book down and listened to Mari recount her story, "If this slime ball completely ignored your wishes to be left alone-in public, what would happen in private?"

"My thoughts exactly. He acted like he could do something bad. He didn't listen and wouldn't go away. At one point in his ramblings, he said that the boss talked to him that day about an accusation that a woman employee had against him. Apparently, she said that he had bothered her. I can't let this go. I'll call the police in the morning. Maybe they know of him. It's possible they've received complaints."

"I agree. He could even be the killer." Fleetingly, Mari would recall that evening; downright scary and unpleasant.

She and Fiona had a little sister, April, and she stopped in her place of work. She owned a pub/restaurant, a real hopping, popular place, and part of the job was to look out for clientele and ferret out the trouble makers. Maybe he'd dropped in there. A few nights after the incident with him, Mari walked in, and heard April call out to her and approached, "Hey sista, how's it goin'?" April gave her a huge hug. They made small talk, and Mari perched on a barstool.

"April, listen, one night I dropped in at the "K", and this man approached my table and wouldn't leave until I left my seat and went to the bar." She described his demeanor, his way of talking, and she said he coldly stared at her. "His eyes are evil." April was wide-eyed.

Mari asked, "Could you have served him?"

"I don't know. What does he look like?" April asked.

"He's ordinary, slim, average height, like five feet eight, and like I said, his eyes were empty, his face expressionless. He was probably younger than what I thought he could be, his face was so soft looking...about thirty, thirty five."

"I don't recall anybody like that, but I'll keep it in mind, and if that creep ever comes here, I'll freeze his ass out. And call the cops."

The serious tone that had opened their conversation didn't exactly fit the physical persona that April had created getting dressed that morning. It made her grin. She was dressed in a black, ruffled skirt, a white crop top, and there was a cute, floppy hat on her head. Her curly hair swung out from underneath. From under the rim, her eyes popped seductively. Her mode of dress was eccentric, but she could make it very appealing. Since she was a child of about ten she would emerge as whatever she wanted to be. She could be flirtatious, moody, serious and studious, or haughty like whoever her favourite movie star might be at the time. It was disarming sometimes, terribly winsome other times. Her personality skyrocketed into her teenage years and clung into early adulthood, and then, thankfully, the drama tempered somewhat. Mari and Fiona would say, "She IS normal."

Mari smiled into her impudent, crazy-haired little sister's face. Once the conversation ended about Mari's experience at the "K", she attempted to lighten up. She smiled, "Hey, tell me about the latest guy in your life." April launched into a tale about her latest boyfriend.

"His name is Brandon, he's cute, and works at that restaurant 'she pointed across the street' as a chef. He's fun. We can dance the night away," she beamed.

Whatever the quirks April owned, her work had sharpened her skills in handling difficult customers, anything from sloppy drunks to bar fights. Mari left knowing that she could handle herself. It eased the tension she'd been feeling before she went in to April's bar.

Leads into the town's brutal murder were as dry as desert air. Like many of the town's people, Mari found it difficult to keep anxious, frightening thoughts from surfacing. They went about their days, the murder in the back of their minds. Fear that it could happen again became foremost in people's minds, especially when weeks went by, and nothing new was reported. People felt helpless.

Picking up the newspaper Mari took it to a café and read that the police were requesting all the adult males in the community to voluntarily submit their D. N. A. She thought: *Can they do that? They're doing it, so I guess they can. Does anyone say no to a request like that without seeming suspect? Probably not. What if I was a guy being asked to do that?* She thought hard. *I'd do it. I know I'm innocent and I'm helping the police narrow their search. Why not help?* She knew her husband though and she didn't have to wonder what he'd have to say about it. He'd have issues with it.

As she finished her restaurant lunch, her thoughts returned to the tasks at hand. April was graciously letting her and Fiona use her cottage for the weekend. She was looking forward to spending time there. The cottage had a roomy living area, light blue walls, and huge windows that faced the lake. The wind and the smell of the water as it lapped close gave it an exotic feel. And Mari could hardly wait to shop for all the stuff they'd need. She'd forgotten to pick up a new beach towel, but that could be done today. They were treating themselves to something they called "unwinding time," and this little vacation would ease some of the stress of Fiona's impending divorce. They were going to soak up sun and drink wine. Soon she was home and she entered the house to the phone ringing. It was April. As Mari talked, she put the flip flops, sunscreen, the new beach towel, and other miscellany in piles that she'd bought to take with her.

"I'm at the cottage cleaning up after my party last weekend. The odor of cigarettes and the cleaner is yucky. And I'M the smoker in the family, but the place will be fresh when you two arrive, even scented. I've got flowery scented potpourri to scatter about in my new baskets." Mari visualized her little sister's grin.

"Thanks. We appreciate it. I'm so glad we can get the cottage this weekend. It's still early but I'm going to swim and enjoy a little sun before I have to start my new job at the newspaper."

"Yeah. We just touched on that, I was so busy, you know, the night you stopped in at the pub."

"I'm taking over the weekly column they have in the editorial section, the one where people submit emails about what's on their minds, or I can choose the material. I train under the columnist who's leaving. She's got some personal commitment this week but she'll be back to work early next week to train me, and then it's mine! I've got a neat little office. My own office. I'm so excited! This little get-away to the cottage fits perfectly, the timing I mean. Fiona needs it too. She is so wrung out from this crap with Warren."

"God, I still can't believe Fiona finally found the courage to dump him."

"Yeah, she's hurting though. She's got a lot to do. In due time, she'll do fine. Her new place is has a homey feel, sort of like a bungalow. Trees surround it. It's covered in white siding and dark blue shutters. The paint is nice. Some walls are covered in terra cotta, but mostly the rooms are finished with muted shades of blue. She's moving her stuff in, probably as we speak."

"How's the depression? You know she won't talk about that much."

"I'll get her talking."

"You're easy to talk to, whereas I'm not." Mari heard her sigh.

"What do you mean?"

"Oh, you know. Some people can hardly take care of their own problems, let alone help somebody else. Especially somebody like Fiona." Mari ignored that statement: *There's a triple edge to that comment.*

"It's always easy when it's somebody else's problems you're dealing with," but she felt a lurch of encouragement. *Was April going to talk about her drinking problem?* It was a huge thing that she and the rest of the family worried about, but she thought: *Oh God, not now. There are just too many things going on.*

"Well, I'd better finish cleaning this place so I can lock up and go home. Oh, one more thing, I'll leave the key under the planter, next to the porch. Talk to you soon."

"Sure, bye, and thanks."

"No need for thanks. Are you kidding, Mari? You're welcome."

Mari fell into cleaning while she listened to the new Adele CD she'd bought for the weekend, and she sang along with Rolling In The Deep and Rumour Has It, banging the words out. Really into the cleaning and the singing, she didn't hear Sonny come in.

He yelled, "It's just the axe murderer. Thanks for leaving the door unlocked!" She turned the music down, kissed him and said, "Smart ass. I forgot to lock the door. I know. Not smart." Laying the duster aside, she suggested they have coffee.

She told him about her plans with Fiona and he said, "Perfect. It's going to be a full weekend for me too. I have extra paperwork to do, lots of work related calls to make, and with you away I'll take a little time to visit my mother." Their plans were set.

Later, he brought up what he'd read in the paper, his voice rising, "The cops are calling for all males to submit their D. N. A. Are they frickin' kidding? Not this guy! They're overstepping their authority and they don't have the right to ask for my D.N.A."

She didn't want to get into it so she faked to being busier than she was. She would wait until he cooled off a bit, their discussions developing a little more productively that way. Muttering something unintelligible, he walked away.

Mari and Fiona took their own cars to the cottage and as Mari drove up she noticed Fiona's car already parked under a shady tree. She also noticed the red and yellow roses set against the white, medium sized cottage. The winding earth path led to the front steps, and she set her overnighter on the porch. A sweet smelling breeze brushed past her as she trudged in and out, taking her stuff in. She took a deep whiff. It was quite warm already and just past noon: *This is so nice. It's already a great beginning for our weekend away.* She entered with the key and found Fiona napping in one of the two mid-sized bedrooms. She'd occupied the upstairs one, so she went into the downstairs, airy bedroom and dropped her stuff onto the white eyelet covered bed. Then she made coffee. Waiting for it to perk, she felt hassle-free. Very shortly Fiona emerged from upstairs, her short hair wet from the shower, wearing white cropped gym pants and a cool white top.

"Hi. I didn't hear you come in. I got up because the smell of coffee wafted up. I was out like a light real soon after I got here. When did you come in?"

"Long enough to unload and make coffee for us."

"Just what I need, thanks."

"Okay, well, my turn to shower. I got up this morning, splashed my face and teeth" 'she chuckled', threw things in the car, and left. When I'm ready we can talk about what we are going to do. Okay?" Fiona nodded.

Mari suggested they take a drive, stop for some veggies to go with the steaks they were going to grill, and maybe pick up a bottle of wine, or two. When they returned they poured the wine, prepared the spinach salad and the potato salad, and placed the steaks on the grill. They turned out so tasty and tender, having been marinated in soya sauce. They ate hungrily, and between bites, they talked about the multitude of birds, trying to remember their species. Suddenly, a cardinal landed in the nearest tree, but the one that followed it puzzled them. It looked like a cardinal, but the body was a bright white.

"Is it the female?" Mari asked.

"Don't know, but it sure is beautiful."

They stopped talking for a bit and simply enjoyed the greenery that was all around them. Over a second glass of wine, Mari plopped into one of the comfy lounges.

"We don't have a television, we may as well talk. We don't do it enough."

Fiona wriggled her rump into her chair, "Eh, what'll we talk about?" Mari eased into the conversation by asking her about her place, only having seen it a few times, when she had helped Fiona move some things in.

"Is it looking like you want it to?"

"The browns in most of my furniture, and the tan pillows against the terra cotta walls, look good. The kitchen sparkles, now that the cleaning is done, and the blue and red bowls cheer it up. I bought a new Keurig for the counter, by the way, like yours. And it's just about over, with Warren I mean. I feel calmer, appreciating the peace I feel, not having to deal with Warren on a daily basis. I have room to think," she smiled contentedly. Her expression sobered, and she spaced her words, "I feel so sad...about the abortion...wondering about whether it was a boy or a girl, and who did the baby resemble. What name would I choose?" Her voice picked up, ever so lightly, "I considered Lorelie for a girl." Mari nodded and touched her hand.

"I wanted a baby for years but he never budged on that, even though, early on, he did say we'd talk about it." Her voice grew determined, shaking her head, "I've learned something very important. Make sure you know the person you're marrying-on the crucial issues. The thing is though, I robbed myself when I had that abortion. I will probably never hold a new born and kiss its fuzzy little head. I'll never grow with a child."

"You don't know that. You're still young. Besides, women have babies later in life now. When you're ready, you'll meet the right guy that will know how to be a great father. And listen. It's always easy in hindsight to dissect your life and think of all the things you could have done differently. Have you been talking to your therapist about the abortion? I'm worried," her voice trailed off.

"Oh yeah, and about the affair that took me there in the first place." Her face bore the pain as she continued, "I grew to be so resentful of

Warren, his constant criticism of my job, well, he called it a job, I view nursing as a career. He always put down my accomplishments. And said things that hurt. But, I puffed HIM up, trying to please him all the time and it was never enough. And, this might sound weird but the less he gave, the more he hated me because it reminded him how mean he really was."

"Doesn't sound weird at all."

"I was so lonely and bereft of any love, any affection. I don't mean to sound like I'm excusing what I did. I would never be dishonest like that again, but I just don't feel that all-consuming guilt anymore. You can only go back so much, to learn, so my therapist tells me." Mari looked into her eyes, eyes that were smeared with remorse. Sadness in every syllable, Fiona repeated, "I just can't get past the abortion."

"You faced this thing alone, and people do things out of fear and confusion, things they'd not normally do, like have an affair. You haven't said who the man in question is." Hearing this, Fiona shook her head, her voice fraught with bitterness, and she said, "I'd rather forget. He isn't important anymore. Besides, he readily agreed that I should have an abortion."

They sipped their wine silently, listening to the night sounds, noting the jarring sound of a screech owl, and when they spoke again the mood had turned to giddiness.

"So, Mari, how do you like the "fruit forward" dry red, that our wine expert suggested?"

"I prefer mine oak forward. Hope that's oak-ay?" enunciating clearly.

They laughed and topped up their glasses.

After a minute or so, Mari said, pointing a finger, "Remember, your life is wide open now, and you'll get what you want. So, what would be the first thing on your bucket list?"

"Well Dr. Phil, I want a baby."

"Oh Fiona, I have majored in Dr. Phil. Anyway, first get a man." They busted up again.

"Oh God Mari, definitely too much wine. I can't believe I'm laughing at that."

"It's all good. You have to laugh sometimes. Comic relief is a good thing."

Taking a break they refueled the fire pit for tomorrow night, polished off the little that was left in their glasses, tidied up from dinner, and finally went into bed. They slept soundly.

In the morning they went to the front porch, a little cool yet, but with their toasted bacon and egg English muffins, and a pot of coffee on the wicker table, they warmed up. The breeze brought the smell of the lake to them, and they were anxious to spend time there.

Before gathering the brightly flowered patio dishes Mari asked Fiona about her treatment plan for depression. Was her medication working well, and was she optimistic about feeling completely normal?

Light-heartedly, Fiona answered, "You mean I'm not normal?"

Mari clapped a hand over her mouth. "Sorry, that didn't come out right." Fiona's attitude reaffirmed again in Mari's mind that her sister was doing okay.

"Yeah, I'm taking my meds, and my depression is lifting a bit. I know that everybody sees me as this mouthy, judgmental person, who probably is as strong on the inside as I am on the outside; a big fat lie. It's a cover. Like I have to tell you that. But, I am going to make my life bright and happy again, like it was before I got married. I do deserve another chance at life." Her face spread into that beguiling close-mouthed grin. Mari smiled too. It was good to hear Fiona being introspective and projecting about a deserved, happy life.

It gave her impetus to talk about her qualms about Sonny. She hedged a bit at first, and Fiona said, "Come on. Out with it."

"When does a person cross the line as far as flirting goes?"

"You're asking the right person" Fiona smirked. "What do you mean, exactly?"

"I mean, Sonny is charismatic, fun loving and all that, but have you ever thought he comes on to women a little too much?"

"As long as you're asking. Yeah, he does. He's with you and he should respect that. Actually, he makes me mad. When he does that he's not even thinking how you might feel. It sucks." Fiona never quibbled. Mari cheeks reddened and she looked away.

"Well…" Fiona's voice rose, and she shook her head a bit.

"You've noticed. It's exactly how I feel. But then again, I don't want to be hysterical. I'm not that insecure and I've never known anything conclusive, you know, that he takes anything further than flirting. I should just talk to him. I mean, if you can't talk to your own husband, who can you talk to? But, I have to tell you this little story." She ran it by Fiona about "Big Hair."

"If he was being that evasive I'd want to know why. Maybe he was just put off by her for some reason. But, if it still bothers you, use "Big Hair" as a way to broach the issue."

"Now that sounds logical. Okay, now what?"

"The dishes, that's what." Fiona took a swipe at Mari.

As their weekend came to a close, Mari brought up how little about the murder was being reported, and how people were getting discouraged.

"I mean, I know they can't divulge pertinent things, but I'd like to hear something," she shrugged.

"Well Mari, it might be that there are no leads yet. That would be worse to hear than hearing nothing."

"I guess. I'm sure you read that the police have called on all the men in town to submit their D.N.A."

"Of course. I'm all for it."

"Me too. Sonny kind of ranted about it. In a nutshell, he says "The Man" is not muscling him into doing that or anything else. They overstep their authority, for the most part, and he has rights. He's an absolutist."

"He does have the right to refuse, so what's the big deal?"

"I made that point, but it was not well taken. He feels that while he still has that right, it could happen that someday he won't. That's valid. Anyhow, no more complaining. This was the best weekend I've had in ages."

"The best."

They packed their things in their respective cars and hugged goodbye.

As she pulled into the driveway, Mari found the house in darkness. She hesitated at the door a bit. Darkness made her tense, especially with the pall of the murder hanging over the town. Turning the key in the lock, she illuminated her way as she walked through the house. Soon relaxed, her face washed, she decided to change into some light pajamas and hopefully stay awake until Sonny got home. Finishing her chamomile tea, she waited. Before long, she drifted off. Stiffly she stretched a leg, slowly waking. She gathered her cup and small plate, and with worry prickling at her, she went to bed. Morning saw her wake up to an empty bed. Signs of life met her in the kitchen and a scribbled note that said: Hi honey, didn't want to wake you, real late getting in. Talk to you tonight Love you.

She pondered aloud, "I wonder what he really did this weekend."

She had a day to herself before starting her job so she decided to call her daughter. Haley picked up the phone immediately: "Hi Mom. I was just picking up the phone to call you. How are you?"

"Great. Fiona and I had a wonderful weekend, just relaxing, talking a lot, drinking more than usual." She touched her head and laughed, "Dave Mathews must have had such a weekend before he wrote: I eat too much, I drink too mu-c-h."

"Mom, I hate it when you sing. It's worse than Vince. How's Aunt Fiona?"

"Ouch. My singing has got to be better than your brother's. Your Aunt Fiona is doing pretty well. Facing divorce and going through it are two different things. It hasn't been pleasant. But, at least the worst is over. She loves her new place and she's continuing with her therapy. She'll get through this stronger than ever."

"That's great. Hmm, I wonder where life will take her now."

"Haley, if you mean, is she dating, the answer is no. It's too early. She has a lot to deal with yet, emotionally and all that."

"I don't know all that went on with them." Mari thought: And, you're not going to.

Silence.

Haley started jabbering, "Anyway, Ducky is finally getting used to his baths. He doesn't run and hide anymore when he figures it's bath time. He sure doesn't live up to his name."

"Maybe he was traumatized by water in his puppy stage."

"I suppose. Oh, Vince and Sally were here last night. They're loads of fun together. She's quirky and funny, like Vince."

"Yeah, they are great, aren't they? They both have jobs they like and they're so involved together with theatre. They are a match."

"Yeah, he's happy. Oh, I called Grandma Emard. She's doing so well. She says her garden is more beautiful than last year's. Actually, her exact words were: it screams vibrancy. Whatever, she sure has a knack. I feel so guilty that I haven't been to see her in a while."

"That's bad. Oh, did you get to say hi to your Dad? He was going there this weekend."

"He didn't make it. Grandma was saying how he doesn't visit enough either, that she hadn't seen him in over two months."

"Really. It's just that he said he was going to drive down this weekend and I haven't had a chance to talk to him."

"Oh."

"Yeah, I wonder why he changed his plans."

"Don't know. You know how Dad is. He gets whims."

"Listen hon, I have got to go. I've got lots to do today, laundry from the weekend, watering, and the housework I didn't finish 'cause I wasn't here."

"Okay Mom. Talk to you soon. Ducky's barking. I'd better go see. Bye."

"Love you." Slowly, she put the phone down as a suspicious thought crept into her head: *Could he have worked all weekend? Doubt it.* Sonny called just as she got some coffee brewing. He said, "Hi. Sorry I missed seeing you last night. I have to rush right now. Listen, I feel like pizza for dinner. You okay with that? I'll pick it up."

"Sure. I haven't even thought about getting dinner. I had lots of stuff to do today."

"Right, see you around six. Bye." Mari showered before he got home and prettied herself up with mousse, eye makeup, and new khakis. Shortly, he waltzed through the door. He put the pizza down, kissed her neck and said, "Hmm, do you smell good. How was your weekend"?

"Couldn't have been better. We really did a lot, have a bit of a hangover though."

"Are you sure you didn't spend the weekend with April?" She tilted her head down and gave him a look of exasperation.

"My weekend was okay. Worked too much. Then, I just sort of laid around here. Had a game of poker last night with a few of the guys, at Rick's place actually. Hadn't seen him for months." Shamefaced, he looked down, "Didn't see Mom after all."

"Sonny. You know she wants to see more of you. I tried to stay up and couldn't. When did you come in? I was worried."

"Sorry. About two. I didn't want to wake you so I slept on the couch. I was really dragging my ass this morning, but, I made it to the office and got some paperwork finished. Anyway, how's Fiona"?

"She's doing great, staying on track, taking care of herself. She's filling her time with lots of different things, especially with fixing up her place."

"Oh yeah? You know, you haven't told me much about what went on there. What gives"?

"Haley said the same thing, and I told her that I'm not at liberty to talk about it. It's the same for you. Fiona will decide who she wants to talk to, and when."

"That makes me think she had affairs, or something. People get into crazy things," a depraved grin spreading over his tanned face. Mari just looked at him with that look again.

Mari picked up a piece of the pizza, then watched amazed as Sonny ate his anchovies. "I'm not in the mood to joke about my sister. She's been through a hard time watching her marriage disintegrate, and then trying to cope with the turmoil and the heartbreak. And, all you can do is joke."

"Wait a minute, I just asked about Fiona and now you're mad. Guess I wasn't sensitive enough," he said flippantly, then regretted it as he watched Mari take her pizza into the kitchen. He finished his dinner, thinking about what had transpired, picked up his beer and plate and joined her, "Mari, I apologize, it wasn't the time to poke fun. I don't think sometimes."

"Yes. You could think sometimes before running your mouth."

"I'm sorry." She accepted the apology, not ready to pursue anything weighty. She nodded, "It's okay. No real harm done."

They spent the rest of the evening leisurely walking around the neighbourhood, talking a bit, and ended their day in front of the television. It improved the mood, and both of them delighted in catching the last hour of Driving Miss Daisy. It always touched them. Yawning, Sonny grabbed her hand before the credits were over and they went to bed.

Somewhat nervously, Mari got ready for her first day at her new job. Surveying the outfit she had laid out, not liking it, she re-hung it. She'd put together a black suit, with a white blouse, buttoned up to the neck. *Too severe, too conservative.* She finally picked a little form-fitting teal suit with cream accessories. I don't present an Erin Brokavich, but I have her perseverance. The full length mirror called to her and she smiled broadly at her reflection, turning a little to catch her back side. Confidently, she grabbed her purse and strode to her car, ending up parking in their lot. As she walked through the wide heavy doors of the gold brick façade, she approached the busy elevator, which opened onto the hall leading to the news room. When she entered, she noticed the line of five desks, two of which were men, one with his tie loosened and a huge smile. The three women wore suit jackets, and when the youngest of the women rose from behind her desk, she noticed that she wore slim cut jeans. She approached Mari and introduced herself.

"Hi, I'm Christina. Welcome Mari." She introduced her co-workers, as Will, Grant, Priscilla, known as "Prissy", and they, including Priscilla, laughed. And hiding back here, is Macie." She said her boss, Stan, wasn't there, and she'd meet him later. She showed her around.

Her first day was great; absorbing as much as she could from her co-workers. Before she knew it, it was lunch time. Her predecessor, Christina, invited Mari to join her. She was elated, "Sure. I'm hungry." Mostly they talked business, and Mari jubilantly exchanged ideas about the possibilities of what she could do with the column and how she would implement those ideas.

Mari said, "I've followed the column. It's pertinent to what is going on in the community, what people are worried about. Of course, the murder often predominates, and you answer their worries and questions the best that you can, with the info you have. I'll do the same. Aside from that, I'll choose issues that I feel will generate ideas and hopefully, some lively debate." She added, "If the boss agrees."

Christina chimed in, "Of course he'll listen and give you some rein. He probably would welcome a fresh approach…"

She placed her hand on her chest, "Oh Christina. I didn't mean that as a put down to what you have done. The column is really good."

She smiled impishly, "I know it's good. But, you can make it better."

Mari finished her day, enthused, and Christina pulled the loose ends of her work there to a close. She told Mari that she was moving into something "similar, but bigger." She was moving to Montreal, and she could barely contain herself, "I love big cities. I can't wait."

Mari watched her clear her desk, symbolizing a veering toward something else, and, with both hands full, she called goodbye to her coworkers. Mari watched Christina walk out. She turned back to look at the space that was now hers. It was a huge moment for Mari. The smooth desk top, bare of anything on it, symbolized for her, fertile ground for something else-for her.

CHAPTER 4

THE BOGEYMAN

Who is that? What is he saying? I look away. I could be in a school yard. It is deathly quiet, eerily dark. I am terrified. I don't scream. I can't find my voice. Suddenly, needle-like drops gush onto the roof. It's so loud, and he starts yelling. I can't understand him. I feel his hands around my throat, like a vice. It makes me gasp. I go limp momentarily, and he loosens the grip around my neck. I gulp in air. Houses, faintly outlined in the distance, are not lit. There's no one there but him and me. I keep searching the space around me, panic stricken. It isn't until I look into his eyes, eyes that I can see in the black. I know…something bad is going to happen.

The dream was the first thing Mari thought about when she awakened in the morning. She re-oriented herself, and shakily remembered a faceless man with eyes hardened like black ice on asphalt. The clamminess of her skin caused her to shiver, so she pulled the covers tighter over her shoulders. Lifting her head she glanced at the bedside clock: *Ah, two-thirty a.m.* She concentrated her attention on the raindrops that formed and slid down the window, and fell back to sleep.

She reached for her journal. The dream seemed real, yet surreal. She titled it: Faceless Black Eyes. She scribbled words: school, rain, black houses, black eyes, hands around throat, going limp, no one else there.

Dreams and memories became constant reminders that there were things to be afraid of in the world. She ventured into childhood, and she could see precisely how one had spoken to her; the crumbs on the table, the scent of tea rising from the teapot when she rushed into the house, frightened by the old man with the shiny stop watch. Now this. The dream of someone, a person not envisioned-yet. She scanned the small room turned into office space, searching her mind for more words: *It's hard if you don't know where you are exactly, or who you are searching for.* She returned the journal to her desk drawer.

Mari studied the framed pictures of her family on the walls, and their cherished wedding pictures, sitting on one of the shelves of the cabinet next to her desk. They were lovely. Tilly was curled up on the russet love seat under the window. She smiled, willing her frazzled nerves to calm, and her thoughts to move forward.

At work the next morning, she discussed with Stan, how she would use her next column. She wanted to tap into the gut reactions of the men concerning the request that they submit to D.N.A. testing. The police were in the midst of the operation and what the community thought about it was circulating around town. Why not create an opportunity for discussion in the newspaper? She said to Stan, "This could reveal if men are feeling imposed upon, or if indeed they feel it's helping to narrow the scope of the investigation, or both. If the public is allowed to be involved somehow, it may help alleviate feelings of dread and helplessness." Without skipping a beat, he said, "And help you too"? She looked into his eyes, "Hmm, yes, you're dead on." Stan looked thoughtful, tipping his chair back. Finally, he moved forward and said, "I know your judgment is sound and that the guidelines would be in place as to what would be discussed. There will be those who will want to berate the police, for instance, or point their fingers at who they think the murderer is."

"Stan. I'd stress what the column is about, and make it abundantly clear as to what I would allow in print."

He nodded, "Go for it", and answered his ever ringing phone.

Mari hurried back to her enclosure that accommodated a desk in front of mounted shelves for the tons of book, newspapers, magazines, and folders she used for her work. She began formulating her column to elicit responses around the matter. As she worked, she couldn't help but let her husband's views intrude. I'm quite sure some men agreed with his position that he was against it.

The subject of requesting D.N.A. from the men who lived in the area did come up the past Saturday night. She and Sonny had met with her usually unruffled, easy-going younger brother, Malcolm, and his wife, Penny. As usual, Penny had seized the conversation with her favorite topic: herself. Her long perfect fingers charged the air as she elaborated about how well loved she was by her friends and co-workers, virtually everybody she had contact with. From experience, Mari let her talk, as did the family. They understood her quest for validation, that constant grasping for attention. Still, for some reason, tonight, it was annoying, as it sometimes was. Mari thought: *It isn't my job to validate her.* She patted her hand.

Sonny was getting loud, drowning Penny out, "I've got a big problem with it. Just because they can't do their job, doesn't mean they can invade my privacy. I'm not allowing THE MAN to just think he can butt into my life so they don't have to do anything that might look like work. I'm innocent. I don't have to do it."

Malcolm resisted, "I've got no problem co-operating with the police. In fact I plan to do it next week. If it helps in their investigation I'm willing to do it. It's murder Sonny. Why not help? I don't agree that they're not doing their job. This is one of the ways they're doing it. It definitely narrows the field. They're not going to have to waste time looking at anybody they don't have to. I don't bel…"

His voice rising quickly, Sonny interrupted Malcolm, "I'm innocent and if I'm not a suspect they'd better leave me alone. They can't be allowed to hassle us like that"!

"Come on. We're supposed to be having fun. There's a good group playing at that new bar in town. Let's go for drinks and dance, dance, dance", Penny wiggled her shoulders. Mari was all for it. She nuzzled Sonny's neck, "Good idea. Let's have some fun. A little slow dancing maybe." Exhaling loudly, Sonny grinned.

They paid their dinner bill and climbed into Penny's car as she didn't drink. Arriving at the bar, they all helped jockey a parking spot in the bar's lot. Sonny opened the door for them and followed them inside. The light coloured walls, except for red brick on the opposite wall from the bar, were decorated with stained glass wall hangings. The contrast brightened the area. Round dark tables were closely placed to each other. People jostled each other when they sat or got up. Inside the parameter of tables and chairs, the dance floor was elbow to elbow with people, mostly women.

The top 40's music blared, and the men were barely inside the bar when Mari and Penny made their way onto the overflowing dance floor. Mari watched as Sonny found a table and strode to the bar to order drinks. She looked back to Penny who was getting really wild, flailing her arms, nearly pushing some poor girl behind her into other dancers.

Mari leaned in and yelled, "Penny! Whoa! Watch that girl behind you. You're not the only one here." She smiled at the person behind Penny and glanced again into the bar area. Her eyes locked onto a familiar face. It took but a few seconds for the realization to set in. It was that guy who refused to leave her table that one night at the downtown bar. He was by himself, looking women over on the floor, then his eyes flickered insolently into hers. She felt her heart jolt but she turned away from him and excused herself to Penny, "Going to the washroom. I'll be right back."

She looked for the on-duty officer. As she approached him, she thought: *What'll I say? I hope he doesn't think me silly or hysterical.* After introductions, she detailed the experience she had with this guy, "There's a man here that bothered me at the K House one evening. He stood at my table, woodenly-it's the only way that I can describe it, except when he moved to block my view of other people. When I told him that I did not want company, he mimicked what I said, word for word, then continued talking in this monotone, almost to himself. And he would not leave. By then I was getting really nervous. Finally, I got up and took my drink and sat at the bar. The waitress noticed what was going on, but she said he hangs out there, and implied he was harmless. I got a very different feel."

"Point him out to me." Locating the spot where he stood, she didn't see him. Frustrated, she looked up at the officer, and said, "He's disappeared."

"Can you describe him"?

"He's about five feet eight, slim, short, dark hair, and his eyes were black, devoid of any emotion whatsoever." The officer jotted all the information down, and he said, "You've provided good info. Can you think of anything else that could identify him? Tattoos and such."

She took a moment to think and said, "No."

"If, at some point, you do, call the department. I'm Officer Robertson." He handed her a card that included his extension on it.

Glancing at it, she smiled, "I will. Thank you."

"No. Thank you. In light of what's happened in this community, it helps us tremendously when the public is vigilant, and they report anything suspicious or different." He reached out and while shaking her hand, he said, "Enjoy the rest of your evening."

Mari walked back to join the others. The night was relatively young and determined to enjoy what was left of it, she decided not to mention it to anyone, just yet. On the dance floor, Penny was dancing with the group around her, her hips pushing against the tug of her skirt. She smiled at Mari and pulled her in. Near closing time they went to a nearby bistro, and after ordering coffee and sandwiches, Sonny piped up, "I meant to ask. Where did you go when you bolted off the dance floor"?

"I saw that creep that bothered me at the "K", so I went to the cop stationed at the door. I told him all about it and gave him a description. By the time I led him to where he was standing, he'd left."

"Why didn't you come get me"?

"I didn't want you mixing with him, and maybe get hurt. The police should handle matters like this."

He asserted, "You underestimate me. I can handle those situations"?

Exasperated, Mari said, "I handled it. I went and told the officer. In cases like this, the police should do it", she repeated.

"Hey guys. We've obviously missed the story. What happened"? Malcolm asked.

"Oh sorry." Mari proceeded to fill them in, and Penny said, "He sounds scary. If it had happened to me, I'd always wonder if he was the one who murdered that girl."

"Yeah, I do wonder. I try to put it out of my mind." Quickly, she added, "You know, it really angers me that it's all the more monstrous that a murder was committed in a small community like ours, where most people know everybody else, where friendliness is easier and everybody says hi. God, it's unfathomable that it could be someone who lives here."

Malcolm commented, "Is everywhere like this? Violent crime is seeping into so many communities, big and small alike."

"It's so scary." Penny said. They collected their stuff, paid their bill and left.

Early at work on Monday morning Mari set to organizing responses to her "questionnaire." She received lots of responses, mostly pro. This, in spite of reports that some feel that this is a serious breach of privacy. It comes at a time when mass surveillance and the accumulation of personal information is gathered through computers, phone records, and dragnets for D.N.A. or "Blooding."

The men who gladly co-operated, explained why. One guy named Pete wrote in: If this happened to my daughter, I would applaud this approach. It would exclude many males in the community. Those that did not co-operate would be 'persons of interest'. And, it would allow police the time to broaden their search inside or outside the community.

Another said: We all understand that police services are understaffed and over loaded. I agree with Pete about allowing the police to utilize all at their disposal, in order to gain time in working to solve crimes.

The few men who disagreed did so stridently. George wrote: I was one of those guys who refused. "Big Brother" has intruded into our lives-through their massive surveillance techniques. And the law still allows us to refuse to provide D.N.A. Time might come when we'll not be able to. They can damn well butt out. Have they heard of the Charter of Rights!?

One police officer wrote in. A part of it said: We're not trying to put any type of shadow on democracy. Requesting that people provide their D.N.A is simply one part of a thorough investigation.

Life just fucking sucks. Mari, be home, please. On the fourth ring, before the machine picked it up, she was ready to hang up, "Son of a bitch, where ur you"? she said aloud. Mari picked the receiver up, out of breath from dashing into the house from the far end of the yard.

"Hello", she breathed.

"Hi, where er you"?

"In the yard, pulling off dead petunias and watering. The yard definitely needs it."

"I wish I had yur problems, sis." *She sounds drunk.*

"What's up April"? Her cheeky little sister grew up susceptible to addictions and her weaknesses were 'dudes and booze', to quote April. When sober, she had a soft, vulnerable side, and she looked it in a sort of skittish, deer in the headlights way. This was her other side.

"My fucking life, that's what. I went to the bar to finish some paper work and it was quiet so I had a drink, okay, so I had a six pack." Mari tensed.

"I started thinking about my life and I got so fuckin' depressed. I still miss Matt, and I can't get motivated to paint. I start en end up scrapping the thing, then I stare at the goddamned easel like it's something I don't even know what it is. Haven't sold or even shown anything in two years. It's 'tupid. Just a sec." April dropped the receiver. Mari could feel herself bristle as she heard her call her bartender to bring another drink. She heard the receiver clunk as she picked it back up, "Hi, guess who."

In spite of herself Mari grinned, "April, good thing you're at your bar. They wouldn't serve you anywhere else." It was out before she could recapture it. She heard an intake of breath.

"Oh great, now you sound sircastic like Fiona."

Mari felt bad about her ill-timed remark, "I'm sorry April. What's bothering you? The last time we talked you were up. You'd begun seeing that guy and things were great. What's his name"?

"What's his name is only in it for one thing, and for one person only, himself, just him."

"So…explain."

"I mean he doesn't really want a relationship, somethin' casual, is how he puts it."

"Oh April, you deserve better than that."

"Like what"!

"You deserve someone who values you, who's proud to know you, who respects you…"

April had trouble getting the words to come together, "What? Like being in love, like I knew…what that was…one time."

Mari interjected, "Yes, like with Matt."

"Oh, now I know what you're thinkin', that I should stop seein' him. He's fun at least, pretty much a dude. An' I need a fuckin' few laughs right now. Fer some reason I think about Matt a lot. I know why he dumped me. It's because I drink too much and I was so mean to him. And, I used to paint. Nothin' happening. I'm just confused."

"You don't sound confused to me. You know exactly what's going on. Listen April, why don't you come over for dinner tomorrow night. Sonny won't be home. Just me and you. We'll talk. What do you say"?

"Oo-o-h, souns real good. It's not busy here on Tuesday nights. Can get away easy."

"Great, so…" The phone went dead. Mari looked at the receiver and shook her head.

She went back to her gardening. Watering always helped her relax and re-group: *I'll have to remind her. She'll forget. This is a good sign though. She's talking things out, at least trying to!*

Mari wondered if April would ever admit that she needs help with her drinking. She knew that it has to be confronted and dealt with, or nothing will change: *She's such a sweet girl, till she gets drunk. Then, I don't know her. Not to mention, the character of the guys she dates. What kinds of situations does she find herself in? It's distressing to think about.*

Then Mari ruminated about the tension between April and Fiona. Deep down, I'm sure they love each other, but April always felt that Fiona treated her like she didn't know what she was doing, that she was scatterbrained, sloppy, and irresponsible. Fiona's body language and tone around April always signaled that she was so much more together. Mari's head swelled: *Wow, if April only knew. What an equalizer.* The struggle that went on between them worried her. She was afraid that they would turn against each other. It could take just one more slight, one more heedless action on April's side that could make Fiona turn on her heel and walk away. Or, April, in an inebriated condition, could say something unforgivable, in Fiona's mind. She loved them both, and the uneasiness she felt increased when they were all together.

Tilly, so relaxed to the point that she seemed to melt into looking boneless, managed to meow when Mari looked down at her. Affectionately, she rubbed her fawn ears. She was a Siamese mix with gorgeous blue eyes, and while she was gentle and cuddly, she could be demanding. She demonstrated that she wanted attention by tapping Mari on the shoulder, lightly-at first. Licking one her white "booty paws", she stopped to look at Mari, sort of like she was waiting for her next cue. Mari was thoughtful, "You're absolutely right Tilly. What this family needs is a barbecue. Just seems right." She surveyed the yard. The multitude of petunias were pushing themselves open almost day by day, and the pink and purple, along with the red geraniums, blended beautifully. The summer breeze was pushing its way toward autumn…and still so lively.

Lots of phoning back and forth later, almost everybody wanted to pitch in, and they finally settled on the following weekend.

Long after dinner, Tilly followed Mari into the garden once again. Mari held a cold Corona in her lap, a lime wedge stuck into the bottleneck. It had gotten a bit cooler and she slipped her arms into her sweater, enjoying the wind that billowed through. She slowly sipped on her beer, and it was getting quite late, but she didn't move. She let her thoughts roam. Lost in her trance, she did not hear the shuffling of feet past her high wooden fence. It brought her too and alarmed, she asked who was there. The voice answered, "Your neighbour. Connor. I was just out for a walk. Sorry to startle you."

"Well, you know."

"Yeah, you can't be too careful. I've been reading your column, interesting stuff, what guys are feeling about the whole question of testing? Sonny and I talked about it a bit. I'm also one of the ones that resents the intrusiveness."

"Really? The thing is, you do have the right to refuse. What's the concern"?

"Innocent people are being hassled. With all the science and technology open to them, why are they doing this"?

"That's right, they're using all they've got to find this guy AND you can decline."

"But that could change. Anyway, this obviously is not a good topic in your house."

"It's not. We don't discuss it anymore."

"It naturally follows that women are for it."

"Not necessarily. Many men cooperated. Most women want it to happen though. I would concede to that. Women are scared and want the killer put away. Too bad Canada abolished capital punishment."

"I can't say that I blame you. It's a cruel and despicable crime. Well, it's a great evening. I'm gonna finish my walk. Besides, I'm talking to the back of a fence here."

Laughing at that she said, "Sorry. Oh, before you go. We're having a barbecue this coming weekend, on Saturday night, and we're inviting a few neighbors. Come on by. Just bring what you're drinking."

"Sounds good, but I'm expecting family from out of town. I probably won't be able to do it. I'll try. Goodnight."

"Yeah, goodnight." She listened to him drag and shuffle his feet. She moved toward the door. *He bugs me. A bit weird sometimes, and chauvinistic. He thinks women should not intrude in male dominated fields, for instance. Thinks they're not equipped to take care of others, or even themselves.* She stood up, held a squirming cat, her empty beer bottle, and headed for bed.

She left work early the next day to shop for the things she needed for dinner with April. Once in the door she called her at the bar and found that April was already on her way over. With a quick shower to pick her up and a glass of wine to inspire her she headed for the kitchen. Sonny, who was required to work out of town sometimes, called while she was sautéing onions. He told her he would be home Thursday night, one day later than what had originally been talked about. Sulking, she said, "Darn it Sonny, you seem to be spending more and more time at work. I miss you. Besides, you seem so tired most of the time. Why are you working more hours?" She heard the strain in his voice: "Mari, I know, but our sales have increased and besides the everyday pace of selling, I'm following up, keeping customers happy. My boss expects it. Just remember, I love you."

"I love you too."

"You're just saying it because I did" comicalness returning to his voice.

"Am not."

"Are too." They both started laughing.

"I have to go. April is on her way over for dinner and I've barely started. I'll see you Thursday night."

"Bye hon."

Dinner with her sister was comfortable, even though their last conversation was fresh in her mind. Then, seemingly out of nowhere came the question: "Mari, why do I have the feeling that a lot of people avoid me at gatherings, at the bar even"?

"Why do you think April"?

"You agree, people do", shot out as a statement rather than a question. Mari snagged the moment, deciding that now that April was asking, she was going to tell her. She thought about how people often reacted angrily when their confronted, and April would definitely feel confronted, but April had brought up the fact that she felt cold-shouldered by people. It looked like she might be ready to hear. Mari felt a barrage of words coming, "Yes, they do. Ever since you were a teenager, you drank more than most of your friends. As you got older it got to be more than a good time. You relied on it to pick you up or to avoid dealing with problems. Whatever, you always end up drunk, like when you called me from the bar last night. It's a way of life for you. They refuse to serve you in bars sometimes, you compromise yourself in certain situations with guys, and you don't remember when these things happen a lot of the time. We worry. And, you're hard to get along with when you're drinking. Your temper flares." She stopped, looking at April. She couldn't tell what she was thinking. "And, what's really embarrassing is when you start to look disheveled and you sit with your skirt hiked up to your crotch, your legs apart, your mouth slack, and you become incoherent. It's ugly April." Mari felt good to have pulled it all out of her.

Mari knew that honest communication is a good thing, but to actually level with someone when the subject matter might get their back up, you wonder if it will backfire. *Will April walk away from me?* She kept eye contact with her, and waited.

"Whoa, can you be more fucking honest? That bad?" She was wide-eyed.

"Yes April, that bad. But, what's even more important are things that happen that are really scary. Like when you drive drunk. One night I ran into you at the bar. I was meeting Syl for a drink. You were at a table alone." April mumbled, "Don't remember."

"I sat with you until Syl came. The bartender came over to take my order, and when you indicated that you wanted another one, she refused to serve you. You picked up your keys and stumbled to the parking lot. I followed you and watched you struggle to find the door lock to open your car door. I tried to talk you into taking a cab, or let me take you home, but you refused. Finally, you got the door open and drove off. I had my cell phone and asked you to call me when you got home. You were ten minutes away. You didn't call. I was frantic. I said good-bye to Syl and drove by your place. The car was there. It was quite the relief. But then, I was upset with myself. I wondered why I didn't wrestle you to the ground for those damned keys."

To ease the embarrassment of her sketchy, almost total lack of memory of that night, and the shame over hearing the truth so frankly delivered, April quipped, "Got a drink?" Mari didn't laugh.

"Okay, not funny. I brought this up because I want to talk, I want to change. And, don't think I haven't been investigating what's available to me, 'she took a breath' I've already had an interview with this person who runs the substance abuse program in the city." Mari shot up from her chair, went to April and gave her a big hug. A tear slipped down April's cheek.

As she watched Mari sit down, she said, "I knew what you guys thought but I excused myself saying, hey, my friends drink more than I do, told myself lots of things, actually. Well, they don't let you make excuses at the rehab place. And I know what Matt saw and I feel really ashamed. He tried to get me to see how much drinking governed my life and how it affected us together. Oh God, I miss Matt so much. He understood so much about me, and he took so much shit." The tear turned into a flood.

Mari waited. "Is he the main reason you've progressed to getting help?" April nodded.

"You know April, straighten yourself out and maybe you can go back there. Matt might be ready to listen if you're taking steps to turn yourself around. I run into him sometimes. He always asks about you. He misses you and how you guys used to paint together. How you two really gelled."

"Yeah, we did. He did say to call him when I did something. I was so pissed off with him then, I said, "Asshole, do this"! she gestured with her middle finger.

"Oh really! That's good."

"I'm not proud of myself."

"Listen, when or if you ever get another chance to get back with Matt, tell him how sorry you are. 'I'm sorry' is a remarkably powerful phrase when it comes from the heart. Tell him as often as he needs to hear it."

"I would. I really would."

"Tell me more about your meeting."

"Well, after the interview I took a test that reveals the severity of the problem. Get this, I have ALL the symptoms of a major drinking problem, 'Mari winced'. She showed me around the center. Then, she took me back to the office and told me that I am a prime candidate for treatment there. First, they detoxify you and after that they determine the course of treatment. Some people can learn to drink in moderation. Others have to abstain."

Mari was getting impatient. "So? What else"?

"The lady, Ginny is her name, with a name like that she's in the right field," she smiled a little sarcastically.

"Stop that. What else"?

"She strongly suggested that I check myself in."

"And"? Mari felt like she was pulling teeth.

"I'm gonna do it. I've got two people working for me who can handle the bar for a short period of time. It takes four to five days to detoxify and determine the treatment. Maybe, you could drop in at the bar to help a bit, you know, check on things for me."

"Of course I would. I'm so happy for you. And proud."

"Happy! It's not going to be a picnic, Mari. Ginny assured me on that score."

"April. You know we'll be there for you."

"We"?

"Fiona, your brother, the family."

"I haven't spoken to anyone else about this, especially Fiona. I get so pissed off at her. She thinks I'm some kind of godless heathen." Mari grinned.

"Listen, don't worry about that now. Take care of one thing at a time. I know she can be judgmental and stubborn, but she'll come around, especially when she sees you fighting to pull your life together. She'll support you. You'll see. She might even take care of some things, like your plants or something."

"I don't want to tell her about this. Would you talk to her? I'd really appreciate it."

"You bet. Anyway, your only concern for the time being is you. One thing at a time." April looked like the world had just been hoisted from her shoulders. She started to cry with her head on her folded forearms. Mari pulled her up and April put her head on Mari's shoulder. She straightened up as she stopped crying, squaring her shoulders.

"Thanks for being here. This was so hard, but I knew I had to tell you soon, before I disappeared from the scene. Didn't want to scare anybody. Listen, I've got to go. I told the girls I'd be back early. I'll call you when I'm ready." Mari walked with her to the door and waited until she got to her car. April called out, "Great dinner, thanks." They waved and Mari watched her crazy, bronze and gold head drive away. As she walked back to the kitchen to begin clearing the dishes she suddenly threw her arms up and thought: *Wow, I did not expect that.* She mulled everything in her mind, feeling hopeful for what April had to face, but she felt trepidation too. She sat with her face in her hands for a few minutes, worried about how this was going to turn out.

After cleaning up she called Fiona. She told her about April. "Whoa, like that'll work. She is so enmeshed in that bar lifestyle of hers, and her crazy friends, and she's never cared about what anybody thinks about it." Mari was fed up and tired.

"Would you listen to yourself? You know Fiona, you're derisive of our little sister at every opportunity. What has she ever done to you? Just be glad that she's taken some initiative and has actually planned this out. She needs support, not insults and criticism. Let's call it a day"! Fiona, silent while Mari talked, was silent a few seconds longer.

"Oh piss off", Fiona sputtered.

"Okay, is that all"?

"Just give me a minute, will you"? ...more silence.

"Okay, I've not realized that I'm that bad about April, and I've never thought of the possibility that I might be letting loose on her that much. Of course, I'm going to support her through this."

"And water her plants, and feed her new fish, Sea Biscuit"?

"Oh Lord, what kind of fish"?

"I think it's one of those Siamese Fighting Fish, I think."

"Fighting fish, oh, that's just great."

"Are you kidding? They are lovely. Lots of people have 'em. They're the size of gold fish, not dangerous, "she chuckled loudly." They have long flowing fins, brilliantly colored. Hers is navy and yellow. Really pretty. They're fed a couple specks of food a day."

"Okay, I've seen them in pet stores. Just call me when she goes."

"I'll call you, or April will. So, are YOU okay"?

"Oh yeah, everything is fine with me. Warren hasn't bothered me about anything and the lawyer assures me everything is going well. Anyway, you can count on me, for April, I mean."

"I know, talk to you soon. Bye-bye."

Rubbing at the furrow between her eyes, she dropped into her chair in the living room, feeling drained. Yet, the recent situations involving her sisters sustained her. Fiona disclosed the hidden aspects of her life, and followed through on her decision to divorce Warren. April came face to face with her alcoholism. She determined that she shouldn't feel irate or gloomy because they are working to make changes. She had to take her own advice fully, about being accepting and understanding. She would support them to the end.

She put the last dish away and climbed into bed, looking at family photos of them as little kids. We were so innocent and receptive to the world and each other. One picture showed them playing hopscotch: *We sure look happy.*

This turn of events made Mari's mood surge. They'll engage each other more, something she had wanted to happen. God knows we all need each other in a world that is tough and threatening.

She put the album on the night stand, dabbed at her eyes with the back of her hand, and turned off the lamp.

CHAPTER 5

HE COULD BE...

Waking from a sound sleep to an insistent phone, Mari squinted at the clock: *It's 5:00 a.m. Who would that be?* She rushed to the adjacent room to pick it up. It was Fiona. She was crying hysterically, "Mari, I've been broken into. A note was scrawled on my dresser. It said **Sorry I missed you bitch!** A nurse called in sick and I replaced her for four hours..."

"Fiona! I can't understand you. Slow down."

"Oh God! After filling in for someone, I went home. I didn't go into the bedroom. I was exhausted. I kicked off my shoes and fell on the couch. I fell asleep. Early in the morning, I woke up and went into the bedroom to change." She took a few moments to catch her breath, and Mari was clutching the phone so hard, her fingers nails dug into her hand, "Okay, go on."

She shrieked, "It was in shambles, things broken, even the mirror, and the screen was ripped open. I was shaking so hard I could hardly phone the police. Mari, why didn't he wait for me to come home? He'll come back, he'll come back. He's playing with me. I know it!"

"Is anyone with you right now?"

"A police woman is here. Carla. And other officers."

"I'm coming over to talk to her. I'll be there as soon as I can."

The phone went dead. Frozen with fear, Mari gathered her keys and left the house. When she got there, she took one look at Fiona and took in the dramatic change in her. She was actually shivering, shaken to the core, her eyes red and swollen from crying. Mari hugged her tight and

51

was so shocked when she looked at the mess in the bedroom, from the doorway, after Carla cautioned her not to go in, the only female officer there. She introduced herself to Mari. In her excited state, she rushed her words, "I'm Mari, as you must know. Have you any idea who could have done this? It's easy to recognize that the murderer could be linked to this. How can this be?"

"I wish I could answer your questions, Mari, but we're in the middle of the murder investigation, and there isn't much we can discuss, just yet. And, of course, we don't know what we have here until forensics can test what's being collected." That either meant that there wasn't very much in the way of evidence at all, or she wasn't able to give her information. It was frustrating, how she was thinking right then, her thoughts disjointed, but she knew that her growing frustration stemmed from fear and her inexperience in such matters. Mari stood there, her hand on her chest.

So scared, Fiona felt her house grow airless, her breathing stifled. She couldn't talk and she just looked around wide eyed. It felt strange to have her house filled with officers, poking around with their gloves on, dusting for fingerprints, and labelling items seized. It seemed to take forever, the minutes dragging by. She listened to the officer explain what was happening.

"If you watch TV, you are aware of forensics. The process starts with the collection of data, as they are doing now. If we find fingerprints, we may have a match in our data base, and we may have D.N.A. Along with the pictures we are taking, well, lots can be determined. Outside, they are looking for footprints, tire impressions, or something that may have been dropped, snagged clothing while he was climbing in. Anything. The screen or window sill could have blood on them as he could have scratched his hands coming in. It'll all take a while. You may call me anytime with questions, or to talk. Please give me your phone number before I leave." Mari gave her the information and Officer Carla jotted it down on her pad. Carla then walked over to speak to Fiona with a hand covering hers. Softly, she said, "I can only imagine how violated you feel, first by the intruder, then with officers milling about in your home, searching through your belongings. It must feel cold and intrusive. But, we must do this." Fiona nodded. Carla made her way out. Soon finished with their poking around and making notes, the other officers also left, except for one. He pulled a card from his pants pocket and handed it to Mari, "I am Officer Robertson, and I urge you to call the station any time. I'll be available to both of you. Whatever comes to you, anything at all, call us." He shook their hands and said goodbye.

Mari urged Fiona to go to bed in the spare room, and she sat on the bed and soothed her until she fell asleep. She brought a chair in from the living room, and dozed off and on. Fiona slept fitfully and Mari comforted her whenever she awoke. When she regained calmness, enough to be left a while, Mari went home to start dinner preparations for herself and Sonny. Periodically, she called Fiona, or Fiona called her, as agreed.

As she was placing the un-dressed salad in the fridge Sonny came through the kitchen doorway. Swinging the fridge door shut she clung to him. He laughed, hugging her. Moments later he stepped back and looked into her stricken face. Not knowing what to think he led her to the darkening living room and sat her down, "What's wrong?" Between tears, she said, "Fiona had to work a double shift. When she got home, she was exhausted and fell asleep on the couch."

"Mari, for Christ's sake, is she okay?"

"Physically, yes, but she's been through quite the ordeal. While she was at work a man slashed her bedroom screen, got in, and destroyed the room. He left a note that said: Sorry I missed you bitch. She called police. I'm not sure how many units they sent out there, but there were lots of police investigating…" her voice trailed off.

"What else?" he insisted.

"I don't know Sonny. Just that they're doing their investigation. They will keep in touch."

Later, still shaken, and not wanting to be left alone, not even long enough for Sonny to shower, she joined him. She winced at the sight of his hands as he scrubbed his soapy face. They were scraped and raw.

"Sonny, what happened to you!!?"

"Jesus, what?"

"Your hands. Did you have a fight?" Rinsing off his face he said, "I had car trouble."

"Where?"

"I was on highway 2, on my way to meet a potential customer and my car broke down. I couldn't find my cell. Nobody would stop, it was dark, but I decided I'd better try to fix it. I got frustrated and banged my hands up."

"You can't fix cars."

"Tell me about it." She didn't laugh.

"Where was your cell phone?"

"Since I usually keep it in my brief case, that's where I looked for it, but it wasn't there. I found it later in my briefcase after all, after the cops drove by, luckily, and they called the tow company. They took me to a shop where it was fixed. Apparently gas doesn't flow well if you have a plugged fuel filter. A couple hundred dollars later, all I know is that it's fixed." He kissed her on the forehead and dropped it.

But, it wasn't dropped in her mind. Fiona's bedroom was destroyed. *Whoever did it may have injured…No! No! What am I thinking? But his hands…*

Her thoughts shifted to Sonny once being described as lion-like, by his mother. He has beauty and strength, is sociable, but he always reminds us that he is king with his knee-quaking roar. She found the analogy funny then. Not now. *Would he hurt anyone?*

Mari thought back to when she was a kid and she was told by a teacher that the devil could get into your head and sway you to do or think wrong things. She was betraying her own husband, even if they were just thoughts. Sonny was kind and good. He was home safe. They would spend the whole weekend together. She threw off the rest.

By Saturday night everybody was outwardly calm and the barbecue went on as planned. The whole family gathered as well as some neighbours. The day turned sunny and breezy by noon, and the only dark cloud hanging over their day was Fiona. She barely functioned. They'd look at her, thankful that she was physically whole. That, at least.

A few days went by, and Mari unquestionably knew how wrong she was when she suspected her own husband of hurting her sister. But, she continued to fret about their relationship. What bothered her was how much time he was away, working or playing with his band buddies. She kept going back to her conversation with Fiona when they were away for the weekend. Fiona made it plain enough what she thought about Sonny's flirtatious ways. It made Mari more aware that she may have something to be worried about.

One evening Sonny took an early evening bath, and as she entered to finger comb her hair, he said, "Wash my back Mari," he grinned. She grabbed the bath mitt and told him about the great lamb chops with mint they were going to have. She also decided she would open up to him about the concerns she had.

"I want to detour through the bedroom." She kissed him longingly and he chuckled through the kiss. He loved it when she was like this.

She ran to check on dinner. Quickly, she lowered the oven temperature to warm. She went to the bedroom, closed the blinds, and disrobed. She felt that once relaxed, through intimacy, he would be receptive to her. A few minutes later they were naked on the bed and their eager hands touched everywhere. Later, after dinner, they took their coffee into the living room and placed their mugs on the shiny coasters on the coffee table, sitting opposite each other. She edged around what she wanted to talk about, nervous about where to begin. He finally said, "Mari, come on, talk." Still a bit tongue tied she came out with, "Sonny, do you love me"?

"What the hell kind of question is that? You know I love you. What's wrong?"

"You're always gone and you seem so preoccupied and short lately, with me, with everything."

"I know and I'm sorry." Taking her hand he continued, "I'm working more and I get tired."

"If it was just that…something has been bothering me."

A little impatiently, he said "Yeah?"

She took a deep breath, "It really hurts when you flirt with other women."

"What do you mean?" he said, suddenly disdainful.

"You watch other women all the time. At parties you make a beeline 'she shot her arm out' for an attractive woman and you spend a lot of time with her, flattering her, being overly attentive. It makes me feel insignificant and embarrassed." She clasped her hands together.

"I look at other women, so shoot me." Momentarily dismayed, she was not going to be dissuaded. Stunned and hurt by his dismissal, she came out sounding angry. "You just don't look at other women Sonny. You flirt. It offends me. It hurts me."

"Well, could it be that you're insecure?"

"Don't turn this on me. You're the insecure one, if you need the attention of women that badly."

He stood up and walked a few steps around the coffee table, before facing her, "What IS this? The next thing I hear is that you're accusing me of cheating!" His face was reddening.

"I am not accusing you of anything."

"That's what it sounds like!"

"Sonny, let me finish. Do you remember Dirty Dancing Big Hair?"

He went back to the couch and sat, leaning forward with clasped hands, "Who?"

"The woman who works at your office and was at that wedding for your buddy. She danced all over you. You didn't put her off."

"Oh yeah, her, she was drunk. I didn't think anything of it. The point is, you were there. It's not like I did it behind your back." He kept looking away, out the window...

"Sonny! Why aren't you looking at me? And that's not the point. You were evasive, not telling me she was married, but separated, and you knew that stuff."

"Why would you care? You did not even know her."

"I know you! Anyway, I asked you questions about her and you put me off." Ready to cry she continued, "Usually we can joke about things like that. You didn't want to talk about her."

"I don't remember that. It must not have been important. I don't know. Even if I do flirt, we come home together. What is the big deal?"

"The big deal is that it bothers me. And, you're not being the least bit sensitive to my feelings. I think you find other women more attractive than me. It gets me to thinking, you know like that other situation, when that guy bothered me at the bar, that really scary guy, and you said, if he acts like that with me in public, what he would do in private. It's not the same thing, but sort of. What would you do behind my back?" Sonny took his time. She couldn't read his thoughts.

He finally responded, "Apples and oranges Mari. Could we discuss this some other time?" He walked away.

She was angrier now and she followed him into the kitchen. Keeping her voice even, she said emphatically, "What! When it's convenient for you. Sonny, what if I behaved that way, flirting men up, and you were the husband at the party?" When he didn't reply, she walked out of the room and back into the bedroom and sat on the bed, still tousled from lovemaking. All the stress that had built up over everything that had affronted her lately, ran threw her mind: Fiona's confessions, April's drinking, Fiona's break in, now this with Sonny. She cried into her hands, not wanting him to hear.

Trying to destress she got ready for bed. And waited. Sonny didn't come in. Her last thought before she finally fell asleep was, in writer's parlance: *To be continued.*

Fiona's ordeal had to take precedence over everything in the next few days, in spite of her own issues. Having spent the bulk of her time with Fiona the past two weeks, she thought: *She's not doing well. She's so pale.*

"Mari, you just don't know what it's like to know that some man broke into your home, someone who is threatening your life. I keep seeing that note," her voice a whisper, her arms folded in front of her weakened body, like she was shielding herself.

"I can only imagine how that feels." She held Fiona's hand.

"Does he watch the house? Could he be watching me when I'm home or at work?" she said, fidgeting with her tea cup, "The doctor has me on a different anti-depressant, one that he hopes will let me sleep."

"I hope so. You really need your rest. How is work?"

"Okay. Management has been very understanding. I needed those two weeks off, but now it's helping that I'm back to work. It forces me to get up in the morning, and sick people have a way of taking your mind off yourself."

"That's good. Speaking of not getting enough sleep, I've been deprived of that these past few days. A half of a sleeping pill helps. But, I know we're not the only ones. This town is scared. It's visceral. You can see it in people's faces up town. Smiles aren't as free, and you can overhear people talking about what the police could know. It's that time of the year that humidity isn't high, but people don't have their doors and windows open as much. It's like outside is evil. But I understand, they can't be as scared as you."

"Or Kristel's family. It's like a shroud has fallen over us, and it keeps getting heavier." Fiona responded. Mari put her arm around her and changed the subject. She didn't want Fiona's situation and the murder to be the last thing they talked about during her visit. Also she hadn't told her about her dreadful dream. It had begun to recur. She didn't want to let on how disturbed she was, because Fiona thought of her as a source of strength.

The dream almost always lay on her waking mind. It spooked her. She felt that if she knew what the man looked like, she would know who the killer was, as farfetched as that was. And, just before dropping off to sleep some nights, she saw the unnamed man slashing at her. Most nights now, she had a cup of caffeine free herbal tea, or a glass of red wine, and she read poetry, until she was settled enough to sleep. She looked at Fiona and thought: *Would they ever find him?*

She stood to go and hugged her sister good-bye. At the door, she said, "The best thing we can do is to keep in constant touch. Call me anytime. You have my work number. Use it."

As she drove off, she made a mental note about talking to Fiona about having the landlord improve the lighting outside her front walkway as the police had suggested. She turned her attention to the leaves that were just beginning to change, a promise of brilliance. *They'll catch him.* Low scudding clouds formed and she sped the rest of the way home. Days passed...

He climbed into his vehicle, thinking: *I have to get a newspaper, see what's in it.* The driver ahead of him was straddling the line, "Stupid fuck, get in one lane," he hissed. Aggressively hugging the vehicle when he passed him, he pulled his cigarette from his mouth and yelled, "What are you looking at, you stupid old fucker! Old man!"

Ah, have to take my time anyway. It's a nice night for a slow drive, he inwardly sneered. Running Fiona's name over and over in his mind, he saw that her car was not there. Squinting, he noticed that the screen at the side of the house was fixed and the window closed up tight. Her doors are probably better secured. "*Fuck!*" He rubbed his left hand, dragged on his cigarette, and picked up speed. He didn't want to attract attention, even knowing that neighbours were not located close to each other out here.

Mari had been thinking about ways to reach out to the public about their feelings of hopelessness about the murderer being found. People talked in vain about the brutal facts of the murder, and many despaired about the possibility that he wouldn't be apprehended. In spite of how forensic science had exploded in scope and was a huge advantage in catching killers, you still had people grumbling about police procedures, and inexperienced small town police seriously lacking capability. It seemed that a good number of people saw the killer as the proverbial needle in a haystack, and she wanted to inspire a more positive light.

Upon arriving to work in the morning, she met Stan in the break room. Over her first coffee of the day, she talked to him about public perception concerning how the police were handling the murder case.

"Yeah, I'm aware of the grumblings."

"Well, it's frustrating. If the police are ticketing someone for speeding, they chant that the police are using their time ineffectively, and just hassling people. If the police are working with persistence around the clock they're either unaware of that or don't care much. One guy who lives on the next street from ours, told my sister in law that he saw some guy in a truck acting suspiciously near Fiona's road, and he didn't report it. He said, "It was probably some curiosity seeker, wanting to catch a peek at Fiona or her house, so what's the point. The cops in this small town don't know what they're doing anyway."

Stan exclaimed, "You're kidding me! He's an idiot. He's the exception. I know it makes you crazy since your sister is a victim. Mari, I know that you're saying you want the community and the police to work together... but I don't know. People are either vigilant or they're not, and complainers will always complain about the police. Right thinkers will always look out for each other, and help. And that is what we both should concentrate on. Not to mention, we have to be sensitive to the parent's feelings about how we say things in the paper, for instance."

"Of course, I'm sensitive to the family of the murdered girl. And, as a matter of fact, I came up today with a broad question that would elicit ideas. What about this approach?"

She pointed to her computer screen and Stan rounded her desk to read the question posed.

In view of the fact that violent crime is on the rise in most communities, how can the police and the public be motivated to work together productively?"

"Okay, that's good. Start with that."

He walked away and then turned back, hands in his pockets, unfolding thoughts that filled his head since the murder. His voice took on a faraway quality.

"Mari, I think murder viciously assaults each and every fiber a human is composed of. I mean…violent death has its own face. I wonder if people who have been murdered ever achieve peace."

"My feelings coincide with yours about violent death, but I worry more about their last moments. It's difficult to imagine what their depth of terror and agony is. Do they wish for death to free them?"

"Maybe. It's unbearable to think about. I've got work to do." He walked away.

Letters destined for her department came in on and off each week, so she walked to her mail slot and pulled a piece of paper scrunched at the back. Hmm, I wonder how long this has been here. It simply had a name and phone number on it for her to call.

She punched in the number and a woman answered, "Hello, Lori here."

"Hi. You left a message for The Write Thing. It's Mari speaking."

She exclaimed that she headed some newly formed group of plus sized women, and proudly announced that they had a play called Fat Pig. They were hoping Mari would help promote it. She thought: *Good Lord. Fat Pig!? What kind of name is that?*

Lori kept talking, "Our group has taught us that as we gain confidence, accepting ourselves fully, with the emphasis on "fully", others would too." Mari smiled at her play on words.

"Furthermore, lots of men are chubby chasers. They find us warm, cheery and we have lots to love to give! They seek us out." She continued to listen to her ideas with an amused but open ear. Really enthused now, Lori exclaimed that they were "fit and in the pink." Mari respectfully balked at that, stating the usual health problems associated with being overweight. Lori didn't comment. Continuing with conviction, she concluded, "We feel that the play can gain credence like The Vagina Monologues. Oh, by the way, the play is called, Fat Pigs." Shaking her head unbelievingly, she couldn't filter what she was thinking: "That hardly conjures up a pretty picture." Her comment was left dangling, with no response from Lori. However, Mari agreed to promote their play. Lori thanked her and they hung up.

Mari chuckled, welcoming the levity, very much needed since her world didn't have much to chuckle about lately.

On the way home her thoughts melded into: *It's Friday already and Sonny is coming home tomorrow afternoon. Maybe I can make reservations at a good restaurant for tomorrow night.* She picked up speed and immediately got on the phone with Enzo's. They loved their manicotti. It was too late to reserve there, so she settled for Moxi's. *Great! That's done.* They hadn't had a date night for a month now, and recalling their argument, she saw it as important to just have fun.

By late afternoon he was home and after a shower he decided to nap. Mari took in the tranquility and worked on a poem that she'd put aside, and it renewed the ardor she felt inside when it came to her marriage. She knew exactly how to finish the last stanza. It was titled: Love

Walking on hot sand
Bare feet kick up desire
We taste each other's mouths
A glance through busy eyes
In separate rooms we're together
One moment at a time, link and bond
Candidly talking, carefree or disquieted
Laughter eases life
We make out, we make time
Little spats, clear as mud

Adversity and sorrow remains wordless
Secrets burrow
The past haunts
Until it's comprehended
Until we trust
Until we know love
Until we know love
We guard, we trespass, we play at it, we barter
Until we're beseeched
Until we're used to giving
Until we're used to receiving

It's lesser than...

Sonny woke up re-energized and she told him of the plans she'd made. A bit apologetically, she added: "I hoped you wouldn't mind."

He kissed her forehead, "Hey, it's great to have plans made for me sometimes. I'm hungry. And, you look amazing." She'd put on her low necked, sleeveless black dress, trimmed in red, and was thrilled by his compliments. He put on a navy suit with an open necked gray shirt and they were out the door, pronto. At the restaurant they found themselves having to wait a little bit because of stragglers so they chatted over a drink at the bar. During a small lull in their conversation, she thought about the fact that he hadn't had a cigarette on the patio before leaving home, as was his usual ritual. She'd never smoked, so that was definitely noticeable. She told him about her observation.

"Right. When you quit you're not supposed to."

"Sonny Really? You haven't even hinted at quitting."

"No, but the doctor demanded that I did. Anyway, smoking causes wrinkles," he grinned boyishly. "It's been two whole days now. I didn't want to say anything until I had a handle on it."

"I'm very happy...but everything's okay?" Mari worriedly pursued, touching his hand.

"Oh yeah, and you're happy because you can't stand the smell on my clothes."

"That's true. I'm not in the least bit worried about you." He lowered his head and grinned at her, "Brat."

She went on, "You've been seeing the doctor more often lately, you know, more than your annual physical..."

"I've had that cold that I can't shake and I've been feeling more stressed at work. I'm just getting checked over."

Mari felt a prickly stab of concern, and said, "You've lost a bit of weight."

"YOU notice everything, but that's good, isn't it," he said as he patted his slightly smaller waistline.

Listening for their names with one ear, she went back to the subject of smoking, "Whoever started the idea that it was sexy to smoke?"

"Oh, I don't know, that Casablanca guy, or later in the fifties maybe, James Dean."

"Well, I think you're sexier than ever. I was just thinking that I'd like to really deep kiss you right here and now."

"You'd never do that in public." Ignoring that comment, Mari quipped, "Hey, now that your lungs can clear, I bet I can even get you to exercise with me."

Sonny gave her a pained look, "I tried that once."

"Goof, think of it this way. You know how you might not be in the mood for sex, but you do it anyway, and the next thing you know you're really enjoying yourself."

"I just endure it." She took a slap at him and they missed hearing their names. When the hostess found them, they followed her to their seats. It felt so good to be having a fun and it filled the whole evening. They got home a little after 1 a.m. and stood in their driveway commenting about how nice the neighbourhood looked with lots of flowers still in bloom. Their pleasant reverie halted when they heard a loud voice. It seemed to be coming from across the street, but there were no lights on that they could see. They waited but heard nothing more. Going in, they hung up their clothes, made a drink, and when they were turning down the bed they heard a male voice again through their slightly cranked window, raised in anger, unremitting in tone. Mari stiffened, and Sonny looked worried. They went onto the front walkway and decided it was coming from the house next to the Smith's.

An oriental man lived there who worked in the city hospital, and every once in a while, an oriental woman came and stayed for a while. Fiona knew him from work and said that he was not terribly outgoing, only talking to her when she approached him, but that he was soft spoken and pleasant. This was not what Mari was hearing. His tone was guttural and threatening.

"He sounds like a killer," she told Sonny and he answered, "Yeah, but we can't jump to conclusions based on this asshole. He's a bully. That is certain."

She'd poked around psychology books a lot and she remembered the supposition the author made about how soft spoken, unnaturally constrained people can be those with the most suppressed rage. They were the ones for whom there is the biggest gap between the public face and the private one.

Mari countered, "Maybe. I've never spoken to the woman, but possibly I can befriend her."

"That's a good idea. Just be careful hon." He went in. Mari stood on the stoop five minutes more, and listened. Nothing. She walked to their bedroom, cranked the window closed, and got ready for bed. Sonny was asleep, but she snuggled close, finally falling asleep herself.

Sunday dawned too early, so she stayed in bed a little longer it struck her that she should know what the date meant. Suddenly, her friend popped into her mind: *It is Sylvie's birthday.* She jumped out of bed and made coffee. While she waited for the coffee to perk, she thought about Syl who was single and working as a massage therapist. Mari loved her because she was upbeat, constantly curious about things and people, and very animated. Her effervescence and caring was contagious.

She picked up her cup and walked to the living room. She looked her up in her contacts, and called her. Syl picked up right away and gushed, "Hi you, haven't talked to you in a long time."

"I know, too long. Happy birthday. Are you free for lunch? It's on me."

"You remembered. How sweet. I can't say no to an offer like that. What time? It takes an hour to drive to your place from London."

"How about 12:30?"

"See you then. I'd better start now to put my face on. I'm turning forty six, and it takes way too long now."

"Boohoo. You're beautiful. And you're forty seven."

"Oh thanks for that. I can hardly wait to see you. Bye."

Mari dawdled away her morning, but she had decided to clean her office and she was making headway when she heard Sonny get up. As she worked, she told him about lunch with Sylvie and he reminded her that he was playing at an event in the afternoon. Just before noon, she slipped on black cropped pants, a loosely woven orange sweater, and waited in her wicker chair on the front stoop. From across the street where the loud voices had emanated from in the wee hours that particular night, Mari saw a faint outline of a man behind the screen door. She kept her eyes down.

Right on time, Syl pulled into the driveway, swung open the car door and ran to kiss Mari, who met her along the driveway. At five foot nine, all of Syl was lean and tanned. Mari admired the bright blue shirt she wore that looked stunning with her long blonde hair. As they walked to Mari's car that was parked on the street, Mari praised her, "It's been too long. You look beautiful."

"Damn, you do too. Check those sexy pants," she said in that rhythmic lilt she had.

At the Swiss Chalet, after toasting Syl's birthday, their liveliness spun. Syl brought her up on the everyday things that transpire in her life, and she ended with, "I love my job, especially when I get to massage the good looking muscular guys. They'll say, it sure feels good to work out the kinks. And, I think, damn it does." she blinked coquettishly. Mari laughed.

"What about you Mari?"

"I'm lucky to have an interesting job, good coworkers, and a boss who is both encouraging and motivational. My column: The Write Thing, keeps me connected with the readers and I'm very busy with family. I'm overwhelmed with responsibility, especially since Fiona's break in. I spend a lot of time with her, just buoying her. Sonny's job takes him away from home more now, so he couldn't really help me shoulder the aftermath of Fiona's break in. He tries his best."

"The murder is incredibly shocking, and I'm sure that Fiona's break in must have everybody believing that HE must have done it."

"Yeah, it's the obvious conclusion. Since it happened, everyone we talk to in town is anxious and fearful, and we're watchful. The whole town is. Like every other woman in this vicinity, I'm careful about where I bike and run." Her face was grave as she peered around the restaurant. She picked nervously at the lint on her sweater. There were three other customers seated, but she concluded that they could converse privately.

"I'm sure you are. A rape happened in my neighbourhood, and I've secured my apartment with extra locks on the doors and windows. I, and others, run in two's, or more" she said miserably. "You just can't let your guard down."

"Yeah Syl, I know. I'm constantly reminding my sisters and my daughter to be ever so observant about who's around them."

"Damn anyway, it isn't fair that we're always looking at who's behind us, and we have to take extra precautions to protect ourselves and our homes."

"Yep, and this guy is walking about freely."

Syl looked pensive, "You know, I've thought about capital punishment since that young woman was killed. I've become more strident about being on the side for it. I mean, there's no such thing as saying, "I'm sorry" for brutally killing someone."

Mari nodded and gestured to the waitress. She came over, "Everything okay?"

Smiling, she said, "Everything's good, I just need more coffee."

"Me too please." They stopped talking until after they received their refills.

"You know, long before the murder happened, I've been concerned about the level of murderous rage that's going on in the states, and spilling over into Canada. Syl, it IS worse. I've wondered about people who are depraved in every regard. How do they decide to kill? Do they break from reality, hearing deranged voices that make sense to them? That the world owes them?" she emphasized, "I don't know. I think that at some point, except for the certified mentally ill, it's a choice they make to futilely overcome a cruel situation of their own, you know, get back at somebody or something."

"Agreed. It's a vicious circle."

"We should put this whole depressing subject aside for now. However, whenever I get upset, I fall back to a television special about a little black boy. He came from a home where he was severely abused and his mother even killed his little brother. When he was little, this boy, he's grown up now, was kept in a closet, unfed, burned, beaten, you name it" she said, looking distraught. "He was interviewed with his adopted family. Syl, his eyes were completely clear of anger, vengeance and hatred. The adoptive parents said he was a gentle person, capable of so much love. You could see that in his smile. He beamed at his parents. And, he was preparing for college. He graduated, one of those at the top of his class. Apparently, he loved the audience applause." Her sadness changed to empathy, "To have suffered so much you wonder what his struggles were deep inside. And where did all that peace come from? Why didn't he go wrong and then justify it, because of what happened to him? Of course, it was a godsend that such good people took him in. In a way, I think success is the best revenge." She concluded with zeal.

"Yeah, well put, and thank God there are positive stories like that one. As for the questions of why and what, you know what is really challenging researchers? They see biological defects in the brains of killers, something undeveloped in the part of the brain that rules judgment. But, what is really odd is that they see the same thing in the brains of teenagers. There's just no way to predict who will kill one day, hmm, we really should change the subject."

"I just got an idea. Most people don't personalize the murdered girl. Look at us. We call her, that young woman. Her name is Kristel. I can personalize her through an article. The paper could feature who she was as a little girl, as an adult, and the parents may appreciate knowing that Kristel is very much in the eye of the community. Of course, I'd have to clear it with her parents, 'she paused to sip her coffee.' Anyway, to change the subject! How's your love life?"

Surprised, she blinked and jerked her head back, "Nonexistent for now. Don't worry, I'll catch you up if anything magical happens."

"I'll give you some pointers, if you need some," Mari laughed, as she dodged the napkin thrown at her. They finished their meal in comfortable silence, and soon it was time to go.

Mari slid up to Syl's sidewalk. They hugged, and Mari said, "We'll talk more often."

With that distinctive lilt to her voice, she answered, "You bet. Take care, and say hi to Sonny!"

On the drive home Mari thought about how she would prepare for interviewing Kristel's parents.

CHAPTER 6

THE LONG ROAD

April rehearsed over and over again how she would confess to her staff. It was the last thing she had to do before she entered rehab. She looked into her bathroom mirror, and mumbled, *"Like, this'll come as a complete surprise. I look forward to the apocalypse more.* She dried her damp face, and tried to put concealer under her red rimmed eyes. Another tear slipped down. She dropped the makeup into her cosmetics drawer: *This is going to be hard.* Picking up her purse and car keys, she slowly stepped out to the car. Crawling to work to delay the inevitable, she got honked at for slowing traffic. Then, jockeying into her parking spot, she slipped into work, using the side door to avoid staff.

They'd seen her drunk at work and she'd witnessed the looks that passed back and forth. Very soon, their boss had to tell them that she was most probably an alcoholic. No, was an alcoholic. Not a party animal, the inane, cutesy thing she'd boast of whenever she was fooling around. Today, April would tell them that she was destroying her body and mind, her relationships, and that she didn't like the person she had become. She had to give herself over to people who would help her get her life back. April hoped she was one of those people who could learn to control the drinking and be able to say "I drink socially." *Not likely.* Being candid was a very important part of getting better. Before coming to grips with this, she'd always told herself the same sad, lame things. Defensiveness in every syllable, she would whine: "Other people drink as much as I do, or more."

Or she'd claim, "I don't have to drink every day." It was time to immerse herself in a program. *No more detouring around the problem.*

She wondered if she would ever have to give up the bar. At the far end of it, a fireplace with a table and two chairs sat in front of it, and the gas lit flames cast a soft glow around it. This is where she worked on payroll during slower days. Two sharply dressed male bartenders in silvery vests over their own chosen shirts, tended bar. Males and females waited on tables, similarly dressed, with the females usually choosing more brightly coloured, fitted shirts than the males did. Opposite the long, sleek bar, a window spanned that wall. She had fallen in love with the place, right off. And, she'd hired the most friendly, outgoing types of individuals. Like her.

Once she called the meeting from the lounge, prepared now with coffee and donuts, she wondered how they would soon react to informing them who she really was. An imposter, a phony. It was she that staff depended on to help lookout for people who drank too much, to eject belligerent drunks, and call the police if they would not hand their keys over.

As they gathered around two pub tables they used for breaks, she summoned her courage, her hands clasped over her knees. She had to be completely honest. She would leave nothing out. She looked at Suzie, and then to Jack, another of her best staff, and she could not begin. Expectantly, they waited. She spilled out, "I called this meeting because I have something very important to tell you. I have a very severe problem with substance abuse. I am an alcoholic. I am entering rehab. It wasn't easy to get to where I am now, but I'm finally here, and ready to go. I've prepared a new schedule. I'll pass it around and we can discuss how it'll work. If there are any problem areas, now is the time to bring them up." She pursed her lips and let the air out, and tears flowed. Nobody said anything. Suzie got up from her chair, walked over to April and put her arm around her. April dropped the paper work and with her hands flattened out on them, she said, "I feel so small, so ashamed." She tried to squeeze the tears back. With all the compassion Suzie had, she told her, "April, you are SO-O not small. You're SO-O big, as big as they get. It took a lot of guts to face this, and then tell it to us straight. You're a great boss, and SO-O nice. Do what you have to do. We'll SO-O take care of this pub, like it's ours. Don't worry about anything." April felt Suzie's bobbing head against hers, with every SO-O, and she looked around the table at seven smiling faces. She thought: *Everything would be okay.* She felt her knees, then her neck, release. She smiled back, grateful. They finished the meeting and opened for business. She called her sister.

"Mari, I did it. I had my discussion with staff. I'm still shaky, "she laughed breathlessly." They took this well. They're a great bunch. Will you still be able to drop in at the pub if they need you, monitor a little? Let them know you're in charge while I'm gone. I mean, Suzie's wonderful, but she could easily take on the position of Head Chick. It could rub the others the wrong way."

Mari heard the overwhelming tremor in her voice, and she felt for her. "Of course April. I said I would."

"I gave them your home number. I hope you don't mind. But don't worry. They're capable and pretty independent. Well. Just two more days to go. Oh, by the way, Fiona called me. She wished me luck and offered to come in and take care of Sea Biscuit. It wasn't the warmest conversation, but, you know…"

"Told you she would."

"You didn't have to twist her arm"?

"April! Stop! She really WANTS to feed your fish every day and change his water and add water conditioner, whatever you have to do for an itty-bitty fish."

"Okay, okay."

"You only have to worry about April."

"I've done a lot of that lately."

"I know this is big, and of course you're worried, but you've pushed yourself in the right direction. We're all SO-O proud of you, 'April giggled', and we have a lot of faith that you're going to brave this out and be great!"

"And how is Fiona doing?"

"She's much better. Naturally, the anxiety about what happened keeps her edgy. She copes."

"I don't even like to think about how close he got. God, if anything had happened to her." The caring tone touched Mari.

"I know." Mari changed the subject, "I'm not prying, but what about Mr. Casual? You still seeing him?"

"He's a done deal. I don't need any distractions, especially not his kind. I admit it. I knew right from the start he was no good for me, a heavy drinker, really full of himself. You know what he said once. He could take but he couldn't give."

"You're kidding. How else to say the world revolves around him. Good riddance and good for you for giving him the boot, and here I thought you were one completely screwed up chick." That Mari had taken up April's playfulness, flippant way of talking made April laugh.

"Shut up"! she exclaimed.

Mari paused. "I always say, you get the best if you think you deserve it."

"Sometimes I think I don't deserve good things, let alone the best."

"That is going to change April. The better you get, you'll get good things. You might even get to be a real pain in the ass about it."

"Enough already", she retorted.

"I'll stop. Did you make a list of everything you're going to need? I'm going shopping tomorrow. I can pick some things up for you, magazines and such"?

"Thanks, I'll do it. I've got to stay busy. I'm not quite as organized as you, but I'm almost ready. Just have to pack."

"Do you want someone to take you there"?

"I'd appreciate that." Mari thought: *I'm spreading myself too thin.*

"I'm pretty sure Haley can. I can't after all. I've been working overtime lately, helping the boss who's going on vacation. I'll call Haley and she can call you. You guys can work it out."

"Oh God, I'm so jittery, frankly scared out of my wits."

"I know, but it's an excellent facility. They'll be good to you. I'll try to pop in before you go."

"I'll be here. Bye."

At work, Mari broached the idea with Stan about meeting with Kristel's parents, and she outlined what she wanted to do. Encouraged, he leaned forward.

"I like the idea of concentrating the story on what kind of young woman Kristel was. It will change the trajectory, from Kristel being an invisible victim, to giving people a full, lasting picture of her when she was alive. Her parents will find it painful, but I hope that they feel that openly talking about her, would help people go beyond seeing her as a stranger that something incomprehensible happened to. And, it appears, through their agreement talk to you, they do feel something good will come from it."

She was elated that he endorsed her plan.

"Thank you Stan."

"Besides, I tend to make everything sound like an interview. I appreciate your ability to build rapport with people. You'll do great." She blushed at his compliment and practically ran to her desk. She pumped her fist and hollered, "Yes!" causing her coworker to peer over her the top of the enclosure. Mari smiled widely as she grabbed her phone and called the Slater's and prepared to go to their home that afternoon. On the way, she made a stop at Tim Horton's and while sitting in the drive through she thought: *What do you say to parents who have lost a daughter who was murdered? I'm sorry about your loss. That is so trite. I'll just say something like: Tell me about your daughter.* She sipped her hot coffee and silenced her thoughts. Before she knew it, she was in their neighbourhood. Their red brick colonial home was surrounded by mature trees. It looked lovely. They met her at the door and she was warmly welcomed in. He was dark haired, peppered with grey, and tall and lanky. She was short and quite petite.

"It's so nice to meet you Mr. and Mrs. Slater."

"You too." They shook hands.

Following them, she perched nervously opposite them at their dining room table, and took in the warm, comfortable room. The walls of the room were a muted shade of gold, but the wall behind the dark hutch was a mossy green.

"Please call us Abe and Hanna", Hanna said. They instantly felt comfortable with Mari and agreed to have a recorder going.

"Tell me about Kristle."

"It's pronounced Kris-tell, you know, like t-e-l-l at the end."

"I'm sorry. Kristel is lovely. She cleared her throat, and looked at the portrait of her on a small table, next to a lamp.

"She's lovely."

"Thank you. May we call you Mari"?

"Your neighbourhood is…hmm, oh sure, call me Mari."

Clearing her throat again, she commented about the street they lived on, how tranquil it seemed and how inviting the homes looked. Kristel's tall, darkly handsome father smiled, ruefulness clouding his dark eyes,

"We moved here for precisely those reasons, and she re-located here to be close to us and crossed paths with her killer." Pausing, he folded his hands looking down at them.

He looked up, "When she was in Toronto, she visited us here as often as she could. More often would have been nice. We missed her. She was still in college when we left home, well, what was our home then"

"So, Toronto was home for you."

"Yes. It's a great city in some respects, but we wanted to live in a smaller community. We were tired of the rush and noise of the city, and often talked about moving into a quiet, picturesque town. We enjoy the atmosphere here. People are friendly and kind. They were attentive after Kristel died. Anyway, she lived with a friend and finished college there and worked at a law firm doing secretarial work. For a while she dated some guy that she took up skiing with. We never had the chance to meet him, only knew of him from talking with Kristel, and pictures. His name is Brent."

Hanna got up and retrieved an album from a drawer of the hutch. Mari looked at the photographs of him, and them together. He was dark, lean, and had a beaming smile. Abe continued, "Then, suddenly she called and said she was ready to move here. She had applied online for a job here and it was hers, in her chosen field, interior design. This job was something she really wanted because she could hone her career with this company. It was perfect. We were elated, especially Kristel. She bubbled over. She said she wanted to be close to us and asked us to find an apartment for her, trusting her mother's judgement about that. We found one close to an area where she could bike and walk. She commented after she'd been here a few months that she liked the peacefulness of this area. It felt easy."

As he continued to talk he kept his gaze direct, as though deciding if this was the right thing to do, inviting a journalist in to talk about their private lives and about Kristel. As they conversed about Kristel, she made a favourable impression on him. She was amiable and he unquestionably found her to be honest and empathetic. He relaxed.

"We didn't ask too many questions about her relationship. It just didn't work out. Actually, we think part of the reason she moved here was to distance herself from Brent, but we never pried. We just loved having her here for as long as we could, because she did talk about moving back to Toronto when she felt ready to seriously pursue her field. Another separation, but not final like this separation." Incomprehension covered his face.

He shifted his position, setting his folded hands on the table. He stopped talking and Kristel's fair, fine featured mother touched her husband's wrist. Looking forlorn, she looked much smaller for a moment. In actuality, she was lithesome and supple, which gave her a youthful appearance. She took a moment to compose herself.

"Once she was here we helped her settle in, and her landlord measured her area of expertise and agreed with her request to decorate the apartment. I helped her paint her living room with one of her favourite combinations, flat dusty gray blue walls, trimmed with a blue almost as dark as navy. We spent a lot of fun time getting her apartment done, quite messily sometimes, but finally we finished." She pressed Abe's wrist. Glancing at her husband she said, "Kristel is very unselfish. Yes, she was an only child, and you know what some people say about only children, that they're spoiled and self-centered and such, but we worked hard to instill responsibility in to regard others. Actually, it wasn't that hard to do. She was naturally good." She appeared to go back to that time, her eyes momentarily alive with memories. "I attribute some of what happened to her as being my fault, wanting her here, especially me." Her husband covered her hand with his and assured her, "You are not in any way responsible for what happened to her." She disengaged her hand and held fast to his wrist, her eyes fastened to his face, her knuckles pink. He exclaimed, "That animal is responsible and he will be punished. He took something so precious from us. Our only daughter." He slapped the table hard, tears filling his eyes. It startled both women, and Mari slowly exhaled, not even realizing that she had sucked in and held her breath, thinking about how devastating this was for them. Hanna put her arm around her husband and they sat quietly for a moment.

"She's gone to another place, but our hearts and memories are filled with her here." Her smile was gentle as she spanned the room.

They leafed through the photo album, "It tracks her life." Mari smiled, not sure of what to say so she allowed them to lead. They looked at a picture of a laughing five year old with her first dog, sitting on the front lawn, her small arm wrapped around the dog's neck. There were lots of pictures of her with girl friends at the age of eight and ten, candid shots of them playing and swinging each other around. There was one quite amusing one where she was in her living room, for her eleventh birthday party, with her cousins and friends, playing some silly relay game with their mouths. One of the pictures showed her with a cute little girl, about the same age, dressed in bikinis as they leaned on her mother's yellow convertible. They were grinning ear to ear. Her high school graduation picture showed a happy looking teen with a mesmeric smile, who was beginning to look more like her mother. Abe said that after she finished college her personality bloomed even more, if that was possible. She was outgoing, confident and independent.

"I'm so proud of the direction she was taking in life and she had fun doing it. She's like me in that respect, and her good looks come from me. Her serious side comes from Abe," a mischievous glint in her eyes. Hanna spoke like her daughter was still with them. Having recovered his emotions he rolled his eyes toward her. Hanna ceased talking for a minute. Growing serious she said, "We need justice. He has to be caught before he hurts someone else, or worse! He already has. Look at what happened to that young woman we read about in the paper. She was so lucky she wasn't home."

"That was my sister."

Hanna put her hand to her throat, "Oh, we're so sorry. How is she?"

"As well as can be expected, thank you."

"Is it him that..."

"That is probable, but we don't know. The police have the note he left. That's got to be a concrete piece of information."

Mari turned to Abe.

"How do you feel about the investigation? Are the police forthcoming with you?"

"Yes. We're satisfied, and they keep in contact, Officer Robertson especially."

"Oh yes. I've met him. He's very nice."

"They're doing everything they can. Of course they can't relay certain specifics of their investigation, but they assure us that they're working very hard for us. They have evidence and they've put together a psychological profile. We know, of course, that there's only so much that they can reveal. It fills me with rage. Someone with a specific genetic signature, committed this crime. It seems he's so near, yet, at the same time, too far to be captured. And, if I ever hear that phrase again about there being closure…" he stopped talking.

Mari decided to wind the interview to a close. The haunted look on his face and the tight clasp of his hands on the table, told her to stop. Memories flowed from his eyes. He excused himself and walked to the window, his back to them.

She turned her gaze to Hanna who had picked up the picture of Kristel posing with her boyfriend. Mari asked her, "Did the police have questions about Brent?" Hanna slipped the picture into the photo album. "Yes, they did. I don't know anything though. They most probably did question him."

With a heavy heart, Mari gathered her recorder and purse, and Abe returned to them. She hugged each one, warmed by having met them. Mari felt a connection, however sad, because she too had a daughter she loved, a sister who was vilely threatened, and because it was evident that they were good people and very devoted to each other.

She turned back at the door, "We want you to be involved before the final copy. We'll speak again before publishing it. Thank you for sharing. Good bye."

She could hardly wait to pull the story together.

After putting the album away, Abe and Hanna moved to the shelter of their cozy living room. She sat in the blue arm chair near the window and Abe sat at the end of the tan couch across from her. Hanna asked Abe, "How are you feeling?"

"That was rough."

"Yes, but I like her. She's very nice, and she knows how we feel in some way. Can you imagine what her sister Fiona has gone through since her break in, what the whole family must have experienced? Mari says her husband is away a lot with his job. She herself could be in danger. After all, he could very well know that she works with the local newspaper."

"That must be, but I have a hard time feeling anything since her death. I can't feel anything, except my grief." His face was ravaged by sorrow.

"I know honey. And I worry about you. That's why I make sure you keep your appointments with Doctor Shui. One day the light will come on again. Not as bright, but you'll see… it'll get so we will be able to talk about the time and fun we had with her, without the overpowering grief. It's what Kristel would want."

"I hope to get to that point."

"You will. It takes anti-depressants a while to work. Four weeks sometimes for them to take full effect."

He looked out the window, "Supposedly. The doctor said to give it more time."

"Honey, I know you're not sleeping. I hear you wandering around the house at night. And your appetite is almost non-existent. You're missing work. You need help to fight this thing."

"What THING. I lost my daughter!" Hanna got up and sat beside him. Gently, she said, "We lost our daughter. The thing I'm talking about is your depression. I'm worried about you. And, I need you. You've tried hard to get through this, but you seem to be getting worse."

"I'm scared. I can't seem to control the crying" he whispered as he swiped at the tears, and continued, "Mari asked you about Kristel's ex. I tell you, I can't bear a thought like that, but it has crossed my mind. What if it was him or someone she knew?"

"I know Abe. It's unthinkable. But, listen to me. We have each other and we have to take care of us. You're important to me and I need you. It might seem unfathomable right now, but you will get better. I feel Kristel near me. She's passed the fear and the pain. She smiles at me and I think of the fun and the love we always shared together. And I talk to her. It helps me. Sure, I'm lonely for her physical presence, but I feel her spirit. I draw from that."

"I guess I have to lean on you. I've been so, um, insulated since it happened that I haven't been much help to you. I've been so self-involved. I am sorry."

"I'm okay. I'm just scared for you, for us. I don't want to lose you too." He pulled her close and hugged her, "You're not going to lose me."

Abe got up and sighed. "I'm exhausted. I'm going to lie down for a while." He kissed her lightly and went to the spare bedroom. She heard the television come on. Hanna sat in front of the living room window, green tea with honey in hand, and watched the glow of the sun sink.

Silently, she thanked Mari because she had cared enough about them to come and talk. An added advantage was that it had helped Abe convey his feelings.

Sometimes Mari didn't want to have to deal with it, but she knew. If she didn't pursue the trust issue with Sonny her resentments would only fester. She put some time aside for them to talk about cutting his long hours back, marked by nights away. The effects of long hours and life on the road were showing, slowly separating them from all the good things. Mari missed the spontaneity in their lives together, such as, long evening walks, time with their kids, cooking together, each with a glass of wine. Most of all, she missed the intimacy of long conversations, being held and made love to. She wanted it to be like the first years of their marriage, where all of these things were spontaneous and natural.

She worked long days herself and there were so many other intrusions, that she knew were partly responsible. Her involvement with her sisters was important, but she felt drained. Still, determined to not ignore the issues that threatened their marriage, this coming weekend would be set aside for them. Talking to him on the phone that evening she told him she had planned the entire weekend just for them.

Puzzled, he'd asked, "What's the occasion? Have I missed something important?"

"We're the occasion."

"Ah, you're missing me?"

"A lot. We haven't had much time to ourselves lately. I need to be with you, and I feel lonely when you're away. Granted, not every second, Sonny, but yeah, I do miss you." She grinned.

"Not every second. Oh really," he pestered her.

"Yes, really, and I won't listen to any excuses about you having to work."

She sensed a little hesitation, then he said, "I'm all yours. I'll be home Saturday afternoon and I won't leave until Monday afternoon, not while you have this "woman take charge attitude.""

"I'm doing it for you."

She knew he smiled that boyishly dimpled way he had.

Hurriedly, Sonny said, "Well, I'm off to an appointment. I'll see you on the weekend."

"See you then. Love you."

"Love you too. Bye." Once that was solidified she decided to finish the day cleaning and shopping for the weekend.

The next day was spent working on her column and putting the finishing touches on the article about Kristel. She reread it, Stan critiqued it, liked it, and gave her a thumb's up.

Mari opened the story by introducing Kristel's parents to everyone, describing them as gracious and friendly. Her afternoon with them found them to be a loving couple, friendly and open. Rounding out their lives as they lived in the heart of Toronto, they glowed about their daughter being born there. At some point Abe and Hanna decided to move to a small community, and they picked Kingsville, describing it as picturesque and peaceful, a haven from the bustling, noisy city life. The three of them drove back and forth for visits.

Sitting comfortably around their dining room table, they described Kristel, spiced with lots of stories of her as a child through adulthood. As a child she had a sunny, bubbly disposition who loved to decorate her room and her dolls. She had comical quirks too that certainly brought out her individuality. For instance, she asked for an erector set for Christmas when she was ten years old, and she designed a blue truck. Begging Hanna to buy her a yellow hard hat, like the ones she saw the men working in the streets wear, she pretended to bulldoze her bedroom. Then, she would rebuild it and re-decorate. She also work at her easel, designing rooms and houses. Her colours were a mix of dark and bright hues that always seemed to work. Hanna praised her imagination and individuality. Their support of her bode well, and by the time she was in high school, she combined colours in clothes, that none of her friends would think of wearing. After graduation, it was natural for her to direct her studies toward design.

Upon finishing college, she worked at her secretarial job in Toronto that kept the bills paid, and she was happy in her relationship with Brent, for a time. Once that fizzled, she felt so lucky to get the position in the Kingsville area, in her field! That was just too good to be true, because it would allow her to be close to her parents. She missed them.

The story had to proceed ominously at that point, but she did not linger long on Kristel's brutal end. She called out the community to do whatever they could to help the police. She directed the citizens to be careful and vigilant at all times, wherever they and their families worked or played.

In her heart, she hoped that Abe and Hanna embraced the story for what it was, a tribute to Kristel as a child, a teenager, and before her parents knew it, a beautiful, smart young woman treasured by family and friends. Her name graced the byline.

The next day Mari went back to April's, presented her with a little trinket for Sea Biscuit, then she picked up meat for dinner. Before going home she decided to drive to the outskirts of town to the roadside produce place she liked, called: The Garden of Eatin.' She picked out a red onion, radishes, and a bunch of red leaf. The stand was close to Fiona's house so she passed by. Things looked fine. Just as she pulled into the driveway Connor was doing the same thing. Mari told him that she'd spotted him coming from the produce place, but that he'd not seen her when she'd tried to wave. He stood there, hands in his pockets, short dark hair, freshly cut, and grinned, "Sorry, I didn't see you. I picked up some fresh tomatoes for sauce. The best way to do sauce, with fresh tomatoes, and they usually have good stuff. How's everything?"

"I'm a little weary. You know, family stuff, but I'm fine." He nodded.

Mari asked him about their next door neighbors, "Sonny and I have heard his loud, aggressive voice coming from the house next door to you, mostly in the evening. He's a bully. It's awful."

Gesturing with his thumb, "Well, yeah, I've heard things going on. He yells at her in their language. Don't know what he talks about but he sounds pretty tough. Hao is always quiet."

"What a pity."

"Makes you wonder if he could be the killer."

"If only it was that easy. Anybody could be the killer. Well, have to get in and start dinner. See ya."

"Yeah." She watched him skitter away, then ambled up her sidewalk, dead heading a few petunias. She went in to fix dinner, shuddering at the last thing Connor said to her about George.

Having topped her meatloaf with a mixture of ketchup and brown sugar, she let the sauce soak in, while finishing the fresh salad she had tossed, tossing candied pecans on top, the final step. She ate dinner in the kitchen. After organizing the dishwasher and wiping the surfaces, she slumped into her chair in the living room. It had been a long week. She rubbed her eyes and closed them, every muscle in her body fatigued. When she awoke, her tea was cold. She took her cup to the kitchen, dimmed the lights even though it was only nine o'clock, and instantly fell asleep.

Waking early and making coffee to bring outside, she made herself comfortable on the lounge. Surrounded warmly under dawn's sunlight she thought: *We're already right into summer*. She surveyed her plants like they were alive and responsive to her thoughts. I wonder what the next season will bring. I wonder what this weekend will bring. *This is bull. Sonny is my husband and he is going to talk to me!* She did not want any of the toxicity to fester beyond what was in her heart now. Determined, she was not going allow him to detract from the matter. She willed herself to relax and finish her coffee. Not idle for any length of time she fussed with dinner preparations and drove off to get a bottle of dry, red wine and his favourite dessert, which was cherry cheesecake. He got home midafternoon like he said he would and they greeted each other affectionately. Over dinner, they discussed the family, the neighbours, other things, then they moved to the living room with their wine. She sat opposite him, legs crossed. She began, "Sonny, remember how we talked about how you flirt with other women..."

"No! 'and pointed a finger' You raised the issue, saying that my behaviour was pretty bad. You don't trust me, that's the issue."

"That's right, I do have trouble with that, and I'm upset that you haven't brought it up...I"

"And why should I bring it up?" he interrupted.

Shaken by his lack of empathy, she was discouraged. "Because I'm your wife and you love me and you want to reassure me. That's why."

He was quiet for a bit. "Maybe I need reassurance that you trust me. And I think that you don't care about meeting my needs."

"If you're referring to that blow up we had about sex some time back, you said something very mean. You said you may as well consider something on the side. How do you expect I would feel if you talk like that?"

"I didn't mean it. I said it in anger."

Thrown off by Sonny minimizing his words, she felt sadness overcome her.

"The words were said and words hurt and you didn't apologize" her voice low.

"I remember saying it, but it's been ignored because you are not responsive to what I want. You are uncomfortable about sexual stuff I want to do." *It's still about Sonny.* They looked at each other, neither one of them shifting away.

With as much patience as she could muster, she kept her voice even, "That's not even remotely to the point, as far as I'm concerned. I'm talking about our lack of communication when things bother us. If I didn't coax things out, you'd ignore them. Unresolved issues just hang there."

Something seemed to click in Sonny's head, "I was cruel that night. Too many drinks, my short temper." Picking irritatingly at his shirt, looking directly into her eyes, he stopped picking, and folded his hands, "I was careless and what I said was mean. That's not an excuse. I'm really sorry I hurt you."

She acknowledged his declaration, but not to be dissuaded she continued, "Sonny, when you flirt with other women it embarrasses me, then I feel inadequate. I want to be the most beautiful woman in your eyes."

He looked admiringly at her, "You with your soft, wispy hair and those gorgeous brown eyes, are beautiful to me. Maybe I flirt to bolster my ego."

A tweak sarcastically, she said, "What ARE you talking about?"

"I need to know that I'm attractive. My ego is kinda big, I guess."

"YOU have an ego, not you." He grinned and lowered his eyes.

"You know how we can begin to resolve this Sonny. You could be less attentive to pretty women at parties. I don't mind that you mingle, but you could find your way back to me more often than you do. I always have to go looking for you, 'she took a deep breath' and I need you around more." She dissolved deeper into melancholy. She waited for him to speak.

"Okay, I can definitely live with that. I'll work on it. Now come here." She hiked up her long gypsy skirt and straddled him. They kissed deeply, "I need to know that I can trust you."

"Be assured on that. I've never strayed." Mari looked into his uniquely astonishing, penetrating gray/green eyes. She needed to believe him, because if she had any doubts about that, she could separate from him.

"You know Sonny, no problem between us has to be insurmountable. Even the stuff you're worried about, your need for experimentation, you know."

"Like with sex toys, and cuffs. Hey, you should see your cheeks. They're red!" He tried to suppress a laugh, unsuccessfully, and up close he looked terribly funny. They roared. They laughed so hard that she nearly pulled him off the chair with her. She knew that in spite of the humour, or maybe even because they could laugh, it might not be so hard to talk about their sex life. She thought: *I'm sure as hell not going to talk about it with anybody else.* They steadied themselves, then he said, "The house has been our own for a time, with the kids gone and involved in their lives, and I get to thinking that we could explore fantasies, our fantasies, you know." She nodded and buried her head in his shoulder. Okay, now shut up about it," her voice muffled. Still, he understood what she said, and he resumed laughing, then stopped. His silly mood evaporated, suddenly exposing his vulnerability, "You know, you're not the only one with insecurities. I've got a few. You have such confidence in yourself, you're so strong. Sometimes I think you don't need me. You could get along without me just fine."

"Sonny, I could get along without you, but I couldn't think of life without you."

Both silent, they lived in the moment. The moments of unity and harmony.

It used to be that tackling any problem with Sonny ended up with him shouting and blaming, and slamming out-obviously something she didn't know about during their dating period. Nothing had been troubling then. She recalled having asked him how he handled anger. He hadn't told her the whole truth, only that he walked away until he regained composure. Tonight though, they'd accomplished something. She felt her entire being swell with optimism. They can build anything together. She said, "Sonny, I love you."

"Me too.""

"You love you too?"

He wrapped his arms around her again and he held her tight. Communication had unlocked troubling things that had been on each of their minds, but he knew that it had taken Mari to steer them this way. It didn't matter. He relished these moments as long as he could, and with childlike wonder, he said, "I've just had an epiphany. I'm growing up." Mari smiled brightly. He thought: *This is not the right time to break the bad news.*

Haley visited her friend Delia who lived in Windsor. On the way home, determining how hungry she was, she'd stopped at a little pub/restaurant, called Mammie's, a place a lot of people frequented; remotely located jutting the lake, away from the city's clamor. Its funky style always gave off good vibes, mostly because of the decorations. The walls were purple with art and not so artsy stuff hanging from them, and it jibed well together. On the upper side of the entrance door to the right, hung a huge portrait of a cow well drawn and painted with all kinds of colours that gave it a happy, contemporary air. On the far wall to the left, past the tables and chairs, almost always full, was a painting that almost occupied the entire wall. Blue lapping water jostled a purple and pink boat that seated the brightest, funniest characters. One had a chicken's head and the other a pig's head. They both had cheeky, happy faces, and were dressed up, the chicken as a woman, the horse as a man. He had a beer in his hand, she a red wine. The rest of the walls were splashed with gooey, sumptuous pictures of food that most people enjoyed. They made the best, the highest burgers she'd ever seen. One topped a big beef patty with pulled pork, and macaroni and cheese with the mac and cheese spilling out the sides of the burger, plus other toppings like lettuce and tomatoes. She could never bring herself to order that monstrosity, and she wondered who could have possibly conjured that thing up. She looked around and noticed that it was unusually quieter than most times, but checking her phone for the time, she saw that it was just before people would quickly begin dropping in for dinner. Having ordered a coffee, she surveyed the menu, and ready to order, she looked around for the waitress. They caught sight of each other, and the waitress smiled, walking over. She ordered a double burger with bacon and a side of onion rings, which were superb here. Right after she placed her order, she overheard two men talking behind her. She hadn't noticed them speaking until then, because her mind had been occupied, but with her selection done, she stiffened, because one had an indistinct, yet faintly familiar voice. She leaned back, pushing against the material of the booth directly behind her, hearing a short remark, "I like some challenge in a woman." She pressed harder into the back of the seat, feeling the sweat that prickled the back of her neck. She wiped it away.

The acrid response to that was, "Not me. I don't need a woman who gives me problems, 'he sarcastically chuckled' I just need those fuckin' dumb shits to follow directions. It's weird because they're...'em, useless. I don't know why I bother. I hate the sluts. Gets me mean. By the time they fight back I really lose it, because they've really pissed me off." He fell silent. Then, she heard the sound of utensils tinkling, and hushed up a bit, but still audible, she heard, "Demonic forces take over. Can't stop myself. I thump' em. Can't help it," he laughed, his voice rising.

Haley rubbed her arms. She sat riveted. Oh God! I have heard that voice before! Seconds later, she heard a rustling like one of them was getting out of the booth, "Hold that thought. I gotta go." She looked down at her cell phone, hoping she wouldn't be noticed. He walked by her seemingly looking straight ahead. She followed the outline of his form until he had to turn slightly to get where the bathroom was. She had no clue who he could be. Haley waited for his return, and when he appeared, walking quickly without looking her way, she instinctively buried her head in the desserts section of the menu. The waitress was directly behind him and she stopped at her booth, letting her know that it wouldn't be much longer for her burger to come. Not wanting to speak, she smiled and nodded at her. However, the waitress, who had begun walking away, stepped backwards, and asked Haley if she wanted to top up her coffee.

"No thank you, bring me a vodka and orange juice, please." She needed something that would calm her nerves.

"Sorry, didn't get that."

Less softly, she repeated her order.

The waitress smiled, nodded as she wrote on her pad, and walked away.

She heard rustling, then heard the clink of a glass on the table, and he said, "Okay, where were we? What exactly do you mean, you thump them?" He lowered his voice on the last part of his sentence, but it was easy to surmise what had been said, and that he was the one back to back with her. She waited for the answer, holding her breath.

"What do you think I mean, man? I make their lives miserable, stalk 'em, thump 'em, stuff like that." He laughed it up.

Haley knew now that it was not the one who had gone to the bathroom who owned the voice. That voice! She despised him without even seeing his face and curled her hands into fists, leaving nail marks in her palms.

"You know what I think about? I'd love to be one of those guys who finds the perfect place to hide a burned to a crisp body, like in a mine shaft, 'cause let me tell ya' I was married to this whack job." The other one said, "Yeah, I've had my share of bullshit from lots of whack jobs. Just want to bang 'em and forget 'em."

Haley thought: *Don't they even think that someone might hear?*

Fortunately, her drink came at once. She unfurled her fist, grabbed the glass, and took a few gulps, spilling a bit on her shirt. Hastily wiping her shirt, her hands shaking, she used both of them to place the glass down. She'd never been so scared. Then, anger coiled up like she'd never felt before, and felt irrationally unhinged from her safe life, like before the murder happened. It was so hard to describe. Her anger boiled. *I have to leave right now!* She gulped the rest of her drink, put money on the table to pay for the drinks, and sat frozen. But, only for a moment. She willed herself to stand and walk by their booth, looking away from them, shaking, but walking not too fast, not too slow.

Please, I can't attract his attention! It is possible that he's the killer.

If the foul mouthed degenerate knew her, the possibility was that she could be his next victim. Thankfully, they were still deep into their offensive, idiotic discussion, and they had paid no attention to her. She hoped. As she exited the restaurant, black devastation bayed at her heels. She half ran, half walked to her car, opened the door, jumped in, and stuck the key into the ignition. Driving home, her hands damp on the steering wheel, her eyes wide with fright, she wanted to call her mother as soon as she got home. When she finally did arrive home, she reached for the phone, but stopped. She couldn't call her while she was still so shaky... and it wouldn't be fair to tell her mother something like this before she went to bed. She'd wait, and call her first thing in the morning. Taking one of her husband's sleeping pills, she went to bed and managed to relax enough to get some sleep.

At 7:30a m. while showering, Mari heard the phone ring. She knew Sonny wouldn't hear it because he usually slept through the phone ringing, and she thought: *Why does the world beat a path to your door when you're on the toilet or in the shower? Geez!*

She dried off, quickly rubbed a coconut scented moisturizer on her legs and arms, got into her housecoat and went into the living room. Seeing Haley's name she picked up the receiver. With one ring, Haley picked up. Startled, Mari said, "Oh! Good morning hon. It's not that I don't want to talk to you, but what's the hurry?"

"I've got to tell you what happened."

She heard the apprehension in her voice, which got her edgy. Her back, still damp from not being able to reach the area between her shoulders, suddenly felt colder.

"What Haley? What?"

"I finally got together with Delia last night and…"

"Oh, how is she?"

Irked by the interruption, she barked, "FINE. Just wait Mom, please. After I left her place, I was hungry, so I stopped at Mammie's."

"Yeah, so…

"In the booth behind me I heard these two guys talking some serious trash about women. One of the voices sounded familiar. That's what really got me scared and so frustrated, because I couldn't pin it down, you know, who he was. One of them got up to go to the bathroom. I've never seen him before."

Frantic, Mari shouted, "And the other one?"

"I don't know Mom. I didn't see him!"

"You didn't see him! Why not!? If he was right behind you."

"I got so spooked that as soon as I saw the other guy coming back, I waited until he sat down, and got out of there as fast as I could, looking the other way. I didn't want him to see my face. Mom, you should have heard what they were saying. The one guy with the voice I thought I knew was talking about how he liked to hurt women, saying things like he liked to stalk them and thump them. He called women dumb, fuckin' shits, and sluts, stuff like that. The other guy didn't say much, but he laughed and joked about what the other guy was saying. It was so creepy."

"Oh no, and you didn't get a look at him," desperation peppering the words.

"No Mom. I was so frantic to get out of there…oh, why I didn't I just look." She'd let her mother down.

Aghast that she'd made her daughter feel like she'd failed her, not intentionally so, and she begged her to understand, "I'm sorry Haley. It just that I'm afraid for you. I didn't mean to sound like you should have put yourself in danger. You did the right thing, honey. You had to get out of there fast. But Haley, look at what you do have. A mountain of information for the police!"

"Yeah?"

"Of course honey. Listen, write everything down that you can remember them saying. And, don't forget to describe the one you did see. Just jot whatever down, even if you don't think it's that big a deal. It might be. We'll go to the station and report it. Oh God, what if one or both of them did see you or know you, and spotted you leaving. Oh God, I hate to even think about it, 'her voice rising.' Struggling to compose herself, she levelled her voice, "I only work half a day today. I can pick you up at one."

"I'll be ready. Hey Mom, steady please. It'll be alright. I thought of the possibility that they might know I was there, you know, listening. But when I walked past their booth, their conversation didn't change any. I really don't think they were even aware of me."

"You feel really sure of that? I'm afraid for you." She didn't want her mother to come undone, so she measured her tone.

"I'm sure Mom."

"Okay Haley, see you this afternoon. Love you."

"Love you too. Bye."

As an afterthought she called Officer Robertson. Her call was put through to his office, and he put her at ease, ensuring her that he'd be in the station, "I'll put on a pot of fresh coffee."

She woke Sonny up and filled him in on what happened. He'd had chemo the day before and he looked white and pasty, his stomach lurching. Mari helped him to the bathroom, and wiped his face with a cool cloth when he was finished being sick. She helped him back to bed. Weakly, he let her lead him, and she tucked him in.

"Mari, you do what you have to do to support our daughter. I'll be fine. I'll stay in bed until you get home. Okay hon?" She smiled to confirm what he said, and kissed him on the cheek. His eyes closed.

Later in the day, quickly leaving work, she drove to Haley's where she saw that she was already outside waiting for her. Mari met her at the curb, and as soon as the car stopped, she jumped inside, anxiety written all over her face. She could see that her daughter had gone through a sleepless night. Her face was pinched and tight, and her eyes were red, as though she may have been crying. Mari reached for her and they hugged. Nothing was said for a few minutes. Slowly, Haley said, "I didn't sleep hardly at all, tossing and turning, and I felt nauseated this morning." Mari patted her hand, and told Haley, "That had to be the scariest experience."

Haley picked at her nails, and her voice sounded taut and strained when she did speak, "I know I said I was sure they didn't notice me, but they could have seen me Mom," her voice panicky.

"From what you said this morning, it seems that they didn't. We'll be there soon. Coffee may be just what you need. Officer Robertson said he'd have fresh coffee waiting for us."

They drove in silence again, until Mari patted her daughter's hand once more and said, "We're here. Take a deep breath and calm yourself. You'll remember things better."

Haley clawed deep for her notes, fishing them out.

"I'm okay. I did write down everything that I could possibly remember, like you said to do. I mean this could be solid info, eh Mom?"

"Oh definitely. You did good, girl. You're prepared." She smiled her most reassuring smile, putting her car in park. Haley regained some colour to her face, and Mari was somewhat more encouraged by the suddenness of change in her. She looked ready to talk to the police.

Officer Robertson came out of his office as soon as he heard them being led there by a female officer. Mari introduced Haley, and he stepped aside to allow them in. Walking behind his desk and sitting down he looked at Haley, pointing to the papers she had in her lap, and said, "What have you got there?" As she started to speak, she handed them over to Officer Robertson.

"Well, I had dinner at this restaurant, called Mammie's..."

"I know the place. And your mother has filled me in on what happened. And thank you for this," he picked up the notes and began to read. Finally, he looked up. Looking directly at Haley, his face unreadable, he conceded, "This 'he held up the papers' is well documented. It's important, adds to the munitions store, so to speak. Info like this is very significant. I'm dispatching an officer to the restaurant, ASAP, to question the restaurant. The staff may have seen or heard something you didn't. And hopefully, one of them paid with a card. We'll have a name."

"And if one did recognize her? Haley is scared. So am I."

"We'll do everything we can to keep your daughter safe. Patrolling her house more is all we can offer."

Thrown and irritated, while at the same time understanding that they couldn't do more than that, she stammered, "Somehow, that doesn't seem good enough."

He gave his cryptic reply, "I'm very sorry, but it's the best we can offer right now."

After a few pleasantries, the officer said goodbye to the women and reread the written text. He picked up the notes, briefed his superior, after which he marked the items and placed the report in the file.

CHAPTER 7

SHADOWS DON'T MOVE

Fiona took a quick shower, and before walking to her room she turned off the bathroom light so she couldn't be seen from outside. In complete darkness, she carried her dirty clothes into the bedroom and feeling her way to her laundry basket, she tossed them in. Blindly walking to her bed she unwrapped the tightly tied housecoat she wore, hanging it on the fancy hook she had screwed in beside the bed, after the break in. Naked now, her vulnerability exposed, she felt for the violet, lace trimmed pajamas laid out on the bed, and very quickly pulled them on. These things were all performed habitually now. The violation she had experienced snatched freedom from her, such as when she would walk from the bathroom to the bedroom, naked, to casually choose which pajamas she would wear. Illogically, she thought that not being completely disrobed as she went from the bathroom to her bedroom would make her less susceptible to menacing outside forces. She wondered if she would ever feel carefree again, able to perform the simple everyday routines she took for granted before her awful experience. It made her angry too, gradually more determined to beat this hideous, life changing event.

But, every night the memory of the state of her room gripped her. No matter how she tried to put it out of her mind, that vision remained. She'd see herself that night, groggy from having fallen asleep in the living room, get up and walk into her room devastated by what she saw. Most things were turned over or tossed, drawers pulled open had been emptied of clothes, strewn everywhere. Her dresser top that had held her lamp and a portrait of her mother and sisters caught in a carefree moment during early childhood, were thrown across the floor, the frame broken. The wall hanging on the wall next to the window, holding her nurse's degree, also shattered. Peace was no longer hers, ripped from her by a nameless, faceless man.

Now, after she had her pajamas on, she'd walk to the window in the dark, look about and, many times think that she'd seen movement in the black forest. Her pulse would quicken to the point that it could have jumped through her skin. She knew that it could be an animal or the breeze moving the leaves on the trees and across the long grass, but that didn't help still her frantic thoughts.

Oh, how she missed cracking the window open, letting the night air move over her as she drifted off to sleep. Now, sleep was strangely confined in an airless room, her thoughts continuously going back to that night; a smear to the trapped air.

He moved about the tree covered area, feeling his way one foot at a time, careful not to make noise. But it was dark and he couldn't avoid stepping on twigs and brush. He wanted to be there when Fiona came in from the bathroom, dressed in her robe. His breathing got heavy with anticipation of her. He always got a charge when he could glimpse her as she stepped into the hallway to turn off the bathroom light. Momentarily, there she would be, shrouded by the light of the hallway nightlight and the window sheers.

He dragged on his cigarette, remembering how easy it had been to gain entrance. It excited him. The barriers she put up fueled his anger, and holding his smoke between his teeth, he clenched and unclenched his fists. *That bitch thinks she can duck me. I'll show her who's boss.* Becoming bolder, he got closer so that he stood at the edge of the yard, still surrounded by the thicket and he strained to see. The windows are locked up tight. *Goddamned bitch!* A muscle in his right thigh twitched. He waited, still as a stealthy wildcat, and watched. He knew that she was walking now from the bathroom hallway to her bedroom. Seconds later, he saw Fiona look out, check the lock, and draw the blind down that had not been there when he'd entered her house. His breathing quickened and he cursed, "Fuckin' bitch!" He dragged on his cigarette, covering the lit end with his fist. With steady eyes he followed the bright lights that illuminated the front of the house and other lights that cast out over the back yard. His gaze shifted to the closest area where he stood, so close to the house. Aggravated, muscles tensed, he paced several feet, tossed his butt, stepped on it, and lit another. *Bitch! Bitch! Bitch*! A dog barked in the distance, incessantly. He backtracked to his truck, hidden deep in the coppice. As quietly as he could he started his engine and backed from the concealed access road.

Fiona listened: *Is that a truck I hear*? She pulled the covers tightly around her, enfolded in them, shaped as a sleeping bag. She imagined him ready to bolt in and attack her, like he did to that young woman he'd so cruelly tortured and killed.

Soon he was home. He walked into the kitchen which was located at the back of the house. The whole yard could be seen from the kitchen sink window, and they could enter the garage by using the door at the end of the walkway. The woman who lived with him was rinsing her coffee mug, expecting him home soon when she saw the garage door open. She stiffened, left her mug in the drainer, and walked into the living room, pretending to read. Willing herself to slow her beating heart, that she thought was visibly thumping, she read the same sentence over and over. He walked into the living room and she looked up and looked into his mean, dark eyes, seeming to change to black.

"Let me know when dinner's ready." Saying nothing else he walked away. Releasing her paralyzed state, she was grateful that he walked away to another place in the house. She stared blankly at the open book in her lap. Terrible questions sliced into her, more often now, since the murder. Could it be that he really did this? Did he furtively stalk the woman called Kristel, until he found the opportunity to rape and kill her? How did he choose her and how long did he stalk her before he mercilessly and viciously killed her?

How often had she heard the tale he was so fond of telling, so vulgarly depicted, about how he and his buddies raped a girl. He'd tell her how they'd punched her around beforehand, just enough to show that she may have been brawling with some girls, to cover up what they'd done. He'd warned the girl that she'd better not squeal if she knew what was good for her. There was always that gleam in his eye when he told her such things, a sick excitement in his voice. Sometimes he'd laugh and say he made these things up. Cunningly, he sometimes suggested that he could hurt her if he wanted to.

She was extremely afraid and heart sick, and she sat stone faced on the couch. Finally, with a glance at the book she was reading, he went to the kitchen. She heard the fridge door open and shut, and she heard the familiar twist of the beer cap. Laying her book on the coffee table, she turned on the TV and watched a program without interest.

After a silent dinner, she could hear him playing with the cat, while she cleaned up. It made her flinch and she wanted to fetch Abby, the poor cat who wasn't as gentle as she used to be. She felt sympathy for the usually calm, playful cat. By the time she'd readied herself for bed, he'd had a few drinks and she could hear fanatical laughter and a screaming cat. She looked into the room and saw him on the floor. His arms were scratched, a little blood bubbling from them. Getting up, he lit a cigarette and leaned against her, his face close. "The cat likes roughhousing." The mingling odor of beer and stale cigarettes on his breath made her stomach turn, and she felt his arm brush hers as he turned away. Revulsion crept deep into her and she pulled back, walking into the bathroom to scrub at the blood transferred to the sleeve of the arm of her pajamas that she'd instinctively held up to protect herself. Clean, she went back into the living room to finish her tepid tea. She couldn't forget how he looked when he'd spoken to her just minutes ago. She'd fixed her gaze on his small frame, the buttons stretching his shirt to reveal a growing paunch, to avoid looking at his face. Not being able to completely avoid it, her eyes met his. A smile squinted his lifeless eyes, and a lopsided smile grew into an ugly twist.

Later, he came back into the living room to pick up yesterday's newspaper, as she was finishing the last chapter of the book she'd been reading. The novel explored two families who lived far from each other, but who traded homes for a time, and became forever intertwined. It seems that she always picked happy, captivating novels like that, where people became close friends. Often, she interrupted her sad, depressing life, by becoming one of the characters, vicariously living through them. It was her deliverance from the feelings of hopelessness she harbored, that life would never change.

She had no close friends left, largely due to the discomfort they felt whenever he was around. And, she could no longer lose herself in the activities that engaged her outside the home, like her penchant for making clay bowls and mugs. He said she had plenty to do to keep her at home. Her days were spent doing housework, reading, drawing, and spending time with Abby, who reacted well to her when he wasn't home to aggravate her cat. Still, she'd changed. She didn't cuddle or sleep in her lap anymore, seeming to avoid human contact.

Crucially, as a teen, the killer did not know that an external locust of control existed. He constantly dealt with the push/pull of the stories created in his mind, and within his development he wanted to believe that he was totally possessed. Nothing could be his fault. And, Satan does not act alone. He works side by side with many evil spirits, such as the spirits of hate, destruction, suicide, revenge, anger, anxiety, desperation, death, and torment. Tortured by his father, his life was hell on earth...and he hated submissive women like his mother. He hated his sister as she grew up. She was seen as being just like his mother. He'd become a man who was consumed by split-thinking. He believed in extremes, good versus bad and powerful versus defenseless. His mind convoluted by his unfortunate upbringing, made sense only to him.

Sonny needed to have more time with Mari, the lack of it distressing his wife for some time now. Mari determinedly brought things up to him that bothered her, and presently her thing was that she wanted him home more. If he didn't arrange his work schedule to include more time with his family, she drove it home that there was danger of them drifting apart. When he thought about her, he understood that she had a way in coaxing him toward introspection, and he realized more than ever how much he loved her. Their talks lately wove around his flirtatious manner with women and his rigid work schedule. He was irked sometimes with her persistence, but he also felt loved and important to her. He'd never really doubted that, but she said that knowing it without nurturing it wasn't enough to keep a bloom on their relationship or further the physical side of their marriage. He smiled. She had a good point there.

In a meeting with his boss, they went through files, looked at territories, and together they figured out how to divide the servicing of clients. The result was that in a few weeks he could begin working in his immediate area with a forty hour work week. Relieved of the long grueling hours and anticipating that Mari would be jumping for joy, he could hardly wait to tell her. He could phone her but he wanted to wait until he was home to break the good news. Slowly driving toward home he spotted the lights of the motel ahead. He turned off the road, into a parking space. After checking in, he read the paper, took a beer into the shower with him and felt his energy picking up. Turned out in clean clothes, he was about to set off for a night on the town. A little music, a few drinks, watching women, was just what he needed. Pushed to the back of his mind, the tests that the doctor had ordered had come back. After taking one last long look in the mirror, he said to himself, "Nothin' wrong with a little bit of fun." Sort of like the last hurrah.

Early on in his life, he'd taken it for granted that women fell all over him. Mom was the first, his number one fan. She loved him unequivocally and she was a proponent of the philosophy that when raising children you ignored the bad and reinforced the good. She had the right idea but she didn't understand that raising children was more complicated than that. His father did. He felt that he needed an honest, forthright appraisal of his positive and negative attributes, and that discipline was part of the equation when he fell short. Sonny always felt their love and praise, but she failed to teach him consequences for bad behaviour. In her eyes Sonny could do no wrong.

His strengths lay in the quickness of his intellect and a strong presence and he used these traits to manipulate and sway people in his favour, even his mother. To compound it all, she fixed things when he fell and she never allowed much intrusion from her husband, telling him he was too heavy handed.

She admired his good looks and personality, forever exclaiming, "Oh Sonny. You're such a handsome charmer." She was endlessly cheery, loving, and provided him with most of his wants. His parents weren't well off, just comfortable. But he expected to get what he wanted and needed to impress his buddies and girls. If he lifted money from her wallet for a date, she pretended not to notice. His entitlement grew. When he was old enough to play in bars, he and his buddies formed a band. Bars were the perfect scenario to pick up women. A guitar player usually had an advantage with women. He took up with many of them, married or not. It just didn't matter that he was intruding on other people's relationships. He simply felt heady that he scored a lot.

Sonny always wanted to shine as being congenial and everybody's buddy. But, of course, his views were so important, factual and logical and he could barely tolerate others with a strong sense of themselves. Overconfident, but immature, he wasn't well liked by most. Blind to his faults, he thought he was loved by all. He never noticed that his school buddies passed bored, dull eyed glances between each other, and often didn't bother to counter his views. When they got fed up, they attempted to contest him with a different view. He reacted with mockery and condescension. They felt it was easier to give in to him, something he saw as superiority.

As a teen he became used to the devoted attention of compliant girls, and he used them, and played around some with drugs. Fortunately, he did not become addicted to hard drugs. He needed to be in control of himself, and allowing drugs and booze to control him was out of the question. Besides, most girls did not like losers like drug addicts. When he partied, which was often, he liked beer and pot. In any case, in college he had felt his way around lots of women, always the one breaking hearts with ease and little conscience.

After college he worked as a sales rep for a few years, something he enjoyed, because he loved closing the deal and because he was good at it. During those years, he met Mari. By then he was stable, had matured, and was ready to settle down. She was attractive, fun to be with, a challenge. But, rather than that dampen his interest, it piqued. Her quickness, her curiosity, and that great laugh, totally pre-occupied him. Pretty soon, shocked as he was by the quick development of their relationship, he was in love. He could tell because, even though he noticed other women, she was the one he wanted to be with, only her, and as often as he could. It felt different and good.

A month or so into their relationship, he remembered running into his parent's house and announcing, "I've met her!"

His mother, caught by surprise, dropped the knife she was paring with, and practically screamed, "Who!"

"Mari, the woman I intend to marry. She doesn't know it yet, but she'll

97

say yes. Mom, she is beautiful, has loads of personality, is smart, and did I tell you she's beautiful."

His mom smiled and shook her head and couldn't find any words. She was surprised, to say the least.

"She knows what she wants from life, marriage, a baby, and a career in journalism."

His Mom wiped her hands on a dish towel and hugged him, "I'm happy for you, but this is unexpected! I'd given up thinking that you would settle down and that I'd lose out at becoming a grandma. By the way, do you want children?"

"Mom, I haven't thought about it. But, sure that could be part of the picture. Little Sonny's running around."

The first time he thought, *I want to spend the rest of my life with her*, he was shocked at how quickly he wanted this woman. She had a softly developed body, curves in all the right places, and she was 'tentatively demonstrative', his expression. She never initiated, and didn't respond enthusiastically to anything beyond the missionary position. He wanted more, but he figured that she wasn't as experienced as some of the women he had dated. In time he felt that could change in his favour. He didn't share any of that with his buddies, and that was another thing that clued him that he knew this relationship was different. If his buddies asked if he was "getting any", he purposely stated that he considered that a private thing between them. His response was, "Don't ask me about that. I respect her. She wouldn't want me discussing that."

He remembered their first meeting. He was at the counter in the small café of the city market and when she took the stool several ones away, he noticed her right off, her butt swelling nicely under those pants. He was reading the paper but he made sure to make eye contact at opportune moments. He knew that if he was attracted he had to be direct and follow through. Chatting cordially, he never doubted that he could win her over. Sure enough, before too long, he asked her to dinner for that night. She was not pretentious or coy, or aloof, something that really annoyed him, so he felt great clinching the date. She'd stirred something up in him.

Before long he got lost in those beautiful brown eyes of hers and he found himself thinking about marriage. He even liked it that she was strongly grounded, independent, and stood her ground, whenever she thought it was important to do so. He'd acknowledged that strength and intelligence are positive things in a woman, if you want to spend the rest of your life with her. That kind of thinking astonished him.

What he didn't know was that this shift in his thinking would prove to be more difficult to actually live it. He was going to have to let go of the idea that he was the center of the universe.

Much later in their marriage, seeing Mari's side when she dropped the bombshell about his flirtatious behaviour, he couldn't see it. He was offended and bristled that that she had levelled a veiled accusation at him that he may have cheated. He thought she was being unreasonably suspicious and that he was completely misunderstood.

One of the women he was recently attracted to...he smirked to himself about how Mari referred to her: *what was it? Oh yeah, "Dirty Dancing Big Hair."* That woman had let him know that she was available and the temptation had been there. Their eyes lingered too long and sexual attraction was strong between them. It puffed him up. But he hadn't strayed. When Mari admonished him about how embarrassed and hurt she was when he flirted, he'd been totally surprised and defensive. And she'd persisted. Forced to recognize how he would feel if she acted that way, he felt ashamed. He was baffled at how dismissive he was. He loved her. But, his need for reinforcement that he was charming and irresistible superseded her feelings of emotional betrayal and hurt.

As Sonny waited to get in to see his doctor, he wasn't prepared for what was about to happen. After shaking hands with Dr. Shay, they sat down and he informed Sonny of the results of his blood, as well as other tests. The doctor soberly told him that he had colon cancer. He blurted, "Say that again!" Dr. Shay did. He had to face that full on and he barely heard what the doctor continued to talk about. Later, he vaguely recalled the doctor chastising him for not taking better care of himself. Sonny had tried to appease the doctor by claiming that the nature of his job made that very difficult, that motel living, fast food, smoking...blah, blah, blah. To no avail. The doctor bluntly straightened Sonny out. Things had to change.

His relationship with the guys in the band was strained because he didn't have time to play like before, so a musician from another band covered for him when he wasn't available. This bothered Sonny. However, he admitted that he drank and smoked more when he was in the company of his friends. Now, with this revelation he had face things squarely, so that he would commit to seriously changing things that would only contribute to his illness, and hinder his road back to health and family.

The rewards would allow him to spend more time with his wife, so important to him now, and also with his kids, Haley and Vince.

CHAPTER 8

THE UNEXPECTED, EXPECTED

Early one morning before leaving her downtown apartment, April held the receiver to her ear, while sipping coffee. She had so much to tell Mari. They'd been having discussions about what she could do for the rest of her long life: *What dumb ass said life was short.* Coming out of rehab and returning to the bar certainly was not the best atmosphere she could surround herself with, the counsellor told her, but she had already accepted that it wasn't the best choice for her. It would be too tempting to drink if she continued to wrap herself around the bar scene, especially since she was "just beginning to work on your sobriety." She agreed and wanted to resolve that. She left the bar tending to her employees and focused her efforts to finding a buyer for the bar.

She planned to open up a little café with a patio attached to the side of it. Also, she wanted to vacate her downtown apartment, a scene that encouraged a certain lifestyle, with clubs close by, as well as where her drinking friends lived. April had decided to move permanently into her cottage, a peaceful, serene environment for someone who wanted to rebound from a hectic, party life atmosphere. Excitedly, she envisioned a bold way to paint the large indoor and outdoor living areas, and she could hardly wait to get started. She wanted to replicate Canada's east coast landscape, loving the red, blue, green, and yellow houses, trimmed with other primary colours. Fidgeting, she waited for Mari to answer the phone. She had to content herself with leaving a message. "Morning Mari.

I need to talk to you. It's important. I have something interesting news. Okay, bye."

Mari roused. Groggily, she looked at the phone before clumsily making her way over to it. It was April. She listened to the message but she had to wake up before she would even think of calling her back. By the time she made coffee and dialed April's number, she wasn't there: *Damn, now I'll have to wait. She said she had news. I wonder what THAT means.*

She was proud of her sister. April had finally faced her alcoholism straight on and she was focused on rebuilding her life. Mari's instincts told her that she was going to make it. She'd thrown herself into doing everything she had to do to succeed. April had informed her staff about her idea of opening a café, and ensured her staff that they would keep their jobs. They understood that she had to spend less time at the bar, expecting them to take responsibility for the bar until it was sold. And, she attended all her sessions with AA. Mari felt assured that April had gumption, was spirited, and loved life too much to keep living it so destructively. She would succeed.

Her thoughts shifted to Fiona. She'd secured her little home, added outdoor lighting, and had purchased a cell phone. She kept in constant contact with family, and Haley and Vince called her regularly too. Rudimentary as these things were, Mari felt a little bit more secure about her sister's safety. And Mari would tell her she couldn't put her life on hold, even in the face of evil. Encouraged, Fiona's spirits had improved a little but she was nervous as a cat. She jumped wide eyed at every little thing, didn't venture out too much, beyond going to work, grocery shopping and buying wine. A glass of wine calmed her at night when she watched television. Bent on getting better, she continued with her counseling, took her anti-depressants, and was able to work to the satisfaction of her employer. During their last conversation however, Fiona had seemed so alone.

"I feel like I'm being watched. I'm forever fussing with the locks, checking the windows, pulling blinds."

"Fiona, honey, why wouldn't you be that way? After what happened to you."

"But I feel like I have no power. I can't get a grasp on finding anything that would help me feel safe. He rules my life, know what I mean? And, that can only be alleviated when he is caught and put away." After that conversation, Mari thought improvement in Fiona could take longer than she thought. Fiona was up and down, mostly down.

Consequently, after Mari's insistence, Fiona had asked the police to comb the area around her home for signs of anything suspicious. The police had been doing so, but they more than willingly complied to do it more often. They'd also repeated their suggestion that she take advantage of the services of their Police Community Support Officers. She eventually agreed that she would. Their efforts helped some, but she couldn't halt her deepest fears. In her mind, he wasn't done with her.

Mari often wondered if Fiona would ever feel safe again. Frustrating the whole family, their calls to the police were patiently dealt with, but they couldn't offer anything that could reassure them. They stressed that they were doing everything they could.

Late in the evening, ensconced in her easy chair enjoying a cloudless July sky, Mari decided to try April. She picked up the phone and without preamble, spit out, "I've been waiting by the phone. I don't know how to say this, but my life will be forever changed about seven months from now."

"Pardon me?"

"I'm pregnant."

"Pregnant?"

Yes, p-r-e-" Incredulous, Mari retorted, "I know how to spell pregnant. I don't know what to say. This is nothing to joke about or throw at me like this."

"Sorry. Joking is the way I handle hard things sometimes, you know that."

"April, I have a question. Did you NOT know enough to use birth control?"

"I know, I know. Don't beat me up. When you drink you're not exactly clear headed or responsible."

"Oh, you're responsible. I just don't believe this. Is this real?"

"Yes. It's real! I have the results of my test. I'm due sometime in February."

"What are you going to do?"

She stammered, "I've gone over it...and over it...have an abortion, which I don't want to do...or go through with the pregnancy. I have never even considered becoming a mother...placing the baby up for adoption seems right. I want to do what's best for the baby."

"Does he know?"

"No, and he's not going to. Mister Casual could never be a good father."

"How are you feeling?"

"I'm as healthy as a horse, in spite of what I've put myself through. It's uncanny that I decided that I needed to quit drinking. I didn't know I was pregnant when I made that decision. I got a thorough medical before I decided to detoxify, and that's how I found out. I had been feeling queasy, but I'd just put it to nerves. I had no clue." She dissolved into tears. Mari gave her time to gather herself, and in the seconds that took, Mari felt the weight of this. Her first reaction was to be angry with her, but her heart went out to her.

"Have you told anyone else?"

"No, I haven't, and please don't say anything to Fiona until I sort it all out. Besides, there are lots of worse things in the world than bringing a sweet little baby into it." She wished April was beside her so she could touch her.

"I can't argue with that."

April pleaded, "Mari, please don't be mad at me. I promise my priority will be to do everything I can to have a healthy baby, and I will do the right thing for him or her. I can't wait to see that sweet little face."

"I'm sure you're searching your heart and you'll do the right thing. And, I'm not angry. Just bewildered and worried. I'll help all I can. Call if you need me." Sounding as though she had the world lifted from her shoulders, April said, "Thanks and love you, bye."

Off the phone, Mari paced and yelled: "Does anything get any crazier?!!" Cognizant of open windows, she clapped a hand over her mouth. *April, April, April. I just cannot worry about that right now, my husband needs me. He's so gaunt. Thank God he quit smoking. He'll be home soon. Hopefully, I'll be able to determine how he's doing. He's been evasive.* She tried to read but could only read two or three sentences at a time before her mind would wander and she'd think her husband's ill health, April's situation, and Fiona's state of mind. She tossed the book aside, and just sat awhile, eyes closed. Sonny came home as she was putting a salad together for dinner. He kissed her and said he wanted to lay down for a while. She asked him how he was. He said, "Okay, nothing to worry about. I've been overworked, that's all."

While preparing for work in the morning, Mari suddenly decided that she was going to take the afternoon off. She felt weary and thought that maybe she and Haley could get together and have some easy time together, walking through the park with the dog. Being with her daughter always lifted her spirits. She got out of her office clothes and got into her tan cropped pants and runners and she ran to work, already feeling lighter. She tidied some loose ends that were still sitting on her desk and told her boss that she had things to do: "I'll make up for the lost time."

"Go ahead. You've been working hard and nothing's pressing. Sorry about that."

"Hmm?"

"Nothing's pressing. A pun?"

"Oh-h, good one. I'm really not with it. Gotta go. Thanks."

She called Haley. They decided to make this another "Walking with Ducky" day, part of Haley's exercise program, her incentive to get some cardio in. Time permitting Mari would then go to Fiona's. Face to face she could see how she was really doing. She ran home, got into her car and zoomed off.

Haley was on the front porch with the dog and he looked ready to go, pouncing on her when she reached the sidewalk.

"Hi Mom. It's a good day for this. Such great weather." The dog ran back and forth between them.

"Yes, it's nice. Ducky, what do you think?"

"Does he look anxious to get going, or what?" Mari patted the dog's head and scuttled past him, "I'm gonna fill my water bottle. Just a sec." She walked toward the front door of the neat Tudor style house, a few blocks showing similar Tudors on both sides of the street. She entered the foyer and continued through the hallway past the living room. At the end of the hallway, she entered the kitchen, noticing the lilies on the table in the kitchen nook. On the way back, she went into the living room, looked out the living room window, framed by dark stained wood, her eyes were trained on the guy standing across the street. She noticed the tattoo on his left forearm, his face was shaded by a red cap, and he was tanned and fit. He was watching Haley. *Who is that?* Mari wondered. She went to the bathroom off the hallway, and by the time she was ready to go and had made her way outside again, the man was nowhere to be seen. Haley started talking a mile a minute. She filled her mother in on Vince and Sally, "I like Sally. She looks like a young Annie Lennox. You know, those bright eyes, those big lips and straight teeth. So dramatic. And, the clothes she wears. She's unique. Anyway, they really like each other and we all get along. Last weekend we went to the pub. Rex brought some cards and we had a few beers and pizza. It was fun."

Mari listened, waiting for her to stop talking long enough to tell her about the man she had seen. But, Haley kept up the chatter and glad that they were spending happy time together, she decided that she'd ask later. She said, "I haven't had time with Vince lately. I'm so happy for him. He's finding his niche. And, he seems to have a great girl."

"Yep, and he's dancing his ass off. They're both auditioning to get into some funky musical."

"That is wonderful! I have to call him. Okay, brace yourself. I have something to tell you."

"What?"

"Aunt April, you know, she's doing well, but, she's pregnant."

"She's what?"

"You sound like I did when she told me. She had been seeing a guy, oh, several months ago, and he turned out to be Mister Casual, as she referred to him. Anyway, April had no trouble forgetting about him, but the relationship with him, left her pregnant." The expression on Haley's face exposed what she felt. She looked stunned, her mouth wide open, both hands over it, closing it only to say, "I don't believe it. Who is Mister Caj?"

"She prefers to not even acknowledge him. So we won't either."

"Fine."

"But yeah, believe it. April is due in February."

"How is she? What is she going to do?"

"She's fine and working to figure that out."

"What a mind blower! I hope she keeps the baby."

"April says that's not an option."

"Ah, it would be fun having a baby in the family." Mari thought how Haley never complicated things. Probably like most young people.

"So you have one," Mari threw out.

"Sorry Mom, we're not ready, might not ever be," looking into her mother's face for a reaction, seeing only slight disappointment there.

"Fine, if that's to be. That's your business."

"Are you disappointed?"

"Don't know. Haven't really thought about it much. And right now, we have to help April get through her dilemma."

"I love her to death. We all do. We'll all help. Don't worry about her."

"Mm, yeah well, I hope your Aunt Fiona takes this as well as you have. They approach life very differently."

"I know, but it'll work out," she said, responding to the worry on her mother's face.

They found a bench and sat silently for a few minutes, basking in the sunshine until they were not even aware of each other. Mari had travelled back to the moment she knew her husband had cancer and how April had stunned her with her pregnancy "news." Haley was worrying about the man who lived across from her, wondering if he was dangerous to her in any way.

Haley heard an intake of breath and felt her mother grasp her arm. She looked at her Mom's frightened eyes and she tracked her gaze. Mari was looking at a man some distance away.

"Mom, what's wrong?"

"See that man walking by the play area over there," not taking her eyes off him.

"Yeah."

"He's the creepy guy I told you about, the guy who wouldn't leave my table at the K House. What's he doing here by himself?"

"He's slowing down to look at those kids coming down the slide," she said, echoing her mother's concern.

"In light of what I know and feel about him, it doesn't seem right. When we get back to your place I'm calling the police. Both of us can identify him now. When your father and I were out with Malcolm and Penny one night at the new pub, he was there and he recognized me. I don't want him to see us. Come on, let's leave. Those kids are with adults.

They're okay." Haley got up from the bench, tugged at the dog's leash, taking a last look at the man, noting everything about him, then she followed her mother who was heading for the street. As soon as they got to Haley's house Mari called the police station and requested to speak to Officer Robertson. When he came to the phone, she said, "Hello, this is Mari Dolan. I wanted to talk to you about that guy who had hassled me at the K House."

"Sure, I remember. I spoke to him. About all I could do was talk about the incident when he'd harassed you. But, it enabled me to put him in my cross hairs. Did something else happen?"

"My daughter and I just returned from the park here in town, and he was there. He didn't see us. He was watching the young mothers, especially paying attention to the children. It was off putting. I decided we should call you."

"Yes, that is something to worry about. I'll talk to him without naming you, of course. I'll say that a young mother at the park reported seeing him hanging around watching the children. We'll keep an eye on him. And thank you for your steadfast attention to things. It goes without saying, that it is so important that people watch out for each other. Call anytime. And, I must say, I appreciated the interview you had with Kristel's parents. You handled it with compassion."

"Thank you. Good bye."

She put the phone down, and told Haley that the officer was going to talk to him.

Haley had started tea and asked, "Mom, do you ever wonder who it could be, the killer, I mean."

"Oh yeah. Sometimes I think it might be that slime ball we saw in the park. Sometimes I think it's that oriental guy, George, who lives across the street from us and takes out his bad temper on his wife. Or maybe it's Connor, so nondescript he is, so pleasant 'she made a face.'"

"I thought you and Dad liked Connor."

"He's just, oh, sneaky like…or, it could be this guy, Carl, from work. He has a way of looking at you. He just stares and avoids making small talk. A little weird."

Haley looked past her mother across the street and pointed out a house that had relatively new neighbours living in it. "The guy who lives in that house watches me a lot. He walks up and down the street, looking over when I'm sitting on the porch, usually after dusk. I try to ignore him. He doesn't say anything to me. Just walks and looks over. Then, the other night I saw him through that little window over there, looking my way. It unnerved me. Once in his yard, he had binoculars. I'm real careful that the curtains and the blinds are closed after dusk."

"I noticed him before we left for the park. Haley, you've never mentioned him," she admonished.

"I know. Rex knows about it. He says to ignore him."

"I'd call the cops."

"Mom, we can't just call the cops on people who stare. If he does anything more than that, I will."

"Promise?"

"Promise." Then, quickly retorted, "Anyway, why didn't you call the cops on that guy we saw at the park, you know, when he creeped you out in the bar?"

"Point taken. I had intended to do that the next morning. Somehow, I neglected to do so. But I did approach Officer Robertson when I saw him again. I'm not perfect Haley."

Frustrated, they talked about how each person in town may have a handful of people they suspected. Haley said that, besides that guy across the street from her, she was concerned about Rex's high school buddy, Pete, that while he and Rex didn't hang around with each other anymore, they ran into him occasionally at the dog park.

"Mom, there's something about him. The look in his eyes as he watches the women around us, 'she shuddered'. He seems to be fuming with his hands in his pockets, playing with his change."

"It's funny how we can attach things ominously to some men who we're only acquainted with and don't know much about."

"Yeah, I know, though this guy I just talked about does have a troubling history. Just before graduation from high school, he was accused of rape by a grade eleven student. Rex doesn't know the outcome of that story, but he did say that some girls didn't like him. That could be why I assume there's something wrong with him. If I didn't know that, would I still be suspicious of him because he seems angry and plays with his change. Just like you said Mom, what happened here could be causing us to be hyper about stuff."

"Maybe so Haley," as Mari looked at the time.

They had whiled away most of the day, so kissing Haley good-bye she made her way to Fiona's. She stopped at the market and as she was paying for her greens and fruit she turned and saw George drive by. Hao was with him. She waved to them. They waved back. It was perturbing to have to be congenial with George, knowing what she knew, but she was hoping to get to know Hao better.

By the time she reached Fiona's she was ravenous, so right after their kiss hello Mari tossed a big, delicious salad, and Fiona set out an Italian loaf and garlic butter. As they ate, she filled her in on her visit with Haley, only telling her they'd had a fun afternoon at the park. She left out their discussion surrounding their suspicions of who the murderer might be, and that they had sighted "the creep" in the park. It would not add to Mari's idea that she would use this visit to lift Fiona up. The conversation flowed about everyday things like what Vince and Haley had been up to recently and how Sonny was, but Mari could tell that her sister was a wreck. Fiona returned the conversation in a monotone. There was no feeling behind the words. Mari pointedly asked her how she was. Fiona was quiet for a moment: "I'm a little better than I have been, but I'm nervous and jumpy, especially at night. Pal 'she petted her Lab' helps big time. If I have trouble sleeping I just curl up to her. She's great company."

"She is beautiful. Aren't you Pal?" Mari petted the sandy haired Lab.

"And so protective. She stays close. It's like she knows something's wrong, But I don't know how aggressive she can be. She hasn't been tested yet." Fiona added.

"What happened to you, I know it's not something you forget easily. But life has to go on. Maybe it is time you got involved with people."

"I guess. It's just that I'm afraid to venture out at night. Sad, isn't it? You're not even safe in your own home."

Persistent, Mari said, "Once you got started with something, maybe having people in for a game night or something like that, you could go from there."

"Yeah, I've been a little stir crazy, and lonesome for company and activity, that's for sure." She bent to pat the dog's head again.

After dinner and washing up they sat on the porch with their wineglasses in tow. This was really enjoyable for Fiona who didn't venture into her yard alone. It was dusk, which along with daybreak, were her favourite times of the day. And it was just cool enough, the wine just dry enough. Fiona shook off her blouse and dressed in her tank top and jeans, she let the breeze drift over her arms. Both relaxed they didn't say anything. Fiona thought about how the density of the trees threatened her. Longingly, she hoped one day that she might find them lush and beautiful, that life would be good again, like now, in this moment. When she was alone in the house, the only time she didn't feel threatened by her outdoor surroundings, was when Pal went to investigate. All things quiet past the trees would let her know that there was no one hiding beyond her view.

Mari was thinking back to the last conversation she had with April about her request that she not say anything about her pregnancy. Quickly, after saying hello to each other and, "What's up Mari?" April had presumed, "Fiona doesn't know, right?" She'd lightly argued, "April, you can't hide this much longer. Before you start showing, it might be a good idea to tell her. How about if I tell Fiona about your pregnancy?"

"Oh wow, I hadn't thought of myself being really pregnant, like big pregnant, if you know what I mean. I do have to get telling Fiona out of the way. And you telling her takes the pressure off me to spill the beans. Say yes. Please."

The next time Mari spoke to Fiona, she started the conversation with, "Fiona, I have news."

Looking hopeful, Fiona said, "Haley's pregnant."

"Hah, that's funny. Haley and I were on that subject today. Nope, not Haley." Reluctant, but determined to get this over with, she continued, "Somebody else is having a baby."

"Mari, no, you and Sonny?"

"Come on. Really."

"Tell me, for Christ's sake." She looked ready to pounce on Mari and shake the news from her.

"April." Instantly, Fiona's face darkened in disbelief. Mari thought: *If she says, "I don't believe it. I'll laugh. I won't be able to stop myself.*

Fiona exploded, "She's pregnant. Well, is that a surprise! I took it for granted that the stupid bitch slept around so much she'd be smart enough to use birth control. What else do you expect from a drunk?"

She gaped at her sister, "Fiona. It's our little sister we're talking about"

"Ask me if I care? How long have I wanted a baby? April doesn't deserve this. She probably doesn't even want it, does she?"

"She hasn't decided what she's going to do."

"That sounds like she's probably thinking about abortion or adoption. Is she?"

"Maybe, I…"

"She's always been so self-centered, doing whatever she likes whenever she likes. She's so goddamned irresponsible. Who's the father?" Mari had been staring at Fiona and didn't answer right away. "You mean April doesn't know!?"

Mari yelled, "Fiona! Stop! Christ, I wouldn't want to be in your line of fire. It's not for YOU to judge April. She's doing great. She's not drinking…"

"So far."

"And you know she's selling the bar. She's been working hard to change her life. She's just been thrown another curve. But you know how soft she can be. Whatever she decides, it will be the best for the baby," her voice moderating.

"I just don't get her. How can she be so damned stupid?"

"She's human, like you." That brought Fiona to a contrite level.

"I'm sorry. God, I am so reactive."

"You think?"

"Yeah, but this really blows me away. I've wanted a baby so badly."

Mari took a deep breath, "I get that you're angry. You're angry at Warren, angry at the world for lots of things, and now you're angry at your sister who's having a baby and you're not. I get it!" Then she snickered and shrugged, "You'll get over it."

In spite of herself Fiona laughed and pointed her finger, "Only you could talk to me that way. Damn you." Seeing how pissed Fiona had been, making light at that moment could have backfired. Mari laughed with relief. She continued, "Anyway, have you always made the right decisions in your life, always done right?"

"Okay, okay, I've been put in my place and I'll really have a lot to discuss with my therapist at our next session, thanks to you."

"Good, you wouldn't want it to get boring. Like those long silences you see between patients and their therapists in movies?"

"It does get quiet like that. They want you to make it your own voyage. Also, they're waiting for breakthroughs in counseling. If that happens or is going to happen they make the session longer, so as not to lose it, so to speak."

"Sounds like you know what you're talking about."

"I've had some breakthroughs lately. My issues stem from what Mom did and who she was as a person. She was so unpredictable when she drank and then she left. She didn't love me enough to stay. It left me vulnerable for a man like Warren. Men like him sniff a woman like me from a mile away." She raised her wine glass and continued, "We talk a lot about women like me."

"Like?"

"Oh, you know, submissive, always obeying, something you wouldn't think I'd be or do. Then, even when I'd had enough, I just stuffed it further down. It turned into depression. When I finally do express anger, it's barbed and inappropriate, like I did just a few minutes ago against April." Mari saw shame in Fiona's eyes, and Fiona bent her head and didn't speak again until Mari said, "Sounds like you're getting something from the counselling."

"Yeah, it might not seem like it, but I am learning. The anger I feel is really at me, and I will never compromise myself in a relationship like I did with Warren. But first, before anything else, I have to get past this latest attack by that maniac, on my life, my peace. And I will."

"Fiona, that's the first time I hear how determined you are to beat that awful thing. Listen, tell you what. Let's get tipsy."

"What?"

"Let's get drunk. I'll sleep over, but I will have to go home early in the morning and change before I go to work, so before I forget I'm going to re-set your alarm." She flounced off.

Bursting into a big smile, eager to relax, have fun again, Fiona scooped up the empty glasses. She made her way to the kitchen to re-fill them. Looking outside, she felt the familiar tightening in her stomach, tonight, as every night when she looked out at the darkening sky. Mari returned to the kitchen to find Fiona standing at the sink looking out the window. She reached past her, closed the café curtains, and together they fixed delicious, somewhat unhealthy snacks. Before long they had mixed a guacamole dip and they brought out the hummus from the fridge, planning to eat both with taco scoops. They settled in the living room. Mari told Fiona about her worries surrounding Sonny; his long hours away from home and how his life style might be affecting his health. Fiona felt relieved that the conversation was not about her. Mari, ready to enjoy herself with her sister, looked through Fiona's CD's and put Serena Ryder on. They sang, well, sort of. It was fun! And, they danced to Ryder's Stompa. Fiona, released from apprehension, said, "It's been so long since I've had such fun." Mari nodded and laughed, as the dog looked on, sitting up as though he wanted to join in.

Looking out at the darkness, Mari pulled the drapes shut. Fiona thought: *Mari is here. I'm okay.*

CHAPTER 9

FUSION AND SEPARATION

M*ari's been looking forward to this…even if I bring bad news with the good news.* Sonny's mind reeled from all the planning that been put into motion. He had informed clients that reps from the home office would be filling in for him. Soon he would be spending more time at home, with Mari especially. Late in the day he ended his meeting with a demanding client and checked into his motel, using the bathroom before stepping into the hot shower. He noticed blood in his stool again. After his shower he put on fresh pajamas. He weighed himself, and calculated a ten pound drop just this month. Closing down and worried about the symptoms he was having, he crashed. Morning dawned beautifully and as he got into his car he willed himself to have positive thoughts. It was sunny and the sky was wide open, as it is in Ontario. He kept the windows down even though it was a bit cool. As he eased onto the highway, he noticed the whirling of dry leaves. He'd seen millions of falling leaves in his five decades, but this time the experience was different, and in a split second, his mood darkened. It was the first time he'd faced the possibility of death and in a strange, tough moment he tracked its path. Doom dominated over what used to be his vision of himself as strong and invincible, and it could be that he wouldn't be around in the near future. He felt diminished and powerless. As he drove he got lost in thought. He wondered if he could do something magnificent, something that would make a mark on the world, before he rotted away…like those leaves that spun, sailed, and dropped. He rubbed at his temple. He had to have a cigarette, just one: *What will I tell her? How will I say it? Can I soften it?* He tried to rub the headache away that was sneaking up on him.

Sonny led Mari into the living room, sitting next to her on the couch. Looking into his face, waiting for him to speak, Mari found her words, "Sonny, what! You're scaring me." He spilled it out, nothing held back.

"I have colon cancer. It's progressing and…

"Oh my God, Sonny, tell me I'm not hearing this," her voice sad and faltering. It quickly veered to anger.

"I'm your wife! How could you not share this with me right away? You don't have a clue how worried I've been. I saw how fatigued you were and I saw you quickly losing weight. I didn't know what to think. And you're just telling me now that you have colon cancer! 'Mari pounded the table', and you sound as though you've given up. You're looking at a dark hole in the ground and you've placed yourself there already. Don't tell me that!" She started to cry, cradling her chest.

He didn't reach for her, his energy dead. Mari looked at this man that she could lose. She was stunned, but resolute. "God, honey, 'she rubbed the tears away', I'm so sorry, but cancer is not a death sentence. Lots of people have been given death sentences and they've lived long lives. Don't give up! I'm not!" He was heartened by the fervor of her words.

Sonny repeated what the doctor had described would happen: "The cancer has grown through the outermost layer of the colon, but has not gone outside the colon. The surgeon is going to do something called anastomosis. It removes the diseased part of the colon and reattaches the healthy tissue. He's done many of them. Doc said he is excellent."

"Honey, that sounds good. Did he say anything else?"

"You don't want to hear this. Last year, Dr. Shay told me that I was at that age when I should have a colonoscopy done. I ignored it. Boy, did he give me shit."

"Oh Sonny. Do you think you know more than your doctor? Had you done what you were told, this wouldn't be happening," she admonished.

"It doesn't matter now." How long would it take before she understood that this was probably the end of the line. His voice breaking, he said, "How can I expect you to absorb all this? I tried to get a grip on the reality of it before I shared all this with you."

"You may have taken the time to adjust to this reality, as you call it, but you'll have to wait for me. I just don't know what to say, what to do. But, I know this. I need to know what you want from me. And, you need to know what I feel. I need to tell you. And when you get better, we've built a stronger gar, eh, what am I saying. I just can't think of life without you." He listened to her quick, breathless sobs and cut in, "Mari, were you going to say that you want to build a stronger garden? Yeah, that makes sense. If I don't make it, you could pluck from it whenever you're missing me. You God-damn poets." She collapsed in laughter and tears. He stared at her. Pulling herself together, she said, "Listen honey, I'm going to take care of you and you ARE going to co-operate. We'll do it together." She turned to him and laid her head on his chest. He held her.

"You know Mari, I've always thought I understood you, but then you get all caught up in the metaphysical, these springboards for getting something, all this mind and body enhancing stuff. It's lost on me." She smiled through her reddened face, "It's what I turn to, to feel better," her eyes sad.

He stroked her back, "What do we do now?"

"We talk, we make plans for the future, but we'll do it a little differently. People spend so much time building for a future that just may not be there, or could be very different than what they imagine. They miss now. I bet if we knew the future we'd make our lives mean more, do more of everything we like, spend a little more money, go away, love everybody more." She looked up at him.

He heard the words, but he finally answered, "I keep thinking of my father and his bout with cancer. Such stark, slow motion pain, terminating with a painful death. I'm so pissed that this has happened to me!" He put his head down. She sat with her arms around him and let him grieve. After long minutes he looked at her: "I am so sorry for all the times I've let you down and hurt you."

"It's okay," she smiled and touched his hair. Then the urgency for knowing how this happened to him took over, "When did you first know that something was wrong?" He remembered the first inkling that things didn't feel right.

"I was at a motel getting ready for bed, phoning you like I said I would, and I felt this pain in my stomach, and it felt a little swelled. I mentioned it to you at the time, remember? 'She nodded' Anyway, I didn't worry about it. I was exhausted from driving and convening two of three meetings that day, so I slept twelve hours, thinking I'd be fine. It didn't go away, and then I started feeling worse, going back and forth from constipation and diarrhea, so I made an appointment with Dr. Shay. He said we'd get tests done, blah blah blah, do an endoscopy. The thing, the endoscope is a long tube with a light at the end of it that allows the doctor to see your insides." He looked at his wife who was nodding, so intent on catching every word, "A few days later he called me at the office, asking me to come in. He told me it was colon cancer. Apparently, with this cancer, there often are no signs and symptoms until the disease is well on the way. That really got to me. I went home and just stumbled around for a while, not believing any of it. Then, it hit me. I'm so glad you weren't home. I punched my fists into the wall of the garage till they were raw." She remembered the night she'd noticed his hands so raw and reddened. "I didn't know what to do. Then, I paced the garage for a while, not knowing what to do next." He stopped talking again. Finally, he said, "While I was there I asked him if he could promise me a few more years with my wife." She smiled wanly, "As if doctors could promise you anything, but you will get past this. We'll beat it together. And honey, you have to take responsibility for how you're going to take care of this, with the doctor's help, of course, and mine." He stood up and walked to the living room window. She felt ready to fall apart again and wanted to hold it together until she could be alone.

"This week I'm feeling weaker than ever. I'm really tired a lot. Sometimes I see blood in my stool. Dr. Shay said that is a serious symptom. He also said that I will probably have to work part time, or not work at all, depending on how I feel. Man, you wanted me to slow down. Turns out I don't have a choice." He didn't say that he would miss this job that represented so much of what he was, a practiced, sharp salesperson, who did well for the company. Looking at her he sensed how unnerved she was, by how rigid she sat, hands folded, and he stopped thinking about himself. He walked back to her, took her hand and smiled through a pale face, "Let's go for a short walk. Maybe we can find some flowers to pick." She smiled and nodded. On the path in the park he told her what had been transpiring at work, telling her that if he continues to work, he would soon be starting his new schedule close to home. "I had to save the best news for last." She hugged him hard, passerby's looking on and smiling.

Dulled by what she had to face, she went through the motions of getting through her work day, and the next. On Saturday morning she let go. She sobbed so hard her insides hurt and when she was rid of the numbing pain, she felt ready to face what was ahead of them. She decided that she will only hold onto positive thoughts: *I will be strong for what lies ahead for him, and for now I'll hold onto the thought that he will be coming home every day after work.*

Information about the murder investigation occupied a small space on the first page of the morning paper. Mari read it. Without giving specifics, the police did say that they continued to work around the clock, and followed any leads that the public brought forth. She couldn't pin it down, but she had the feeling they had something they weren't giving up. She also pondered that the lack of updates probably meant that they still had very little to go on. Thrusting the paper aside, she felt that if she was frustrated by reading this barely informed article, others must be too. Her coffee cold, she got up to dump it in the sink, startled by Sonny who'd come up behind her. He hugged her and she turned to hug him back. Checking the coffee she found that it had become strong, having forgotten to turn the coffee maker off. It was so hard to stay focused lately, feeling overwhelmed by Sonny's cancer, not to mention how her sisters relied on her. She hoped to be able to meet everyone's needs.

"Why don't you look at the paper and I'll make some fresh coffee." He walked off into the living room, taking the paper with him. Joining him with coffee and a small tray of orange sections she lounged opposite him in the recliner, offering him fruit.

"Just coffee, thanks," he nodded toward the paper, "A little bit of news here, nothing much. Sometimes it takes years to solve this type of crime. Sometimes they're not solved."

"I know. It's unthinkable. By the way, you look rested, not so strained."

"Yeah, I slept well. The weight's off and I won't be away working days on end. I feel so light."

"Me too." She smiled softly.

They moved through the morning just relaxing, munching on fruit and her favourite dark chocolate covered biscuits. Needing to be doing something on this sunny day, they tidied up the yard, discarding the browned flowers and primping the ones that still looked new. A lush burnt orange gerbera looked ready to open up. Mari thought they were amazing. Some bloomed late into the fall season, like this one. She touched it. It gave her hope, continuing to abide by her idea of being positive, even if it was only over a flower. But it wasn't just a flower. She told herself that it was there to show her that their world would heal.

Later in the day, midafternoon actually, they settled down in the sun dappled yard with light sweaters on. Over their late lunch they talked about the tough chore of telling family and friends, and they decided that they would have everyone over and tell everyone at the same time.

Having Sonny come home every night proved to be a joy. He helped with chores and they spent a lot of time together. Even watching television took on a new quality because he got home much earlier and they could decide together what to watch.

And, she noticed that each of them fluctuated from being hopeful about Sonny's prognosis, to being unable to rise above their sadness. When this happened they shored each other.

Fiona heard the phone ring. Putting her rake down, she rubbed her hands together and went in. She pressed the button to get her message, and listened for the message to begin. It didn't. She felt her throat seize up.

"Hey BITCH, the sex I had with Kristel? It was the best sex I've ever had. You're next. Are you as excited as I am?" Next, she heard muffled laughter. He hung up.

She stumbled back and reaching back for the arm of her chair, she slumped into it. Hardly breathing, she got up and walked back and forth in the living room. Her heart raced. Fear dominated. What to do! What to do! Call the police! Calming her hands, she pushed POLICE on her contacts list. A voice said, "Police headquarters. May I help you?" Shakily, she said her name and asked to speak to Officer Robertson. He lifted the receiver, "Hi Fiona. What can I do for you?"

"Hello. Someone left a message on my phone. Please come."

"We'll be there shortly." Within ten minutes Officer Robertson and a female police officer arrived and listened to the message. They replayed it several times attempting to pick up any distinctions in the voice. "Fiona, is there anything significant in the voice tone or the words used?" It was useless. Fiona couldn't come up with anything that might help identify him. They told her that surveillance of her home would be stepped up again. Also, they would rig up her phone that would immediately trace probable future calls.

They left, and she had to think about how to proceed. A victim for most of her life, first of a compassionless mother, followed by a domineering, controlling husband, her depression, now this evil thing…it had to stop. This madman would not win! Fiona felt her old self bouncing back. Anger propelled her. This emergent attitude had taken change after listening to that vile message and she held onto it. It felt better than the awful depression she'd been dealing with. While she waited for the officers she came to the conclusion that being a victim would no longer dominate her catalog for living life.

After the officers left, she called Mari to tell her of the awful message she received, and what Officer Robertson proposed what they would do. Mari, terrified for her, hoped that Fiona would accept the idea of having someone live with her, an idea that surfaced recently when she'd been thinking of her. This latest threat made it all the more important.

"Fiona, would you consider having someone live with you? You have that extra room that you could convert into a bedroom. And we have the guest room that you can occupy for as long and as often that you need it."

"Thanks. I may consider bunking with you sometimes, but a roommate? Even the best of friends can't be expected to agree to living in this house, with this situation," her voice catching. Hurriedly she continued, "I need to gather my wits, think how I will face this moving forward. Can I come over this coming weekend?" Mari answered, "The room will be ready." She said nothing to her about Sonny's illness? It didn't seem like a good time, and being that she was staying over the weekend, she'd know soon enough. Mari informed Sonny of the phone call Fiona had received, and told him how she was spending the weekend with them.

Sonny concurred, "That's the best thing we can do for her now. That dirty bastard! I want to do something, but what? It's frustrating not to have any recourses to help her. And the cops. There's nothing new being reported. How long will she have to live with this maniac making dangerous threats like this? That, I'm sure he'll continue to do."

At the same time this was happening to Fiona, they had invited his parents, Haley and Vince, and the rest of the family, over to their house the coming weekend to break the news. It was time, and because Mari didn't want to alarm anybody ahead of time, she just told everyone it was time for everyone to get together. Fiona had been the only one left to call, but with this vicious incident that had happened to her, a call wasn't necessary. She'd be there to hear it.

On Friday Mari baked a cake and an apple pie to serve. The next morning they cleaned a bit and put fresh flowers in the guest room for Fiona. Mari felt as prepared as she could be. As the morning progressed she noticed how worried Sonny had become as he tried to prepare himself for what loomed ahead of them. She took something for her own tension headache. During a rest period and over their second mug of coffee it dawned on her that with all that had occurred she'd neglected to tell Sonny about April.

"Oh, by the way. April's pregnant," she blurted, feeling her mouth twitch.

"Wonderful. Who's the father?"

"Mister Casual." They burst out laughing, and finishing their coffee, that became the topic of conversation. They wondered how that perplexity would work out for April.

On Saturday afternoon, their relatives seated, Mari told them about the phone call Fiona had received and that she would be coming soon to spend the weekend. Disbelieving, they were incredibly angry and sad for her. Silence hung in the air. Finally, Sonny said, "There's something else Mari and I have to share. I have colon cancer." The living room became quiet again. It seemed as though they'd all been struck deaf and mute. His mother was the first to break the silence. She cried, his father held her, tears in his own eyes. Then they each clasped their son. Crestfallen, the kids hugged their father in unison. He hugged them close and smiled bravely, murmuring to them, "It'll be alright, I'll be fine. You know me. Nothing holds me down." The dark cloud over the living room hung and he looked at his family, "Listen to me, I want life and I'm going to fight for it. I am going to be alright." Determination emanated from him because his family's presence had stoked him. He outlined the prognosis and options for care and he said that he was committed to taking good care of himself.

"I'm very proud of him. He's working near home again, his hours have been cut, and he's not smoking. It's a great start," Mari pronounced.

"Dad, that's wonderful and I'm so happy you're going to be home lots. Vince and I miss you." Vince grinned, "Yeah, we do."

Having gotten through it, they settled down to coffee and sweets, and the knock on the door told them that Fiona was there. Mari put her coffee down on the coffee table and headed for the door. Entering, she hugged her sister who looked over Mari's shoulder, "Oh, is this party for me?" Seeing their wooden attempts to smile she hung her sweater on the hook and stopped, "Hey, what's wrong. I'm okay, really." Mari said, "Sonny has cancer." Not knowing what to say, she made her way past his parents and hugged Sonny. She said, "I'm so sorry Sonny." Wearily, he nodded. It had already been a long, emotional evening. Shifting the focus, Mari brought Fiona some coffee and pie as Fiona answered their questions about the recent events surrounding her. Mari and Sonny, through eye contact, acknowledged that they were relieved that it was done. She watched April go over to Fiona and touch her hand after being told about what had happened to her. That little gesture was unexpected and tender. Like the gerbera daisy had done, it made her optimistic about what was to come.

The next morning as Sonny slept in Fiona walked into the kitchen, and now that they were alone, asked Mari how she was. Mari answered, "For now, the best I can. Having Sonny home every day makes such a difference. I can take care of him." Taking their coffee from the counter to the small kitchen table, they sat facing each other.

"You're sounding positive and courageous. That rubs off on me. I have something to conquer also, and I'm using this latest attack on me to keep me motivated."

"We both have something to conquer and we're going to beat the odds," Mari leaned toward Fiona, touching the planted ivy she had in the middle of the table.

"Yes. Sonny WILL get well. Working in a hospital I hear a lot about the increasing success rate involving cancer. Many surgeons stay connected to the patients they've performed surgery on. Follow ups and medical science show that many patients live long and healthier lives. It'll happen in this house too." They held hands.

While Fiona lounged in front of the television Mari told her she was going to call close friends and inform them of Sonny's cancer. Setting the phone down after talking to the last person, she sighed. That ordeal was done. She went back into the living room with a cup of chamomile and relaxed. Soon Sonny was up and they shared a small lunch, Sonny finishing his coffee in the living room. Mari was bewildered, watching them as the day progressed. They reminded her about how babies under a year old played parallel to each other, not giving and taking. They knew the other occupied the same space, but each was absorbed in their own universe. Mari felt like she was suspended between each, answering their bids for attention as it surfaced: *My sister thinks she can lick this thing that was happening to her, and my husband stuns me with his ferocity, a ferocity he doesn't even know he has yet. They can't help but win.*

Sunday dinner was livelier. They sat together, talking and enjoying the camaraderie. Soon, the dishes done, draining her coffee, Fiona announced, "It's time for me to head home. It's going to get darker soon." After packing up her things, they bid their goodbyes, and about to get into her car, Fiona noticed eyes on her from across the street: *Many townspeople knew about her break in. People look at me curiously now.* She sped away.

CHAPTER 10

THE CONNECTION

The phone rang. Fiona thought: *Who's that?* She was in the front yard with Pal who was following her around the area where she was cleaning up her geraniums, pulling off the dead leaves and flowers. She wiped her hands soiled with dirt on her pants and walked into the living room. Anxious, she looked at the screen and let her breath slowly out, seeing that it was Police Services.

"Yes?"

"This is Officer Robertson. Listen, I wanted to let you know that we've made some progress in your case. I have something that may help. A woman called the police station to inform us that the person she lives with is behaving very suspiciously. It's strong information. Among other things he leaves their residence at all hours of the day and night, for short or long periods of time, unaccounted for, and he behaves aggressively toward her. Especially before he leaves the house. Too, she describes his abuse as getting worse and his behaviour is especially strange when he drinks. I can't tell you who we are looking at, of course, but we feel it could be helpful to give you a description. He is about five feet, seven inches tall, small in stature, has thinning dark hair and he walks fast, with sort of a bounce. He looks to be about forty years old, give or take a few years. In ordinary conversation he speaks rather softly. Do you know anyone like that? Even if it's just a feeling."

"I can think of several men who fit that description, and I see men on the street like that. I look at men passing by me or walking behind me, wondering if he could be the one. I must tell you though, that I am encouraged to get this report, but I'm scared. You guys suspect someone, but I'm not privy to this information. But, I understand why you can't tell me who you are looking at, but it feels eerie nonetheless."

"I understand how you may feel. No one more than you and Kristel's parents want him identified, but until we confirm that he is the subject, we just cannot state who the individual is. I can assure you we're working hard and steadily for you. This person is under surveillance."

"Oh, I know that must be and I appreciate your efforts. Thank you."

"Sure thing. Before we hang up, I want assurance that you have done ALL the things we've suggested you do to augment your safety."

"Getting him in custody would augment my safety. We've done a lot though. I've added outdoor lighting, have better locks on the doors and windows, and I keep my curtains and blinds drawn, even during the day, something I hate. My dog, Pal, stays in the fenced in yard overnight. It works because he only barks if there's something to bark at. I communicate a lot with my sister Mari. And, someone will be moving in with me shortly. Our schedules are such that neither one of us will be alone in the house for more than an hour and a half at a time. Both of us will be sleeping at home every work night and our weekends are free so that we can be together. If she or I are going to be spending a night away, the other will be bunking at Mari's."

"Great! It's an excellent plan."

"I refuse to live in constant fear, and it really helps that my family and I are in constant contact."

"That's what family is for. Okay. Bye for now, and you know where to reach me."

"Yes I do, bye-bye."

Aloud, Fiona repeated, "That's what family's for" as she walked to the bedroom to change into her light flannels. That familiar refrain really did mean something to her...now. She smiled, remembering how Mari had coaxed her to meet with April and attempt to ease their alienation. At first she was averse to meeting with her sister. She thought: *We're so different on things, and she is so unpredictable. Last thing I need around me right now is April.*

Fiona had told Mari that she had no patience for her "screwed-up" sister and would rather not, really pissing Mari off. She would co-exist with April and keep her mouth shut.

"Isn't that enough?"

"What do you think? No, that is not enough. You are sisters!"

"We've managed to live okay without having had much to do with each other."

"Oh, but I have a novel idea. Talk! Get to know each other better. You two have to be more than simply okay with each other. Fiona, what if one of you developed a chronic disease or was suddenly not here, then what?" She had her with that one, especially since she'd had a close call with her break in. She wondered how long April would miss her if she wasn't here, having been murdered. She grimaced: *I should be open to rediscovering my relationship with April-even though my heart isn't in it.*

"Well, I do need people around me right now, as self-interested as that sounds. I'll call her, okay?"

"Thank you very much! Let me know what happens." Mari got her to agree that she would do this soon, and they hung up.

Fussily gathering her thoughts over the next few days, she eventually left a message for April on her answering machine. April finally returned her second call a few days later. Fiona was pissed about that.

"Gee April. Thanks for calling back. It's so good of you."

"Sorry, I was really busy. What do you want?"

"I'd like for you to come over for brunch on Saturday."

"Why! Are you having a little do?"

"Yeah, really little. Just you and me."

"Oh, and why would you be thinking of doing that? I'm surprised to say the least."

"Yeah well. What do you say?"

"Hmm...'pause.' Okay. What time?" sounding less than keen.

Awkwardly, they made small talk before hanging up. Both sat afterwards wondering what the hell to think. April felt guilty about not asking her how she was doing. No matter what, she is my sister, and she had such an awful thing happen to her.

Early Saturday morning, through a cold wet window, rain weighing down the leaves that still clung to the trees, Fiona watched April drive up. She stopped in the driveway, and apprehensively she forced her gaze toward the left side of the property, wondering if he was in there watching her. The undergrowth and the trees blew an eerie sound across the front of the house and she clasped her arms and shivered. She remained as she was long enough take in the expanse of trees bending and blowing around. Fiona waited. Another minute later, April turned the ignition off and got out of the car. She looked at April's stomach: *There's a baby growing in there. God-damn her! I should be the one bringing a child into the world.* Momentarily angry, but pasting a smile on her face, she opened the door and greeted her. April felt a confused mixture of disquiet and discomfort as she closed the door behind them. Fiona's feelings turned to annoyance as April looked around and pronounced that her place looked nice and intimated that it was probably because Mari had contributed to decorating it. She didn't know if April meant that she was jealous that she and Mari were so close or if she was saying she had no decorating style. She stifled another stab of anger even though what she really wanted to do was tell her what a snotty little bitch she was. But, because of Mari's insistence about the two of them getting together, she clamped her lips shut. She had to start this off on the right foot.

"Come into the kitchen. I've got coffee on. I'm assuming you'd like some?"

"Perfect. I'm still cold from being out there," she looked out the kitchen window. They fixed their coffees and carried their mugs into the living room. They'd been quiet doing this and then Fiona found herself facing April curled up on the love seat.

"Nasty out there, isn't it?" Fiona said.

"Yeah, pretty nasty, but it is cozy in here." Concern in her thick lashed eyes, she said, "How you doing?"

Wearily, Fiona answered, "Yeah, well, I try to keep it together, waiting, trying hard to see each day through without feeling too afraid, or depressed, or jumpy. Officer Robertson phoned me. He said they were looking at someone. He gave me a description. He's slightly built, has dark thinning hair, about five feet seven. He's about 40, walks quickly." She looked out the living room window where the wind was really picking up. Silence again.

April said, "About every third one who comes into the bar, looks like that, young and middle aged alike."

Fiona shrugged and nodded and put on some calming music, thinking about how to start, "I'm glad you came April. We need this time together to get to know each other again."

"It's not because I've never wanted to. You stopped liking me a long time ago, thought I was a flake, or worse."

Fiona forgot how straightforward April could be. It startled her, and she could feel the consternation rising in her. She kept her mouth shut, and determined to not become defensive. "Why do you say that?"

"Oh, just the way you've always acted around me. You tolerate me. You pretend to not hear me when I talk to you about what I've been doing or the things I'm interested in, my painting specifically. I'm getting back to it. Anyway, I get that look, like this." She stood up, crossed her arms and she slid her eyes sideways at Fiona, that look that can cut you down in a split second.

"That bad." She looked at the floor.

"Oh yeah. Nasty." When Fiona did that, it would render her wordless and unable to defend herself, as though Fiona was superior. April was sure she knew how small she made her feel, and she'd waited a long time to tell her sister this. While waiting for eye contact, April remembered, "Long ago it stopped being like when we were little kids, even with four years between us. There was a time when we played and sang and danced together. I loved those times. Then, when I was fourteen you stopped paying attention to me. You were mean." Fiona knew what she was talking about, but being outed like that, she could feel a flare up about to erupt. She pushed it back. "How?"

"You and your friends made fun of me, my clothes, the way I talked, stuff like that, and even when we were home together you never let me in your room."

Fiona heard herself making excuses, "April, you borrowed my things, ruined them, didn't return them, stuff like that. Fighting IS a normal part of growing up for most sisters. I was struggling with my own things and I did not want my mouthy little sister around. Anyway, you couldn't do the things we were allowed to do by then."

April retorted, "You were going through your own things!? It hardly excuses how you treated me. It's wasn't all about you. When Mom left and Dad checked out, I couldn't cope, thought I'd lost my whole family, because you deserted me too. And Mari was on her own by then. Then Dad died, and I felt like I had no family." Fiona felt her sister's sadness, something she hadn't felt before. She shifted forward in her seat, seeing the tears that April held back. Irritation melted away, and finally she said, "I turned my back on you when you really needed a sister. I'm sorry."

Fiona stopped to look out the window as though she could see beyond the pulled blinds and listened, something she did constantly now, becoming still and cocking an ear like people do who feel threatened. She decided that everything was okay and came back. Fiona continued, "I am sorry. But, you know when I started thinking differently about you. You developed Mom's style of handling problems. You learned to drink. By the time you were fourteen you hung out with kids who did the same thing. It was a bad mix. I could have helped but by the time Mom left I was so desolate and hurt that you were the last thing on my mind. I was impatient and I did take a lot of things out on you." She stopped and sighed, searching for words, "I internalized things, hiding the anger I felt toward Mom, hiding how hurt I was. It was easy to put you down. A kind of release, I guess. You handled things by acting out, getting into all the trouble you could." She put her hand out, "Those were bad years for us and we didn't handle it too well, did we?"

"No Fiona, you didn't. You were the older one. Still, there's no getting away from it. I admit it. My way out was to hang out with friends and drink."

Fiona pulled her hand back, "I wish now that I'd talked to you April. But, growing up with Mom I learned to hate anything associated with drinking and honestly, you just reminded me of Mom. You acted like her when you drank." Fiona felt herself beginning to talk really fast. "If you could have seen yourself when you were partying, when you were really drunk, which is, was, pretty much every time you drank." Shifting positions on the couch she spit out, "April, you could get so drunk you didn't know where you were. You became incoherent, your eyes glazed over. It was embarrassing and so pathe."

"You were going to say pathetic."

Fiona grabbed her forehead and hid her face. April got up from her chair and went to Fiona. She touched her leg, "Hey, it's all right. I've had enough group counseling to know how we can turn people off. Besides,

I've seen a few of my screen performances on the family videos. Not too pretty." She made her quirky little face, widening her eyes and quickly nodding her head up and down. Fiona smiled, and April continued.

"I'm beginning to realize how things affected the whole family, and well, everything. Anyway, when Mom left I hated her for a long time. She had always been so demonstrative with me, she spoiled me and let me get away with a lot of things, until I got too hard to handle." She went back to her chair and sat forward, "She left without so much as a goodbye. After she deserted, I went even wilder, just to show her how I didn't care."

She couldn't believe how sorry she felt for April, such a foreign way to feel, but she could feel her eyes tear, "I regret how I handled things, especially how I treated you. I feel bad about that now..." she paused, sifting her thoughts.

"I lost my mother too though, April. When Mom left I thought she left partly because I was so demanding. I needed her approval so much and I was always working to get it. As a kid I never felt loved like you did. I was the more serious one, more into myself. She took that for self-sufficiency, I guess. Her neglect left me wanting and self-absorbed, and I had nothing to give, not even to you. Then, I made another really big mistake, I married Warren, and..."

April cut her off, "You know Fiona, I never thought of how it could have been for you. I thought you were okay, you had your friends and stuff. You were so busy living life. And you always said exactly what you felt. You were the boss. But now, looking back on it, you were just pissed off a lot, and I never realized how hurt you were. Something just came to me. Remember when Mom would pit us against each other. She'd say I'd been in your room trying on sweaters and get a self-satisfied look on her face when you whacked me. The thing is, it was true, but I'd have done that the previous week, and Mom, because she was in a frickin' bad mood, would bring it up. She did those kind of things. You know, she never did love us without conditions imposed, and she hurt us on purpose. Then, she would carry on, lofty and self-centered. Those traits really reared up when she drank."

"Yeah, I don't like to think of it, but she could be those things. I learned the loftiness from her, 'she chuckled,' not an excuse though. The thing is, we've worked against each other, and we've made our share of mistakes, haven't we?"

Tongue in cheek, eyes mischievous, April said, "You don't make mistakes."

Fiona thought: *Oh God, what she doesn't know.* She pronounced the obvious, "Oh no? If I'd have had the self-esteem I have now, or I'm trying to build now, I wouldn't have married a man who said he loved me, but, who really thought he was the center of the universe, who wanted complete control of how things went, who put me down, and who gave me the barest of attention, especially when I became depressed. He thought I should have just snapped out it. When I couldn't he withdrew. He couldn't be bothered."

April sympathized, "That isn't love. I thought of him as some kind of pompous, bigheaded jerk. Wasn't he though! I always felt we were supposed to concede to him all the time, whatever he said or did. And worse, he never minded his own business. Things that should have been handled by us, the immediate family, he always put his nose into, and he was always sneaky about it, cornering me sometimes when nobody was around."

"Really. Yeah, he always thought he knew everything about what other people should do. He used the phrase, "you should" a lot. Guys who need to control, like Warren, marry women they feel are inferior to them because it gives them that edge they need. That is so pathetic, eh?"

April raised her finger and leaned forward, "And he seemed to be bothered that I could have had more wild sex than he ever had." Cheeky, she emphasized, "Notice I said-could have had. He always acted like sex was the male domain or something, and I, a woman, was slutty if I was the least bit provocative. But, at the same time he invited that kind of thing, he needed the strokes or the proof that women are sluts, or both, I don't know. Just wanting to keep peace I swallowed the bait when he teased. Being a woman, I understand everything so much more. I'd speak up."

"No doubt. Certainly, your premise about him, or men like him, is pretty sound." Fiona smiled.

April accredited her evolvement to the counseling she was getting, and Fiona really noticed how April had a better grip on things. She was stronger. Fiona hoped that insight would also extend to what Fiona was about to reveal. Trying to put the right words together, she knew she had to leave nothing out so that she could gain her confidence: *We'll see how you respond to this.*

April was about to extrapolate more, but she couldn't help but notice the flickers in her sister's eyes. Fiona had suddenly pulled her back ramrod straight, avoided eye contact and she was nervously nervously at her bottom lip. They looked at each other. Seconds passed.

"April, there are things I need to tell you. I told you about my mistake when I married Warren. I've got more, lots more. A few years before our divorce I had an affair, got pregnant and had an abortion." April was dumbfounded!! She gaped at her older sister, "What? Oh shit!" and stomped out of her seat and walked to the living room window. She laughed out loud. "I'm frickin' astounded. Whoa!" She tried to digest what she'd just heard. Fiona held her breath.

Looking stricken, April gushed, "There's lots of stuff I want to know, but first I have to ask. You've always wanted a baby. Why in the hell did you decide to have an abortion?" That was a tough one, but she was relieved that April's first reaction hadn't been to mock her.

Fiona answered, "It was hardly the right time or the right circumstance to have a baby. Warren never wanted to have children, you know that. I couldn't bring a baby into an unhappy home where the baby wouldn't feel loved by both parents. And really, deep down I knew that I wanted out, but I just didn't know if it would happen, always wondering if I'd ever have the courage to leave," her voice fading to a whisper.

April listened and she felt all kinds of things at once, mostly feelings she'd worked hard to keep bottled up. She wanted to lash out accusing her of being so critical and judgmental of her. The perfect one, so much so, that she never felt that she could relate to Fiona in a meaningful way. But...she couldn't hurt her, especially now. They were on the precipice of something new building between them. The confidences they had just shared had revived feelings of closeness. She didn't want to destroy that. April thought about how sad it must have been for her to live in a marriage so devoid of warmth and acceptance. All she could do at that moment was hug her big sister. She pulled Fiona up, smiled, and hugged her tight. Fiona, relieved and spent, responded likewise.

"Boy, are we fuck ups! No, were." April walked to the couch and flopped.

"Yeah, we were."

"You know I am pregnant."

"Yeah. Mari told me."

"What did you think?"

"I'll admit it, I did not take it very well. I wasn't convinced you'd quit drinking, wasn't convinced you'd be a good mother. You've never wanted a baby."

"Fiona, I can see why you'd feel that way. I wasn't a responsible person. I've grown up. Getting sober allowed me to take a good look at myself. Not having that boozy haze has opened up an honest look at myself. I'm going to do the best I can for this baby. You know, just a few months ago I wouldn't have been able to communicate like this, with you especially. It feels good," 'she smiled triumphantly', "and you know what else?" Her knees folded up under her as Fiona asked, "Tell me. What?"

"I'm looking for a little café to manage. That really excites me. And, I want to give up my apartment and move to my cottage to live. I want to paint again and the environment there inspires that. I want all of that so much."

Fiona couldn't help but smile indulgently and she told her sister, "You are so bubbly, and you seem so motivated. Something tells me you'll do what you've been talking about. I hope you get everything, absolutely everything you want." She walked back to the kitchen with their mugs. Carrying fresh coffee back, she said, "Hey, I'd love to know. What was the deciding factor that made you decide to stop drinking?"

"A combination of things. Even if I was living in a stupor, I knew my self-respect and dignity was in shreds, I knew I was losing respect from others. I was vain. My looks were going. A drunk doesn't look good for long. And when I lost Matt, I really became unhinged. Mari, seeing how bad things had gotten, bless her heart, wasted no time intervening when she could, when I allowed it. But, it really came from me. I was ready," the flat of her hand touching her heart. She frowned, "I was a mess and I knew it. The worst thing I did was date Mister Casual. He was so callous and jaded, just taking whatever he could. Something I heard in group really stuck with me. Never invest more in a relationship than you can afford to lose." Fiona raised her eyebrows and nodded in agreement, and April finished, "When I finally held fast to some hard decisions the first thing I did was end it with him. Not soon enough. I was pregnant."

"You do have quite a situation there. You have decisions to make on lots of fronts."

"Shit, tell me about it. And you Fiona, what's important now?"

Suddenly on the brink of tears, she said, "I want to feel safe. Is that too much to ask? They have to catch him. I feel like everything is on hold until they get this bastard, 'she scrunched her hands into fists.' I don't know who he is, exactly what he looks like, where he is, but I feel his presence-every-day." She rubbed her eyes hard. April didn't know what to say. They sat for a while petting the dog, catching up on Sonny and Mari, discussing the painting Fiona had recently purchased for her living room. It showed a serene water-side setting with a little girl feeding some baby ducks. April understood why Fiona had chosen it. It was peaceful. Their new-found ease with each other enhanced their good feelings. Suddenly, April's face lit up like a beacon through a fog: "Fiona! You adopt my baby!" She couldn't have stopped the words, but she wondered where and how those inexplicable thoughts rose up. Where would the baby fit in this world? She felt right about what she'd just said. Wanted to know how the baby was being brought up.

"What?!" She didn't just hear April say those words! Fiona wanted a baby, but did she want to mother this baby? They looked at each other, and it was like their questioning thoughts passed through each other.

"You heard me. You've always wanted a baby and I have one to give you. We can both benefit. I will know where the baby is and that it has a loving mother and the best of care. And, you will have something you've always wanted. What about it?"

"Slow down. You're scaring me. These are big steps. Besides, it's not something we can keep secret from the child, unless we moved away or something. And, another thing, what if you change your mind? We're just finding each other again. Could we both bear to go through the fallout and everything else that could be involved?"

"Fiona, it doesn't have to be a secret. We can decide what to tell the child when he or she starts asking questions about not having a dad, for instance. Please, I think it would work. We'll do it up legal. We'll make it work. That child will have a good mother and a damned good Auntie.

April 'shook her crazy head', and we do have a good family. What more can a child ask for, except a dad. Anyway, we both know that a family can consist of just about anything besides the traditional Mom and Dad thing. Like that always works. Listen, just promise me you'll think about it. Think of it this way. Having this special thing to look forward to might just be the thing you need right now. You n-e-e-d something to look forward to."

Listening to April say this, Fiona laughed with joy, and it thrilled her. It had been a long time since she'd laughed like that. She'd gotten caught up in the spontaneity and passion in April's voice. Before she even knew what she was about to say, she gushed, "It could work. I could watch the baby grow and help you in delivery, and make plans. We have so much to work out but we can do it! And Mari will help-after she recovers from shock." Both laughed.

"I know in my heart this is a good solution, and I've thought of something else."

"What?" She watched April bounce up and down excitedly.

"Until I'm settled career wise, and my cottage is finished, why don't I live with you. Your situation has us all scared and I've thought of how it must be living alone out here, especially after he broke in. You'll feel safer. Say yes." She bent and clasped her hands between her knees.

Fiona said, "Mari said she wished I'd find a roommate. Wait till I tell her this." She couldn't stop the tears now and both of them were unable to contain themselves, laughing and talking a mile a minute. Fiona kept thinking how happy she felt to be with her totally crazy little sister again, and that it was happening at this important juncture in both their lives. They finally quieted down and attacked the brunch Fiona had prepared. After they had their chai tea April left, telling Fiona she would phone Mari as soon as she got home and inform of their unbelievable morning.

Fiona quipped, "Great. Have her call me as soon as she picks herself up off the floor. I'm going to start rearranging the house. It has to suit us both." Totally wrung out now she shooed her out. Fiona thought: *Darn, they hadn't talked about what furniture April would bring.* Oh well, she had her sister's number. She remained on the porch a few minutes and closed her eyes, the most peaceful she'd felt in a long time.

Mari couldn't contain herself after her talk with April. Excitedly, she called Fiona: *Answer the phone, answer, answer, answer!*

"Hello sis!"

"Fiona is it really so?! April told me about you adopting the baby!"

"Where to begin! Mari, it wasn't as hard as I thought it could get. April is phenomenal. She's grown a lot. I trust her sincerity and for me that's the most important thing. She made me see things about myself I don't like, like how I can be judgmental, or jealous, or cruel. In my defense, I've certainly become better than when I was a teenager. Anyway, she talked about what bothered her when we were kids. It was especially enlightening when we talked about how we each of us handled Mom leaving. And, as far as her moving in here, it just makes sense. She's needs support. We can help each other."

Fiona was telling her important things, but she wanted to hear about their plans about adoption. She couldn't get the words out fast enough.

"It's all too much! But it's all too good. Especially, that April is moving in. You'll be safer. April is being selfless in that regard. It's wonderful!" Mari's response nailed it. They HAD done something phenomenal and now that they'd all expressed the same excitement, it was as good as done.

Fiona asked, "Well, what about Sonny? What's happening?"

"I'm waiting for him to get home from his doctor's visit. They're outlining treatment. He's doing okay, feeling pretty good, and the part time schedule works well. He's trying hard, walking a lot, eating the right things. It can only help."

"Good. He'll do fine. How are you doing?" Their conversation continued to fill the air, hopeful and strong.

"It's not easy. I'm worried as hell, but I'm okay, really. And, I can hardly wait to tell him about this, hmm, miracle."

"Yeah, I guess it is. Mari, I've already rearranged the furniture. I'm almost done. I gotta say, that was fun."

"Call me when you're through. We'll get together. I've got to go. I can't wait for Sonny to get home, and I want to get ready. Talk to you later. Bye." Fiona said goodbye.

Mari soaked in a bubble filled tub and her head filled with a million thoughts whirling through, and even the long bath failed to calm the butterflies in her stomach. But, by the time Sonny got home she was relaxed and dressed. Coming in with mixed flowers he kissed her forehead and pulled her toward the living room.

"These are beautiful. It's a sure sign of optimism. Tell me what happened."

"The cancer is seated in the lower part of my stomach, apparently where you have a greater chance for survival. He said that he'd told me that, but I didn't hear it. He said that while it has spread to the second layer of the stomach, there are five layers, tests show that all the cancer can be removed. I'm going ahead with the surgery. I just have to be ready for when they call." Mari was jubilant, and she jumped up and hugged and kissed him. It sounded good because he sounded convinced that it was. For the first time since he told her that he had cancer, she felt upbeat and positive.

"Well, they say attitude is everything. I'm happy if you are." Sonny was smiling and he said, "It's all I can be right now. The doc sounded pretty optimistic about the outcome."

"God, that's good news honey. Now, wait until I tell you about the Miracle on Eighth Concession." She was all but bursting to spill the news. With no comprehension about what she was talking about, he had a quizzical expression. She laughed.

"April is moving in with Fiona while she is in the process of finding a little café before she moves into her cottage that needs some work before she moves into it."

"Fiona, April together. Wow. Holy shit. You're kidding me!"

"There's more. Fiona is adopting April's baby. There it is in a nutty shell. And they say people can't work things out," she said as she threw her hands up.

"Well, they certainly know how to keep the fun in dysfunctional."

Faking consternation Mari said, "Shut up! It took a while to absorb it all but I feel that it could work. The moving in thing is such a good idea. Fiona needs someone there. They can look out for each other. And, she's offered her baby to her sister who wants one so much. Fiona had concerns, certainly, but they talked it out. It'll be all legal, and they've even worked out how the child will be told one day. It's a wonderful solution. I mean, they went from being poles apart, to pulling together to work out some pretty serious issues."

"This is serious stuff. And what if they don't agree on things concerning this child…" he threw his hands up.

"They'll be co-parents and they'll work things out. April will know that she can offer her opinion on things but that Fiona would be in charge."

"You have faith in this. Both are strong headed and reactive, especially Fiona. And you have faith that this is a good solution."

"Yes! And a new baby breathes new life into this family in more ways than one. We can all share in raising her."

"You are so amazing." He knew that Mari felt that she may never become a grandmother, so he understood that that was part of the reason she felt so positive about this baby being raised in the family. He or she was going to be so welcomed.

"I know," Mari said, grinning mischievously. She saw a cute, goofy leer appear in his eyes.

"Before I forget, I don't know if I mentioned this but the doctor said to have all the sex I want."

Their positive mood ignited inside her. "What are you waiting for?" Salaciously said, she sauntered into the bedroom. Their elation and need captured them both. She joined with him, deeper this time. Her body tensed as her smooth legs clenched him. With her open lips against his, she met him with a fiercely demanding energy that awakened him to her even more. The experience was richer, deeper. Afterwards, their eyes met, and they shared a new knowledge of each other. Free from past insecurities and distrust, their love swelled. Sonny thought: *Why haven't I felt this much intensity with my wife before. Why haven't I known this much love before?* He decided to ask her.

Mari replied, "Because we're going through things that have never challenged us as much as now. We need each other. And we trust each other more. And you know, Fiona and April working things out…it's energizing. "

What fuckin' luck I have! That little bitch is living there. Slut. Could be a problem. I WANT Fiona. Now her little sister is there. Maybe I could do both. Like I did Kristel. God, that cunt was scared. Did anything I told her to. Stuck her as hard as I could. I could feel her shaking. Definitely my type 'he grinned'.

CHAPTER 11

JUNCTURE TO FEAR

Sonny was standing at the kitchen window noticing how autumn was beginning to show it's splendor, when he got the call informing him that the date for his surgery was set. Opening a kitchen drawer, he picked up the pad in it and set it on the counter. While rummaging for a pen, he said, "I've been waiting for this call. I have a pen. Go ahead." The receptionist provided the date, told him to not eat breakfast that day, what time he needed to be at the hospital in the morning, and the time of the surgery. Writing it all down, he heaved a sigh of relief. He thanked the receptionist and was anxious but elated, "This is great. I'm ready to get it over with."

He thought about how he had been feeling lethargic and lonely in the throes of his illness, but also knowing that if he made it, it would be because he believed he would. He tried hard to stay strong, for the most part. To compound his emotional roller coaster, he also felt sick after treatment. It drained his energy the first two or three days afterward, keeping him in bed. Those were the times he'd give in to dark thoughts, like he may not make it and that he was not as contributory to his family as he felt he should be. He agonized about how Mari shouldered her sister's woes while she took care of him, and how he just didn't have the energy to partake in family activities. When she needed him to be strong he was weak, and feelings of guilt pervaded his waking moments. It was during those moments that he thought: *When I'm well, I'll shower her with everything that's in me to give.* They'd go on romantic and adventuresome annual vacations and he'd take her out on date nights more often.

He put a smile on his face and went into the bedroom where Mari was making the bed and told her the news: "My surgery is only three weeks away."

"Oh Sonny, that's good to hear. I know how you've been waiting for this." She told him how much she loved him, and that his surgery was going to turn out "just super." He wrapped his arms around her and gave her the biggest hug. Mari felt the emotional turmoil that surged through him as her heart beat against his chest. They didn't have to say anything to know what each was feeling.

Getting up the next morning, after getting dressed, Mari walked about the bedroom, picking up her pajamas and robe, hanging them behind the closet door on their hooks, and she stood her booty slippers next to her dresser. Similarly she tidied the living room of an empty bowl of popcorn and two and empty beers. She returned them to the kitchen and placed the dishes that also littered the counter into the dishwasher, and turned it on. Sonny walked in, and over coffee and toast, they chatted. He placed his plate in the sink, refilled his coffee, wandered into the living room and read the news off his cell phone. Mari washed his plate and put it in the cupboard. Carrying her coffee in to join him, she sat herself opposite him and when he looked up at her, she spontaneously asked, "Sonny, if we had to say good-bye to you, what would you want?" Equally unpredictably, he answered, "A farewell party." Once uttered, the wonder in her eyes was amusing. Actually, it was a wide eyed look of amazement, and it made Sonny laugh. She sputtered, "Did we just say these things?"

"Yeah, we did, and I'll tell you what I want. Not that I'm going anywhere. BUT, if I did, I'd want people around me. Seth has avoided me since he knew. I need my friends now more than ever."

Mari understood completely, but she pointed out, "Honey, Seth may not know what to say. People are always afraid of saying the wrong thing. Like, just a few seconds ago. I didn't know what I was going to say. I just said it. I don't believe you're going to die…"

"You just can't help but think it."

"I guess… yes. That has gone through my mind. Just like it's gone through yours. But, we know that the survival rate is high for this particular cancer when caught in the stage that yours was. And thank God for that. To get back to Seth, maybe you could make it easier for him. The party you

want could be a conversational opener. Just don't call it a farewell party."
She laughed and raised her eyebrows.

"Haha. Okay. I'll approach him. I could ask him to come to my maybe going away party."

"Cute."

"It wouldn't be being selfish, would it?"

"What? Having a party?"

"Having a party because I'm sick. God damn it, Mari, I wish I didn't have to reckon with any of this. So, am I?"

"You're not being selfish, and it's interesting that you use the word reckon. Maybe the reason you want a party is to have those around you that matter...but you have to make right with. Most of us look beyond ourselves as we mature, and we try to make up for things we've done or said. You, sweetie, had to get sick." He smiled, chastened, not because she spoke the truth, but because in spite of her honesty, she had a calming effect on him. He asked her if he'd been better at being a husband.

"We have gone through life together 'she searched for a word'... valiantly. I'd do it all again, especially with you."

"I'd do it again too. And, I do want to make things right with the people I care about. Lord knows, I haven't always been easy to deal with." Mari tilted her head away from him and raised her eyebrows again. Facetiously, he harassed her, "Didn't think I saw that look, eh? Well I did." Mari dashed away to start a fresh pot of coffee before he could grab her. He followed close enough to slap her behind and said he'd let the guys at work know about the party: "Is it okay if I invite Big Hair?" Mari hissed.

"Sit down for a minute," his expression changing. Slowly, she sat down at the table. He reached for her hand and said, "Mari, I need to get something off my chest. You're the most important person in my life and I have to make everything right with you."

"What?" She wasn't sure about what he had to say, and she tried to quiet her thumping heart.

Quickly, he said, "There were times when I thought about other women, but that's as far as it went."

She pulled her hand away, "Oh, well, that makes me feel just great. Thank you for that Sonny, but I KNOW you thought about being with other women. Did you think that getting it off your chest would make you less guilty? If that is why you told me that, it was selfish."

"Mari, please, I want to straighten everything out with you. I didn't want to be with them. It's about how they made me feel; left over from when I was growing up and Mom fawned over me constantly. I'm trying to explain to you that I wouldn't want you to go through life thinking that I WANTED other women…"

Pausing, throwing up her hands, she said, "Oh God, Sonny. In your own damn way, I know you're trying to make me feel better." She heaved a sigh of exasperation.

"I just want to make sure you understand. Those women I flirted with? It was ego. It meant nothing else. You mean everything to me. Only you. Believe me." His eyes plead for understanding. Mari softened. He was well-intentioned, and she had to do everything in her power to see to it that he felt her unstinting love. He needed her, and she said, "Thanks for that Sonny. I know you love me and I love you."

April opened the can of beer she'd brought. Heck, one beer wouldn't hurt the baby. She was very involved in one of the tasks that would brighten up her cottage, and she was applying the final touches of the dark maroon she'd picked to accentuate one of the bedroom walls. She hummed happily. Sitting the paint brush down, she backed up to survey the room. It's perfect. She heard the phone ring, grabbed a rag to wipe her hands, and ran to the kitchen to grab it.

"Hello."

"Listen slut, I'll get you too. You can never have too much fun." He muffled a laugh.

The phone went dead.

Fear invaded her body like a frigid stream of ice water, and she shouted, "You dirty son of a bitch!" clutching her swollen tummy. With trembling hands she hurriedly found her purse and keys and ready to leave, she got the door locked ahead of the mess she left behind. Her mind numb, she drove home. As soon as she got home she called Officer Robertson, making an appointment with him to meet at the cottage the next day to listen to the message.

Fiona walked through the door just as April had finished her conversation. She dropped her sweater on the closest chair and the look on April's face as she gripped the phone stopped her cold. She asked, "Did something happen?" April put the phone down.

"He called, said he was going to get me too. I called the police right away."

Fiona slumped into a chair. "God, I'm sorry, it took me a little longer to get home from work. I got that oil change and a turning signal light replaced. It ran into an hour before I could get out of there."

"Don't apologize. Besides, I wasn't here when it happened. Remember I told you I was going to the cottage to paint my bedroom wall. He called there. Anyway, we aren't always going to be exact about how we spend time. That's fucking impossible, isn't it?"

"At the cottage!! It's someone close. He knows too much!" Fiona shuddered and held her head between her hands.

April walked to Fiona and rubbed her back. Fiona grasped April's other hand.

"Officer Robertson and I have an appointment tomorrow to meet at the cottage so he can listen to the message he left."

"God April! There must be something else we can do to be safer here. I mean, he could lurk in those trees back there. Maybe we could fence ourselves in. I mean, the coward can terrorize us on the phone, but if we strengthen the fort…"

"Fiona, I don't want a fence. It's like we're giving everything away. Our freedom, our view…and, it would set my teeth on edge looking at a stark wall."

"Okay, okay, let's get a German Shepherd to help Pal. He'd be company for him too. I'll be in charge of hmm, what'll I call him. Hercules, that's a good name. Together they'll guard the house and the yard. Dogs hear anything that moves."

April looked calmer. "Hercules. I like that."

Fiona smiled tremulously, scared and worried about April having to go through all of this in her condition. Still, a definitive plan eased their mood and they yammered on about how much fun it would be to have a new dog.

The next day was a busy one. Almost home, driving up to her driveway Fiona gazed at the trees shading the house; trees that initially had drawn her to look at the little house. They were so beautiful in the light of day. She so longed to walk the pathway. Tall blue spruces, oaks, and maples edged the thicket. Foxtails rimmed part of the left side of the house and along the road. Wild flowers of varying colours, edged the worn path leading into the forest.

When she was making appointments to go look at dogs, April drove up having finished her day of looking at several options for a café, as well as looking in on the pub, where she visited with the staff. Happy to see them and they her, they got caught up on tons of things things, business and personal. All was well.

After a quick coffee with Fiona, they determinedly set off, wanting to take their time choosing their new pet. They met with some private dog owners, but not thrilled with the conditions, they drove to the humane society. Sure enough, Hercules was waiting for them. April said, "Just look at that smile." Fiona had to laugh. He had beautiful soft dark brown eyes and the shepherd took to them right away. Enlivened by him, they took turns hugging the huge dog. On the way home they buzzed about how they hoped he'd get along with Pal. They were picking him up the next day.

April sat petting Hercules, not forgetting to give the same attention to Pal. She smiled, thinking about how they had fretted for nothing. It wasn't instantaneous, but Pal finally forgave them for bringing a contender into his territory and having to share affection with Hercules. Good friends now, they caused a lot of mischief, and filled the house with laughs. If they played ball, they jumped and jostled each other to retrieve it. If one caught it too many times, Fiona and April made sure the other one had the same opportunity. They "practiced their game again with our damn shoes," April would comment whenever they came in to see them scattered all over the kitchen floor, shoes that were usually neatly lined up at the back door. Even so, it was fun watching them click their paws on the kitchen floor, hoping to get the first treat.

She stumbled to her feet. There was still room for another drink, just one more. The need pushed aside the self-loathing and the fear. Fear of? Of the unthinkable, of hurting the baby, of not being able to stop drinking. She thought about how she'd been able to conceal this from Fiona, but it was getting harder. She swallowed the drink, trying to sell herself on the bullshit that she could control her drinking, like she could control her life.

She smirked, rubbing her face. She remembered how she would derisively talk about a few of the guys that came into her bar, the regulars, some of them real bull-shitters. She looked toward the microwave that sat atop the stand, and picked up her glass to toast her reflection in the glass door. Ashamed and pissed at herself, she said, "Get ready for another load of bullshit!" The phone rang and she got up, stumbled, walking away from her slack reflection and looked at call display. It was Fiona. She didn't answer.

She thought about the stories that two of the AA members admitted to about relapsing. One woman, about forty, had relapsed several times. She admitted that whenever she spent time with her large family, most of them drinkers, she got caught up in their cavorting, partying lifestyle. She didn't want to lose their affections, which was demonstrated with hugs, loud laughter, and dancing. It was fun. But, the self-loathing kicked in the next day. At the sessions, she said that she had finally faced the fact that they purposely sought to derail her quest for sobriety. She was in counselling trying to determine what she could do to keep her sobriety and her family. If she would even be able to do that.

One young man in the group had to face himself for what he was, after mowing down a little girl in the road outside her house. He had chosen to drive when he was way over the limit. His personal agony was profound. He too was in counselling.

Looking at her empty glass, she could actually visualize the pride and trust in Fiona's eyes fade away. In Mari's too. Guilt stabbed at her as she visualized the little being growing in her. She wondered if she too needed counselling. I'll see about that tomorrow. She poured herself another drink and hid the bottle.

Fiona drove to Mari's. She'd called her from work so April wouldn't be around to hear the conversation, but she hadn't shared with Mari what she wanted to talk about. Hustling her in, Mari fussed over her and gave her a big hug. She told Fiona that their little sister had recounted how content she was to be living with her and how proud she was over how well Fiona was doing. She did not add that April had also said that she was always "skittish, like some nervous cat." Between meeting April at the door to when Fiona was seated in the living room, Mari sensed that something was wrong. When she had hugged her, she'd felt the tense shoulders and had taken in her worn out appearance. Her eyes were dull.

"I want to hear how you're doing?"

Fiona got agitated being asked that unbearable question again and said, "That fiend is still out there. I am doing as well as I can."

Heading for the phone, she said, "I've got to call April and tell her I'll be late." Mari got some mugs from the cupboard, waving one at Fiona. She nodded. While Fiona added cream to her coffee from the tray that Mari had placed on the table, she waited for what was about to come.

"April is drinking again. I know it. She gets that look like she wants to hide how much she's had, you know, trying to control how she moves, like we used to see all the time. And, I smell it on her. Sometimes, coming in from work, I detect tooth paste, and the other day, the mouth wash was on the counter, the cap off, like she'd just hurried using it."

"Oh God. The baby." Mari sat with a thump.

"I'm so goddamned mad. I'm livid actually..." her frustration building.

"Don't! Sometimes they have relapses. She can continue with treatment."

"More treatment? For what? For being such a dumb pitiful selfish bitch. I can't count on her for anything!" She looked at Mari seeing that familiar glint form.

"You talk like that and you can do it from the other side of the fence." They eyed each other. Fiona didn't say anything.

"How long do you think she's been drinking?"

"Not long. Probably about the same time she got that phone call from that sick bastard. Maybe longer. I'm not sure."

"This has to be handled real quick. You have to tell her that you know. She's going to need you to support her."

"I'm not babysitting my alcoholic sister." Fiona picked up her coffee cup, then set it down with a thud, her frustration building. She wiped at the droplets of coffee that landed on her hands.

"It's not babysitting. You just have to level with her and be there. No temper tantrums. Go to Al Anon. They're experienced with this stuff and they know all about how drinking affects pregnancy. You may be able to influence April. And, they'll tell you how to take care of yourself. One of you has to be rational and focused." Fiona heard everything she said, but she reacted to Mari's prickly comment, "Is that what I have? Temper tantrums? You know, that really kicked in through my divorce, but it's better than what I used to do. I'd just stuff it down."

"I know, but spare April. I'm sure she hates herself enough as it is."

"Okay, well, I feel a little better now that I've talked to you. I'll work through this somehow. I'm through with my coffee. I'm going home. It'll be okay. Promise."

"Stay for sandwiches and salad first. I know you don't eat well enough. It won't take me long. Difficult situations are always easier after a nice meal and a glass of wine. I got a new one. It's quite nice." Fiona felt hunger pangs. She stayed. They mostly ate in silence and shared some of their salad with Sonny when he came in. Finished with his meal, he excused himself, sensing they had been deep into some discussion, and he didn't want to be in the way.

When she was ready to leave she felt grim again, and she absent-mindedly placed her empty wine glass in the sink, already deep into her thoughts about what she would say to April. She hugged a very worried looking Mari, "I know what you're thinking. Don't worry. I'll watch my mouth, 'she made that locking thing you do with her forefinger and thumb against her lips.'

Fiona smiled, "Call me if you need me."

April had wandered outside. She finished her drink, lazing in the lounge in front of the house
because it was an unusually, mild, sunny day. Totally relaxed, she fell asleep in the lounge. Soon she was thrust into a fitful dream beginning with seeing a deep, foggy, snaking, lake. Fiona was in it too. They clutched at each other, their cold bodies sinking into the black water over and over. When they were tossed up, they coughed and heaved violently, each of them fighting the current, seeing bodies all around them thrashing about as though submerged in a tsunami. Then, swiftly, they were in a car blindly driving beneath the water, on a road that kept resurfacing and disappearing again. She fought with the steering wheel, then the car disappeared completely. They sank and the dream got blacker. They clawed the air for breath, and couldn't keep their hair out of their mouths and eyes. April scratched at something over her mouth that was smothering her.

From a distance, she heard barking. Gasping, her eyes opened and she slowly turned her head, seeing the back of a man vanishing, and feeling as though she was still dreaming. Both dogs noisily chased wildly in pursuit, and this brought her to: *Oh God, I'm not dreaming this!* Still not fully aware, she stared wide eyed following their direction. Deep into the forest, she could hear them growl and bark furiously. Following this, she heard an engine turning. She listened to the distant vehicle speed away. Frozen, she was met by Hercules who licked her face awash with tears of self-hate, fear and revulsion. The man had touched her mouth! She could still feel his rough, gloved hand. Pal raced in and after walking them back into the house, she went into the bathroom and frantically splashed her face with water that mingled with tears. She steadied her breathing and dried her face. Dropping the towel she went to get her phone, and called the police.

Fiona approached the house, quickly parked, alarmed that the police were there. Running toward the front walk she saw the toppled chaise and her eyes moved to the empty glass beside it. Angry and terrified, she picked it up, grasping it so tightly she thought it could break.

CHAPTER 12

A STRENGTHENED COMMUNITY...

Fiona ran into the house and found her sister in tears, her arms folded in front of her chest with her head down and her hair hiding her face. When she knelt beside her, April didn't raise her head.

"What happened to you? Are you all right?! Did someone hurt you?"

She placed the glass on the table and put her hand to the side of April's head, pulling her hair back. April pulled away and turned her head further away.

"April, look at me. Tell me what happened?" April looked at the glass that Fiona had just placed on the table, and fixed her eyes on it. She wouldn't answer. Directing her attention to Officer Robertson, Fiona emphasized her words.

"What happened to my sister?!"

"Your sister fell asleep in the lounge. Someone tried to attack her. She woke up to see him retreating with one of the dogs in pursuit."

"Oh my God!" she said, putting her arms around April. They shivered.

"I felt his hand over my mouth. Hercules chased him off."

Fiona looked up at the officer as she began speaking, "Your sister wasn't harmed. Physically at least. The smartest thing you two did was to hide that dog door behind the shrub, and that it was left open. Certainly, he was not expecting the dog to get out."

While Officer Robertson talked to Fiona, April watched them and cried. When Fiona made eye contact, again, she looked away. But not before April's face bore a mixture of fear, shame and remorse. She put a hand to her face, covering her eyes. Fiona felt sad for her and hugged her, then directed her words at Officer Robertson.

"Let's hope you find something in the woods that will help your investigation."

Turning to look at April again, she wondered how much booze she had consumed and what had spurred her to drink again. But this attack was very stressful for April, and as upset she was about that, it would wait.

"She's pregnant, and having to deal with something such as this is unbearable. Something has to happen soon. We can't take much more of this."

"I understand completely. We want to solve this. We'll keep in touch. Before we leave, we'll give the yard another go around." Awkwardly, the officers bade them farewell as they shuffled their way out.

Both sisters were so shaken and drained that they decided to go to bed immediately, but not before Fiona placed the empty glass in the sink that she'd picked up from the table. Tense, April watched her and wondered if Fiona would confront her about her drinking again.

"Get some sleep April. I'll call Mari in the morning."

On the way to her bedroom April stopped her, "Would you sleep in my room with me?" Fiona got her throw off the couch and followed April into her room. She couldn't be alone either. Lying beside April, she literally zonked out.

April stared into the dark room. She'd never felt such fear and repulsion. She could still feel his gloved hand over her mouth, stifling her breath. It was visceral and stinging nausea rose from her gut. She clasped Fiona's hand and intermittently fell in and out of sleep, still feeling that monster's hand.

Sonny sat, once again, stewing about his approaching surgery and about how tired he was, a useless vocal exercise, yet, there he was. Sure, Mari and he talked openly and honestly about his cancer and his anxiety about the surgery, but it only helped so much. Often, he scuffled about the kitchen and living room at night, trying to relax, usually nursing a glass of wine. Unseen from the outside, under the dim glow of night, he saw things that sent shivers up his arms. Their neighbors go out at all hours. Last week was no different. Connor runs out of cigarettes a lot, it seems. One night he entered his front door with a newspaper tucked under his arm. Tonight, George stood on his walkway and stared toward the house. Sonny thought: *Odd, the way people's habits are.* He rubbed his arms and shut out the fearsome thoughts that rumbled around in his head. But, no matter how much he wanted to drive the upsetting thoughts away, he would think: Did the killer drive to Fiona's and April's home to watch the house? Was he planning his next attack? Eventually, Sonny would go back to bed and fall asleep.

Reaching over to silence the alarm, he thought: *Christ, I just got to sleep.* Mari loudly echoed similarly, "Damn, I forgot to unset the alarm. I'm staying in bed for a while." Sonny smiled, pecked her cheek over her bare shoulder and announced, "Well sure. It's the weekend. I'm up. Just sleep. I'll take care of Tilly." He stretched and wriggled free of the blankets. Awakened a little later, she got up to the smell of coffee perking and poured a cup. Throwing on her housecoat she joined Sonny in the yard. She said, "Thanks for making coffee. It's good." Sonny answered, "You were tossing and turning a lot last night. I knew you'd appreciate it." She didn't answer. Sipping on his coffee, Sonny said, "Mari, I've been up a lot nights, can't sleep, and I see our neighbours going out, oh, probably, it's been three or four times that I've seen them go." She stopped and looked at him, baffled.

"First of all, who?"

"Connor and George."

"Connor and George! Maybe they can't sleep either and they go out for a drive. Some people do that."

"Yeah, I thought along those lines, like maybe Connor runs out of cigarettes or something."

"You're not thinking what I think you are, that he could be…come on Sonny. I think he doesn't like women much, but it hardly makes him a killer. You know, Haley thinks it's her spooky neighbour. He positions himself inside his house and stares at her. She's even seen him outside in his yard with binoculars. And, you know what? I couldn't sleep the other night and I saw George go out, quite late. Not to mention how he rages at Hao."

"Guess that doesn't make him a killer either. I'm more worried about that asshole that lives across from Haley. You've never mentioned it. I'd like to know these things."

"We were just talking, wondering about the same kinds of things we're talking about now. Okay, I know I'm being evasive why I've not told you about Haley's neighbor. I worry about how all of this is affecting you. I'm sorry."

"I know. It's okay. Connor stood on his walk last night looking over at the house. That was spooky."

"Connor couldn't be...I can't even say it."

Sonny gulped his coffee and clumsily set his coffee cup down, not moving his eyes from hers as she repositioned herself in the lounge, "Well, I'm saying. It's not so wild that the killer could be living right across the street. You hear about that sort of thing all the time. I think we should tell the police about Connor's comings and goings and Haley should mention her neighbour to the cops. And George, what about him?" Mari didn't say anything and they stayed silent for a while.

Sonny muttered, "There's not much in the paper about the murder anymore. I wonder what's going on."

"I don't know. It's getting so that I can't go a day without wondering how the investigation is going. Has it stagnated? I get letters asking about the same thing."

"I've read them."

"Sonny, if they have a person of interest, they're leaning on him by now. I mean, they must have enough evidence to be able to move in on somebody soon."

"Let's hope so."

She blurted, "Sonny, I'm so scared. He's honed in on both my sisters. Why not me?" She looked like a caged rat, her eyes darting and panicked, and the air seemed to thicken with fear. She felt hopelessly trapped.

Looking into her startled face, he made an attempt to reduce her fears, "Honey, April moved in with Fiona. It makes sense that both of them are targeted. It doesn't follow that you will be. Come here." They stood up and hugged.

"If it was Connor, WAS Connor or George, they wouldn't attack me. It's too close." She said the words, muffled by his shoulder.

"Right. I'm sorry I said things to upset you. It doesn't do us any good to speculate. I don't want you going crazy about this."

"She looked up at him and smiled. "Let's talk about something else."

"I'd love to do just that. You seem extra edgy. I've been meaning to ask you what your problem is."

"What do you mean?"

"Like I can't tell when something is bothering you? You didn't hear a word I said last night. And then, you were so restless. And, you said you had trouble sleeping."

Abruptly, she answered, "April is drinking again."

Sonny sat down, "So that's why Fiona was here at dinner time. Does she know for sure?"

"She's sure. She smells it on her. And April tries to cover it up. Lots of teeth brushing and mouth wash, stuff like that. I told her we have to expect a relapse even if this is the worse time for her to do it, being pregnant. I suggested that she ask Al Anon for help. They'll guide her on how to NOT get sucked into her problem, or worse, enable her. Ruefully, Sonny said, "There's hardly a chance that Fiona would enable her."

"Yeah, well, that's true. Anyway, she was going to talk to April last night or this morning. Okay, now it's your turn."

"My turn to do what?" Sonny waited.

"Why aren't you sleeping?"

"I worry about my surgery, what else?"

"You are going to do fine honey."

"Yeah, you keep saying that, but I've seen your face sometimes."

"I worry about what you're going through. I know you feel helpless about not being able to help all of us get through this stuff. Sonny, you wouldn't be able to do anything about any of this anyway, even if you were the strongest man in the world. I know what else you worry about. You wonder what'll happen to me if something happens to you."

He felt his stomach tighten, "Yeah. You've got too much to worry about without…"

"You're my first concern. I'll always make time for you. Promise you'll keep talking to me about whatever's bothering you," she implored.

"I promise." Devilishly, he smiled, "You know what you can do you to cheer us up. Make some homemade brownies. Plea-s-e?" he sweet-talked.

"About as homemade as it gets is Betty Crocker." She giggled, "Actually, if people ask, I tell them, if it's made in my home, it's homemade."

"Good answer. Never mind. If instructions are on the box, I can probably make them. How's that?"

The phone rang. Mari's face tightened as she walked away into the kitchen saying, "Okay, go ahead and start. If this is Fiona I could be on awhile."

He hollered at her retreating back, "I told you. I can read directions. I can make brownies."

He started looking for a large bowl, feeling a little lighter after his talk with his wife. She had that innate quality that helped him feel brighter and grounded. It was only a few minutes into their conversation that he knew something was terribly wrong. He abandoned the search of looking for a bowl to listen to Mari, trying to connect with what was being said. She was getting frantic. Quickly hanging up after telling Fiona that she'd be right over, she briefed Sonny about April's ordeal, and was out the door. He collapsed in a kitchen chair, his emotions rumbling around again. He wondered where it would all end. Folding his hands, he promised himself that he would get better and he would be strong and robust again, both physically and emotionally. But his incapacity to do what needed to be done for his family now, saddened him. He could feel tears well up, and he completely forgot about his idea of baking brownies. He wiped his tears, walked to the living room and stared out the window.

Walking into her sister's living room Mari looked around and said, "Hi. Where's April?" Fiona put her finger to her mouth, gesturing to Mari that she should keep her voice down.

Her own voice quieted to a whisper, she said, "She's resting now. It was such a hard night, probably has a whopper of a hangover too." She walked down the short hall to close the bedroom door.

"She's asleep. I got her relaxed with a little chamomile. There's some left. Want some?"

"Yeah thanks." Mari dropped her purse and fell in to a chair. Adding a little sugar to her tea she listened to Fiona's story. She finished with, "It was too much. So I didn't call you. We just went to bed."

"Does she remember much?" Sounding hopeless Fiona answered, "She saw his back as he turned the corner of the house and disappeared into the woods. By the time April could shake sleep off, and get this, try to chase after him and Hercules, they'd disappeared into the woods. She heard Hercules barking like crazy the whole time and she heard the engine roar as he sped out of there, but, that's all."

Frozen with fear, Mari clasped her hands together and pushed them against her chin as she spoke, "It's incomprehensible to think that this mad man had his hands on her. What did the police have to say?"

"They got as much as they could from her. She said that the man was of average height, had a dark hat on and was slightly built."

"That's not much Fiona."

"Like we all know."

"I hear you…maybe she'll remember more later on. Forget the chamomile. I need a drink. Got some vodka and orange juice?" Fiona moved to the cupboard to get it. There was an ounce left. She lifted the bottle to show Mari its remains and raised her eyebrows. Neither one of them said anything.

Aggrieved, Fiona kept her voice down, her words sounding like a hiss.

"If there was enough alcohol left, I could get blind drunk, but what good would it do. She said she wasn't drunk. But she was, and it nearly cost her life! What if Hercules hadn't scared him off?"

"Thank heavens for that dog. And that they're both safe. Damn, what was April thinking!?"

"It's obvious she wasn't thinking Mari. I could be mad as hell at her right now, but it just isn't in me. I'm thankful she's safe." Mari thoughtfully looked at her sister and took a sip of her drink. She winced, *'some breakfast'*, and let it settle. Both sat for a bit, each in their own mind. Mari raced over the conversations she'd been having with people concerning the crime that had struck their town. What if she used her column to focus on what people were feeling and doing without talking about the murderer? She wanted to focus attention on the community whose lives had been affected by the crime. What were they doing to unite with each other to decrease the danger they faced every day, prominent because he hadn't been caught. Attention is what these sick bastards want. They relish the twisted kind of notoriety they get that gives them the power to create such paralyzing fear in people. She looked at Fiona who was deep in her own inner ramblings.

"Fiona, what are you thinking?"

"Oh, different things, and that today, because of this awful thing, I feel protective and closer to April than I've ever felt in my life. Being angry at her is just not important anymore."

Mari knew she was on to something. What if she could inspire people to be thoughtful and forthright about this long miserable ordeal and less about being fearful? If being fearful was the only emotion they felt, it didn't make room for heightening ideas and actions that could help people unify, and work with the authorities. She intended to speak up at work about her idea on the next work day. She told Fiona as much and was spurred on even more by her concurrence with the idea.

A short time later she sat in the car and looked toward the density, hearing the leaves rustling. The rush of the leaves seemed to lean into the house and hold it in its grip. She closed her eyes momentarily, then started the car. Once on the road she took a deep breath and wondered how she would urge people to write. She couldn't help but think that it could spur the killer to react, something she thought about each time she summoned people to respond, but, again, she pushed that fear aside. Mari felt confident that her column would elicit sound, altruistic responses from the public. It could also serve as catharsis for people.

At work, she prepared the following:

Due to the fact that a young woman lost her life, our community has become fearful and suspicious of each other. Being fearful is a gnawing feeling that something may happen to us or to another member of the community. Being suspicious makes many of us look at our neighbours, friends, and other family members. That takes its toll.

You know about the separate attacks on my sisters. One had her home broken into. She responded by safeguarding her home extensively, and she invited her sister to move in with her. They also adopted another dog to help augment their feelings of safety.

Still, the other sister was attacked in the front yard while she was asleep in her lounge. A cowardly killer snuck up on her. The dogs chased him off.

I ask you this. Are we really so damaged and helpless in the face of these very dark events invading our community, perpetrated by a cold blooded killer? We are not. In some unholy, unintended way these loathesome acts have pulled the entire community together and it has deepened our respect for the police. They understand the far reaching effects murder does to people, and they are doing everything they can to solve the one that happened here. Our family knows this firsthand. The police have been nothing but caring and effective in the way they have treated us and collected evidence. He will be caught and brought to justice.

Please write. No one will be identified
Continue to be vigilant and protective of one another.

Mari Dolan

On a beautiful early autumnal Saturday morning, Mari spotted the little Chinese woman, Hao, coming out from the back yard. She pulled a few weeds, walked about here and there, and picked up a discarded paper cup. It appeared to Mari that she was surveying how much outdoor work needed doing. The house was one of the smallest houses on the block, and one of the most attractive. It was red brick and had white window boxes, which were the lengths of two front windows that held large, red geraniums, still blooming. Mari and Sonny especially liked the metal sun that hung from the top of the house, below the peak, with its spindly rays and a smiling face that projected happiness.

Mari had stuff to do in the house, but for now, with the sun warming her back, she stayed put. On impulse, she shooed the cat in, grabbed her coffee, and walked across the street. She smiled, "Hi Hao, I've been meaning to introduce myself. I'm Mari. Your husband works at the hospital with my sister Fiona. That's how I know your name, 'she extended her hand,' while thinking: *And I know your husband's name, a Chinese guy named George'* she inwardly smiled.' Aloud, she said, "I'm having some coffee. Would you like to come over and have some?"

Just like that, Hao made a little bow, extended her own hand, and accepted. Sitting on the front stoop while Hao sat on a folding chair that Mari fetched for her, they quickly blew away twenty minutes, chatting and laughing. Listening to Hao talk, Mari marveled: *She's a little shy, but her eyes have spark. She must pull from somewhere to be able to cope with the bullying she gets from that man. Does she ever stop to think that the neighbours hear what is going on in their home?*

A few days later she and Sonny were cleaning the front yard, when they saw George and Hao come out from their side door and get into their car. He backed out of their driveway, drove past them, and Mari stood where she was, expecting a wave from Hao. She didn't even look their way: *She couldn't not have seen her?*

CHAPTER 13

THE MAIL

Mari headed straight for Stan's office on Monday morning. She gave a little knock before letting herself in. His tie, already loosened, and holding a paper cup filled with the usual black tea, he said, "Good morning Mari, what's up?" She walked to the love seat set off to the side of his desk and he put his cup down. A little amused, he noted how she always looked so eager, sitting on the edge of it, hunched forward. *"She's so cute. Those eyes, the thick lashes. When she blinks you can practically feel a breeze."*

"Yes Mari?" he said in his business like, professional tone. Smiling inwardly at the boyish mess he was, and the mischievous look he had on his face for some reason, she didn't answer right away. She was looking for a place to set her Tim's coffee down. Every Monday morning it looked like a hurricane blew through, toppling the piles of paper haphazardly all over the desk. By Wednesday the piles would look worked on and straightened, but by Friday it looked like it did on Monday, and by then he was so anxious to leave, he left it as is, only to begin again the next week. She walked to the love seat set off to the side of his desk and he put his cup down. Finally settled, she chirped, "Good morning Stan. Please hear me out on this idea. I want to start a column that would allow people to send in letters about how they take care of themselves in the face of tragedy; like we have here now. I want to know how people react to and how it affects their lives. Besides that, people need to know that they're being listened to, that somebody cares and that they're not alone. I'll use the letters, mostly, that have an encouraging bent to them, the ones that offer coexisting ideas and hope. What do you think?" She sat back.

Stan didn't say anything at first. He loosened his tie even more, and he said, "It's a good idea. These fucking sickos get a rush knowing that they're the center of attention and that somehow they're controlling the show. They gloat. It's even fun for them to be able to orchestrate this hideous cat and mouse game they play with the police, the families of the victims, even the neighbourhood the crime happened in. It makes me sick. The idea is good. How can it not make people feel better to know, for instance, that your sisters have pulled closer together 'he paused' I don't want to constrain you in any way, or dampen your spirit, but I'm also thinking that when the killer reads this stuff it'll fuel his rage..."

"Stan! We know the depth of his rage. Kristel knew! Fiona knew when he broke into her home and left that note and now April has felt his hate and rage. His hand touched her face. Everyday...he's planning his next attack. We're not fueling him. He's fueled! We're left trying to find a way to get through all of this without cracking. We need to know that we can take care of ourselves and each other. I don't want to waste time wondering and worrying about him. I just want to provide an avenue where people can talk about things that worry them." She took a breath.

After what seemed like a long time Stan started to talk. "I failed to imagine the depth of fear and anguish people suffer through these things. It's like if you don't experience it firsthand you don't know. You think you do but you don't. If you feel this way, my God, what are Kristel's family and your sisters experiencing. You've given this a lot of thought and I'm behind you, 'he stood up.' Let's go see Carl. I didn't mention it to him last time you reported in the paper and he said that if something came up again, like that, he wants to know about it before it hits the news. I mean, he is the senior editor." Mari followed close behind, "Oh, sure."

Carl was busy reading something as he stood by the large window that looked over the winding roads outside of town. He put it aside, listened to her ideas, and put a protective arm around Mari's shoulder. He didn't hesitate to give her the go ahead. She thought about how lucky she was to be working for such good, open people.

After lunch she headed over to the police station to speak to Officer Robertson. She was certain that her idea was sound, but she thought that the authorities would know best what the repercussions could be for doing something like this. Mari checked in at the front desk, and the officer on desk duty ushered her in. Officer Robertson met her at the door of his office. "Hello Mari. Come in." She explained what she wanted to do. He offered, "The public needs a place for that kind of dialogue. Allowing the public to express their grief for what this community has lost, and perhaps make suggestions to others about what has helped them, well, it's a good thing. I've read your section of the paper. You're astute, discrete, and compassionate. Nobody could do a better job. I only want to caution you about the fact that he may lash out at you, but somehow I don't think that would deter you. Please keep safe."

"I will. Thank you so much." They shook hands. She was smiling as she exited the building.

Stopping at Tim Horton's on the way back to the office, she bought a peanut butter cookie. Sitting behind her desk, she rubbed her neck. This assignment was just the thing that would her take her mind off the things that ate away at her. Sometimes she felt like she was losing it. She couldn't keep up. Sonny's upcoming surgery worried her more than she would admit, April needed a shoulder to lean on and constant support and Fiona was just getting through each day. Mari's tolerance for supporting her family was slow to dissolve, but her strength was withering. Sonny perceived her anxiety and her dwindling patience when he'd heard her on the phone with April one recent afternoon. He asked if he could help.

"How? What could you do or say that I've not!?"

"Probably nothing more, but I see how heavy this stuff is weighing on you, and I wish I could help, if you'd let me." She heard the worry and frustration in his voice, and she felt ashamed that she'd been short with him.

"I'm sorry honey. You need your strength to take care of yourself, and I think I have to take on everything for everybody. But, this is your family too and I'll unload on you when I need to, and I'll get your feedback on things. Even if I don't listen, 'she laughed.' Okay?"

He felt encouraged and grinned, raising his eyebrows, "Okay."

She re-shifted her attention to work and did something before starting anything else. She called Abe and Hanna. They should know about her plans. It wasn't unthinkable that they may want to respond. Hanna answered the phone, they warmly exchanged greetings, and Mari explained the reason for her call. Hanna formed her response by first telling Mari that some days were better than others and that her husband was being treated for depression. Abe would tell his wife that he was in a huge pit of despair, "a dark hole" is how he mostly described it. Hanna told Mari that the psychologist explained that the depression was so enveloping because he felt that it was how he should be feeling. It was oddly a safe place to be. He could curl up around it and not move beyond, something he was afraid and ashamed of doing. He would ask himself things like: What if he didn't think of her every day? Would he forget what she looked like if he didn't keep her image fresh? Worse, what if he found something to smile about sometimes, when his daughter had met such a painful, unmerciful death? The psychologist was working to help him see that his daughter would not want that for him. Kristel would want him to remember her happy and fulfilled life, instead of her hour of death. She would want her parents to smile, to feel her light in the room, comforting them, and leaf through picture albums with them. She wanted to hear them laugh about the way she had always expressed curiosity and joy in life, giving them joy. Not just tears, and unbearable pain. Mari felt tears sting her eyes as she listened to Hanna talk about how helpless she felt trying to help her husband, and she told Mari that the psychologist had enlisted her help to help her husband. This journey they were on toward becoming whole again "was the most important thing they had to do at this time." She thanked Mari for her good intentions but she declined to submit a letter. She couldn't bear the thought of sharing her inner thoughts with the killer.

Waves of affiliation came over Mari, and before concluding their call, Mari suggested that they meet for lunch sometime. Hanna said she'd like that. Mari had not known anyone who had lost a child to such tragedy and it affected her deeply. In her mind's eye she saw Haley when she was under two years of age. She'd run around laughing and toppling everything, folded laundry even, and how "Mo-ma" really looked forward to the little imp's evening bath. Soon she would have quiet and Haley would enjoy her favourite pre-bedtime activity. They made fancy bubble-bath hairdos. It soothed Haley and made her sleepy. Then, she turned thirteen. She shook her head, remembering. One day Haley was late coming home for dinner and when Mari approached her at the back door, she sauntered backwards chomping on this ridiculously large mouthful of bubble gum. Mari supposed she was trying to hide something and she had her empty her mouth. Well, the huge sticky bubblegum lump reeked of stale cigarettes. It made Mari chuckle out loud. Now it did, anyway. Not then.

Mari's conversation with Hanna increased her understanding of what their life was like now. Before hanging up Hanna expressed, "When Abe learns to reminisce with me, about our daughter, it will be good for us, but I know that it'll swing in painful, bittersweet, and joyous ways. I want that for us, so much, to heal together." She concluded, "This psychologist possesses deep insight and such warmth. She is really helping us." Mari smiled tremulously, and they said goodbye. Their talk brought to the fore how they might handle it if one of their own children met a gruesome death like the one that claimed Kristel. Could she be as brave as Hanna, she asked herself. It made her appreciate what they had. Her family was alive and healthy and everyone was working hard to deal with their situations, as upsetting and stressful as they were.

Mari completed what she could at the end of her work day, and earmarked the rest. She could hardly wait to get home to Sonny. She told him everything that had materialized that day and she melted into his body. He didn't say much but his touch was consoling.

The article took on life like she couldn't believe. Mostly, the letters came from females. They expressed sorrow for Hanna and Abe, and for what was happening in Mari's family. Many of the writers said that they found it helpful to read about what people were doing to cope with and conquer their fear, the latter difficult to do. It dragged them through a difficult stretch of life, putting it in striking view what was criminal, violent, and evil, in the world they lived in. They couldn't look away anymore or think that it couldn't happen where they lived. It was in front of them every day. However, many people shared that they were doing the same things that Mari's sister had done. They had added lighting, gotten dogs, and were forever watchful and suspicious. At times their doubts about the people they had known for a long time, reared up. Trying to be sane about it all, they attempted to dismiss their doubts about individuals who were family, their friends, or their neighbours. People were upset that they were forced to live that way. One lady wrote, in part:

I am very alarmed if my teenaged daughter is only a few minutes late. I report anything that looks suspicious, regardless of how paranoid or trifling it may appear. Our windows and doors are double locked now, and the only window I leave open is the kitchen window, which I lock up at bedtime. I always walk with my daughter after dark. We didn't do these things before, because we didn't need to. We loved our town, a peaceful environment. Now it is tarnished and every dark corner is ominous.

Some wrote about the fear that dominated their nights. Their dreams were darkened with ghoulish, black forms. Sometimes, they chased them into wakefulness. Alarmingly, there were a spattering of letters that pointed fingers at their neighbors, even relatives. Mari handed those over to the police.

Mixed in, were letters from young girls. One came from Alicia, who, upon turning fourteen, had been finally allowed to go to the mall with her friend, taking city busses to get there. Now they couldn't do those things unless the most stringent of rules and instructions were followed. The parents made arrangements to pick each girl up at their homes, and they had to wait at the mall for whoever was picking them up and taking them back to their respective homes. Sometimes, the parents shopped with them. Arguments erupted between parents and children. Alicia knew that her parents worried about her and her friends, but she didn't think it was necessary to be with them all the time. "All the time" meant that she and her friends weren't allowed to walk alone to their friend's houses, or anywhere else, for that matter. But, going to the mall was the thing that really got ruined for them. They felt that they could look out for each other. Especially lost for them now, was the fun they had flirting and talking with boys while they shopped. They loved putting on samples of lipstick, eye makeup, and bronzing gel for their cheeks. Some of her friends were restricted from owning make up beyond lip gloss. The last thing they wanted was to experiment while parents seemed to be forever looking over their shoulders. She was unhappy at home too, and her friends complained about the added restrictions imposed on them. Some parents stepped up their watches in what the girls thought was a little over the top. She and some of her friends had been allowed to go out summer evenings, just walking about until 9pm or so, but that was strictly out of the question since the murder. They had to hang out in each other's rooms, dens, or yards.

Alicia's letter bothered Mari, because that time of life for a young girl was precious learning time and it could be so much fun. They were learning how to grow up, they were forming lasting friendships, and they were learning how to be strong and independent. Now they were afraid, dependent, and angry. Still, even Mari couldn't see any other way to keep their girls safe.

A letter from a twelve year old girl concerned her the most. Paula said that her parents ignored her for the most part and they went out a lot without her. She was left to roam about the streets or stay in alone. She felt neglected and scared. The darkness in her home always loomed frighteningly and she would leave the lights on when she went to bed at night. Her father chided her for being afraid of the dark and so she didn't talk about any of her fears, even to others. She didn't want to be vulnerable, but she felt very alone. Mari shuddered thinking about how lonely this girl would be. What kind of parents were they that they could be so detached?

Within a week of the letters appearing in the newspaper, a poem appeared at the office. The envelope had typed print, but the poem within was put together using magazine and newspaper clipped words. She brought it to Stan, who did not know what to say to Mari to comfort her. He lay his hand on her shoulder, "I'm so sorry about this. I'll deliver it to the police." Mari thanked him, feeling shaken by the threat the man bragged about. The rest of her work day continued in a shadowy haze.

The poem reverberated repeatedly:

I THUMP AT NIGHT

THEY SPASM THEY FIGHT

TO MY DELIGHT

TELL THE BITCHES I'M AROUND

I WILL HUNT THE GROUND

UNTIL THE NEXT ONE IS FOUND

At his worst, the killer exhibited psychopathic traits, convinced of his grandiosity and superiority. He looked down on women and violated their boundaries. He was callous and remorseless, although he carefully hid those tendencies. His destructive behaviour first exhibited itself when he became interested in girls. He could falsely charm them into becoming sexual with him, then, when the sex was over, he would pull their hair, slap them hard on the face, or punch them. If they resisted sex, he roughed them up, and laughed at them, poking fun at their refusal to give in. Briefly married in his early twenties, the woman sought a divorce due to his predilection for torturing her emotionally. She recounted this tendency by telling the following story to her lawyer. It was an event that occurred when they'd made plans to go camping. Trying to gather all that he wanted and needed, he'd accused her of hiding his pot, a silly notion, since she never entered the dresser drawer that held his personal items. Nevertheless, he told her that she'd probably gone on one of her stupid tidying forays and had invaded his stuff. She told him that he made up with her later at the camp site and he invited her to take a bike ride with him. She was grateful for the reprieve from his dark mood and followed him. On a fairly quiet section of the bike path, he put the brakes on, and she careened into him. She fell hard. While she was not seriously injured, she was struck by the fact that this had been done on purpose. Nothing had been in their path. She reported that other things like this happened on occasion, in public and at home. Also, he drank excessively which exacerbated his vile mood swings. Increasingly, his angry tirades became viler, and she left him. She sought safety by living with her mother. In short time, she left town. He wanted to hurt her bad, before he killed her, but he was smart enough to realize that he would be the first suspect. He directed his hate and blind, hot rage toward other women.

By the time he'd encountered Kristel one morning at a local blues festival, he had decided that she would be the first one.

After work, Mari popped in on Fiona, thinking that if she concentrated on someone else, she'd regain some equilibrium. Fiona was in a pretty good mood and offered to whip up a light supper. Mari called Sonny to let him know where she was, and Sonny said, "Take your time. I'm playing cards with Vince."

"Great. Say hi. See ya' later."

Fiona was chopping green pepper for a salad as Mari ended her call, so she helped herself to a cold beer, and began setting the table. April wasn't there. She had come to the conclusion that she needed to enter rehab again if she was going to save herself, and, foremost in her mind, keep the baby safe. Everything was fine in the pregnancy, so far. Fiona told Mari that she'd been there to visit her the day before and that April had told her everything about the direction her treatment was taking, and that since she was pregnant they would keep her longer.

"I'm actually furious about her relapse, but I did not scream at her like some crazy woman!"

"Thank you for that. If it makes you feel better, my patience is slipping when I'm with her or talking on the phone. She knows the gravity of the situation, but..."

"I know she's scared about her circumstances, but I can sympathize only so much. She can't threaten the baby's life!" They ate in silence for a few minutes, then a calmer Fiona resumed speaking.

"She is learning a lot about chemical dependency, and that can only help. The first thing they did, of course, was to detoxify her again, and they meet daily in group. She learned that babies born of alcoholic mothers can develop a condition called Alcohol Fetal Syndrome. It causes brain damage." 'Mari's eyes flickered nervously and Fiona reached out to touch her hand.' Affected kids have learning deficits and can exhibit behavioural difficulties. They remain small and have large eyes. Essentially, they are mentally and physically handicapped, not called mentally retarded any longer. That term has become too negative, people in the field point out. They also say that the forces that keep recovery on track is the bond that forms between alcoholics. So...they're working on finding a good friend for April. I'm feeling the strain and I'm all for April finding a friend who's been there, excuse me, is there."

Mari remained quiet as she bit into her taco, then congratulated Fiona,

"You know, you've learned a lot, and your presence and persistence is exactly what she needs until she moves past this."

"Yeah, but like I said Mari, let somebody else have that responsibility, like you." Mari smiled unapologetically, and catching that certain firm glint in her sister's eyes, Fiona stated, "Mari, I am there for April, but first, I am our baby's caretaker…and I'm determined that we're going to bring a healthy baby into our family."

"That's the spirit. For sure. And, by the way. Have you two decided on the names yet for this beautiful healthy baby that's coming much sooner than we think?"

"Yes! I chose Katelyn, if it's a girl. April loves the name Elliott for a boy."

"Oh wow! April has mentioned those names, amongst others. Beautiful choices." They talked baby stuff for a few minutes and Fiona diverted back to discussing April's setback.

"A good way to think of the experience of rehab is to call it basic training. The counselors teach coping skills so they can deal with their stressors. They broke it down to me by explaining that just like soldiers need a rapid course to give them the basic knowledge and skills they need to fight in a war, alcoholics need the same kind of thing. It needs to be practiced so well that that they can replace destructive patterns with good ones, and be able to carry them out. So, like I said before, people are matched up with each other, and when April comes home, she'll have that friend for support. They'll support each other. They call each other when they're tempted to drink, you know, stuff like that."

Mari felt encouraged and told Fiona, "Wow, I mean, April has filled me in on some of that stuff, but hearing it all together like that, I'm satisfied that the center is a very good one." And, although she didn't say it aloud, she found it endearing that Fiona said "their baby" whenever she mentioned the pregnancy.

Almost immediately following their discourse, Mari noticed an almost imperceptible, yet key shift in Fiona's attitude. She had folded her hands, rubbed them together, and it looked like she wanted to say something else. She hesitated.

"What's the matter, Fiona?"

"I'm alone in the house without April there. It has made me extremely nervous. May I spend the weekend with you and Sonny?"

"Of course. We'll do something together, a show maybe." They got up from the table, and began clearing it.

"Thanks Mari. I'll shop for the fixings for a good dinner for us and I'll be over Saturday afternoon."

"Don't bring wine. I have lots. Need help with the dishes?"

"Nope. You go."

She drove home thinking about Sonny. He was doing great, but Mari could tell that he was especially more nervous about the surgery that loomed close. For instance, he was often lost in his own mind, like when they watched television. He never knew what was going on, he'd apologize, and ask her to fill him in. Religiously, he followed all the doctor's orders, he read everything he could about his condition, and he exercised as much as he could. He appreciated Mari's constant attention. He joked sometimes, things like, "Really hon, I need you to whine to."

When Mari got home, he was in his shorts and laying on the bed on a bunch of pillows, absorbed in a book. She changed into her jeans and a t-shirt and told him that Fiona was spending the weekend with them.

"That's fine, and guess what? Vince dropped in today, like I told you, and it's a miracle we could spend time together. He and Sally have just begun to travel about to perform with that dance troupe they're part of. They're not going to be home much in the future, so we talked a lot, and I beat him at cards, big time."

"Oh honey, that's great. I'm going to miss him. It's been so hard to get hold of him lately, but I'm so happy for them. It must be so much fun."

"Yeah, it is, he says, and he'll call next week sometime, when he gets home."

Mari was glad to see him so lighthearted, but she was feeling tired and as soon as she could, she headed for the bathroom. After lining up her candles and splashing lavender bath foam into the tub, she disrobed and put a creamy cleanser all over her face. When the tub was full and just the right temperature she got in. While she soaked she thought about April and vowed to call her later. She heard a slight rustling outside the bathroom window but decided that it was just the wind pushing at the shrubs. She closed her eyes. Finished with her bath, she dressed in blue polka dotted flannel pajamas and decided she would make tea before calling April. When she emerged from the bathroom she headed for the kitchen, just in time to see Sonny hang up the phone. He was breathing a bit heavy and he looked very agitated, his face set.

"Honey, what's wrong?"

"I went to the recycle box to unload those cans we had on the counter and I thought I heard someone at the side of the house by the bathroom window. I didn't see anything, but I'm almost sure somebody was there. I didn't say anything to you, so as not to get you panicked. The cops are on their way." Mari felt sick in the pit of her stomach, and said, "I heard some rustling outside the window but I just thought that maybe the wind had picked up or something."

"Honey, they'll be able to tell if someone's been there."

"I'm making tea. Do you want some?"

"Yeah, please," but he was walking away from her toward the bathroom. He checked the window to be sure it was locked and he readjusted the blinds to close a slight crack in them. Mari's hands trembled a bit making the tea, and she spilled a bit on the counter when she took a sip. Her heart beat wildly. She walked into the living room just as the police were coming in. One burly, muscled officer and a slimmer younger man, about thirty, with close cropped blond hair, were shaking Sonny's hand. She offered tea but they politely declined. Sonny led the officers to where the noise had come from. They flashed their lights and looked around and they told them that nothing seemed amiss. Sonny walked them to their car, and Mari watched them while she sipped her tea. As Sonny re-entered the house, she told him how unnerved she was to have had cops in their house, and that they had been looking around outside for someone who could have been peering in the bathroom at her.

"I'm so scared, Sonny." Sonny held her, "I know baby, but you heard them. By all appearances, no one was out there."

Later, they sat comfortably together in front of the fire, but neither one of them said much. She didn't call April.

By the time they spoke a few evenings later, April was upset.

"When I didn't hear from you, I thought you were so angry and ashamed of me that you didn't want to talk to me. Believe me, I hate myself enough. I needed to talk to you."

"I'm sorry, but yeah April, I was angry for a while, but I was not ashamed of you, never could be. It's just that so many things are pressing in on me right now, and I can only spread myself so thin! I've spoken to Fiona though, and I know you've worked so hard there. I'm proud of you for that" 'April inhaled' Thanks Mari. I know how much you have to worry about. How's Sonny doing?"

"Oh, okay. He's mentally preparing himself for surgery, which is soon. He worries, of course."

"He's going to do fine. He's so strong. And, I'm going to work extra hard to get to where I was. Please believe how sorry I am, for being such a dumb ass."

"It'll be okay April. Just keep your nose to the grindstone. I know you can do it."

"I will. Say hi to Sonny. Love you."

Mari got off the phone grappling with the fact that she found it so difficult now to calmly deal with April. She would never lash out at her. But, she was angry with her, like Fiona was, that she had to talk to her in that place. What if it wasn't the last time that she had to be there? What if she continued to put herself and the baby in harm's way? What if Fiona became addicted too? Addicted to having to fix the wreckage that was April? Because April was carrying a child for her, for them. I love her. Still, her goddamned relapse put herself in a place where she was almost killed in her own yard, and the danger she put their baby in was unforgiveable. Deep down, she did blame April for her happenstance, and without warning, she slammed the side of her fist onto the kitchen counter. She stared into the dark outside the living room window, having ended up there after aimlessly walking about the house.

CHAPTER 14

THE NEIGHBOURS

"**D**amn anyway!" Mari shouted at the clock that told her it was 9:30 a. m. and kept flashing it. "Damn, Damn!" Fiona would be here early this afternoon. Mari had lots to do. She was totally irritated as she kicked her leg to untangle herself from the blankets. Blindly, she felt for her slippers, finding one, then the other, and gazed out the window as she put them on, thinking it was pretty nice out there. She managed to trip over the cat who had to be blocking the doorway to the bathroom, as usual. Tilly protested, and Mari somewhat sweetly murmured, "Sorry Tilly. Morning." Emerging quickly from the bathroom, feeling clean but not too pretty, she pulled her jeans on, a loose oversized top, poured some strong coffee into herself, picked up her purse, grabbed her half-filled coffee mug, and left. Before noon she had made progress, having picked up a cream cheese chocolaty dessert, a small block of havarti heavy with garlic, and a vegetable tray for balance, she told herself. Fiona was due to be there early afternoon, so she scurried home. After putting her purchases away she slowed down and sat on a chair in the kitchen.

Suddenly motionless, she stared off, at nothing distinctive, as the foreboding that lived with the family hit hard at that moment. While she loved having her sister visit, she wished that it wasn't because Fiona didn't feel secure in her own home. She moved toward the linen closet where she got her dust cloth and lugged out her vacuum. Her gaze shifted toward the living room window. Outside wasn't as fresh and sunny as it used to be before the murder happened. Hao walked by, and Mari watched her until she disappeared. It's not like their town hadn't ever experienced crime, but murder is different. Peace was absent. Once dusk fell, kids were kept inside, their parents not trusting the solid fences that surrounded them. She remembered how in summers past, she often enjoyed hearing the little kids laugh and shriek in nearby yards. Not so much anymore. If she had to describe it, she would say that their town was cobwebby and people didn't want to be caught in invisible webs that wouldn't allow them the freedom to enjoy their surroundings. After dusk, their ventures outdoors were shorter, and they went in long before they used to. It was like they needed to go in and touch the soft places, the wood surfaces, their kitchen counters. People needed assurances that they were safe.

She refocused to the present and ferociously attacked the housework, working until the carpets showed very straight vacuum lines and surfaces shone. She pushed her bangs away from her damp forehead and moved the furniture back.

Later, after a quick decadent snack of dark chocolate and jujubes, Mari glanced out her foyer window and saw George's car pass as Fiona's car screeched up the driveway. She ran down the walk to meet her, where Fiona was already bent over her back seat to get the groceries. Turning to greet Mari, she looked good, like happy had fallen on her from the heavens and nothing in her world was wrong. Mari delightedly took the moment in and helped her with her bags. Fiona beamed, "I bought big steaks. They were too beautiful to pass up. I know, red meat, but…" Mari didn't hear the rest. Her eye had caught movement in the curtains across the street, coming from George and Hao's house. Fiona was still talking her usual mile a minute about the drive to Mari's, a quick stop for a six pack, and about meeting George in the beer store with his waif-like wife, "Hao's her name, isn't it?"

"Yep, they were behind you."

Fiona glanced at their house, "I know. Did anything ever develop with her?"

"Nope. There wasn't much of a chance after that little visit we had."

"Yeah, when I chatted with them earlier, she was quiet and didn't say much. Little eye contact too. It was uncomfortable. And, I wanted to get away. You know how I feel about George."

"Yeah. After that one visit with Hao, which was really nice, she wouldn't even look at me. I asked her over sometime after, but nothing. And, she wouldn't even wave when they drove past the house. I told you how he rants at her sometimes. The Smiths hear it more, being right next door," 'she waved her hand toward Connor's house.'

"George is so soft spoken and polite at work. What an asshole." She shivered.

"Anyway, come on in. We deserve a nice weekend. I may run out to pick up some wine for the evening. I checked just before you came. We only have enough for dinner. I'm getting sideways tonight. And so are you."

"Sideways 'Fiona laughed,' that's April's expression. Speaking of which, she and our baby are doing fine. She's contrite and lonely at times, you know, misses the bar, her staff, her connection to people she regarded as her friends. But, she has distanced herself from her drinking buddies. She's different now, so much more confident that she'll create a new life for herself. I know she'll do it this time. I feel it."

"I'm encouraged by your optimism." Secretly, Mari had nagging doubts.

"Plus, I have been in touch with her counselors. They say she's stronger, that her relapse was stress induced because of all the changes she's been through. And, I do like that when she leaves the facility, her AA buddy will be there when she needs someone."

"Why didn't have a buddy the first time she left?"

"She did Mari. But she didn't call her."

"Hmm."

"It's...well, that arrogance she's always had. It's obvious that she thought she could do it on her own."

"Again, hmm."

"Where's Sonny?"

"Napping. He'll be joining us soon."

The potato salad was mixed, the kale salad prepared, ready for the poppy seed dressing, and she checked to see that the white wine had been slipped into the fridge for chilling. They took a break, beer in hand, slowly sipping it as they settled themselves in the yard. With her legs stretched out on the lounge, Fiona breathed deep and exclaimed, "Hey, let's barbecue those steaks. Please? It might be the last time we can do it this year."

"Well then, why don't we?" Mari said. Fiona's eyes sparkled at the anticipation of it. Mari was reassured by the fact that Fiona and April were not nearly as fearful and suspicious of every noise they heard, like they had been for weeks after they moved in together. On some occasions, they even enjoyed playtime with the dogs in their yard, and they sunned together on hot afternoons. But, Mari also knew that these activities were enjoyed together, never solely anymore. There was more work to do, or, better yet, the killer needed to be arrested and locked up.

Sonny got up, shaved, and remarked that he had to go to Vince's for a few minutes. Mari jumped in to say that she wanted to get red wine, and that she'd go with him. They told Fiona that they'd be fifteen, twenty minutes at most, and to please get the barbecue out of the garage, set the table and get the condiments ready.

"Anything else Mari?" They all laughed.

After they slipped off, Fiona busied herself in the kitchen, gathering placemats and tumblers. She wandered into the garage and looked around. It was so neat and clean, everything in its place, and she grinned because the interior had been freshly painted with bright colours. It surely was unlike other garages she'd seen, where this and that was everywhere, without a coordinated effort made to help facilitate finding things when they were needed. Their shelves were a shiny red, the cabinets were dark blue and white, and most of their stuff was hung on hooks and nails. On one of the tops of a cabinet, she found an attractive old vase mixed in with pots for planting flowers, plant food, a hand rake, and the like. Near the back wall, she spotted the table's umbrella. After mounting it she arranged the mats and the tumblers, and she went back into the garage for shears. Walking about the yard she tore off the browned leaves and cut the flowers that still looked fresh-to show in the vase. Then, armed with a sturdy wooden tray that carried barbecue sauce and spices, she carefully carried it and the water-filled vase outside. She felt a sharp pang of pleasure as she did all this. I don't feel so free at home, she thought, with their house being as secluded as it is. Confident that Sonny and Mari would be back soon, she felt carefree. Sublimely, she took the time to taste those feelings of freedom and safety. With time at her disposal still, she got the plates and the silverware, while reflecting about the fact that she truly needed her family. The warmth and the support she got from them had lifted some of the terrible depression that had seen her buried after the attack in her home. Everybody needs a sanctuary from things and people that prove to be dangerous. She finished setting the table and went back into the kitchen again. Immediately, she heard a knock at the door: *Hmm, I wonder who that is.* She walked toward the screened door, where a head appeared.

"Connor…hello." She waited for him to say something. Intent, he looked into her face, and she couldn't look away. It was oddly unnerving, and instinctively, she took a step back while his eyes raked over her. She wanted to slam and bolt the door, but she forced herself to remain composed.

"Is Sonny around?"

Behind the screen door, she replied, "No. He and Mari went out for a few minutes."

"Oh. See, I lent him a trowel earlier this summer, and I need it. It's probably in the garage. I'll just go in and get it."

"Sure, go ahead." He moved toward the garage. Then stopped.

"How ya' doing?"

"Oh, okay, you know." She didn't want to talk to him, let alone discuss her life, being little more than acquainted with him. He took his time walking to the garage, talking about the project he was working on in his yard. He looked around the garage from the doorway, not really intent on finding the God-damned thing, it seemed to Fiona. Relieved, she heard a toot from out front. She stepped out and waited for Haley to walk into the yard. Suddenly, there she was, the dog a step ahead of her.

"I knew it was you. I know that toot anywhere."

"Mom hates it when I do that. She says it's like I'm summoning her. Her car is gone. Where did she go?"

"She and your dad had a few things to do. They left me to set things up."

Connor had disappeared from view and he came out of the garage, saying, "Hell, I don't see it. Oh hi. Been a while since I last saw you."

"Yeah, at the barbecue. How are you?"

"Good. I was just rummaging for my trowel. I need it for something I'm doing."

She turned to Fiona, "I'll keep you company until Mom and Dad get home. Anything I can help you with?"

"Yeah, Ducky just took a dump," she said, suppressing a giggle, one hand over her mouth.

"Oh God. Sorry. I'll get a bag." She went to her car to get a doggie bag. Connor just stood there. Fiona wished he would leave, and he finally took a step toward the side of the house.

"I won't hold you up any longer. I'll come back some other time."

"Bye. I'll tell Sonny you were asking for your trowel. He would know exactly where it is." Haley, who'd gone in to the bathroom to wash her hands, was back in the kitchen where Fiona was doing something at the sink. She grabbed the dish towel and dried her hands, turning to look toward Haley. Abruptly, Haley stood still. She looked stunned, her mouth open slightly, and while she was looking right at Fiona, it seemed that she didn't really see her.

"Haley, snap out it. What's the matter?"

Slowly, she began, "Remember when Mom told you about this experience I had at the beginning of summer. I had visited Dee, and on the way home I stopped for something to eat at Mammie's…

"Yeah, I remember."

"They were really trashing women and the one I didn't get a look at said something like forces take over and I hurt them." She stopped talking. Unsettling seconds passed.

"Yeah, I know, what?"

"Just hearing Connor talk right now. It sounded like him."

"Are you sure?"

"No, I said it sounded like him. I can't be sure."

Fiona sat down, feeling panicked, a far cry from the serenity she had felt mere minutes ago.

"I'm reporting this. You okay?"

Fiona nodded, and without another word, she went back to rooting through the cupboards. By the time Sonny and Mari got back home, setup was finished. Walking into the yard, Mari noticed their somber expressions. No smiles. No greetings.

"Is everything all right? Did anything happen while we were away?"

"Mom, Connor was here when I got here. His voice. It sounded like that guy's voice I heard that day, remember when I stopped at Mammie's for some dinner. I can't be sure, but there's just something…" Mari nodded.

177

"His voice gave me a creepy feeling. I'm probably being paranoid, but I reported it to the police just before you got home, not ten minutes ago."

"Well, we have to report everything. I'm glad you did that. Listen, we'll tell your dad and then we forget about it. We're not going to let this spoil our barbecue. Do you want to join us for dinner? It won't take long to prepare another steak."

Just then Sonny joined them and Mari filled him in. He put his arms around Haley, hugged her tight, then released her and slumped into a chair.

In a rush of words, she said, "I can't be sure of course but his voice was so familiar 'worriedly she peered at her Dad' I didn't upset you, did I?"

"No-no. I'm fine."

Mari cut in, "Haley, what about dinner?"

"What, oh sorry Mom. I'll phone Rex and tell him I'll be late." She got her cell phone out of the car, told him what had just happened, and told him she was staying there for dinner. She rejoined her parents in the kitchen, "Rex says hi. He hopes we're okay." Sonny put an arm around her and looked at Fiona who was dishing out some sour cream, "That trowel Connor was looking for is leaning on the far wall. Anyway, we can't let this rule the day. We have too few of them together. Let's enjoy it." He smiled. Following his lead, they went into a flurry of activity, sat down to eat, and their evening became comfortably cool. At about nine thirty they started to feel chilled, and decided to call it a night. Haley rushed home, Sonny went in to watch a little television, and that left Mari and Fiona in the yard, pulling on hoodies. Fiona suddenly started talking. "Mari, I have to tell you this. I really enjoyed this day, the taste of the food, the conversation, the shelter from the reality that life has become. I am truly happy at this moment. But, there's something else. I realize how important you are to the cohesiveness of this family, even with how impossible we can be, not me, April 'laughter.' If you hadn't refused to let me ignore April's existence, or listen to me knock her, and if you hadn't stuck by me after knowing what I'd done with my life, well, where would I be?" Tears stung her eyes, and Mari reached for her hand, her own eyes brightly moist. Fiona continued, "Where would April be without you? You accept us no matter what? 'She extended her arms,' "I love you." Overwhelmed by the tones of wonderment and gratitude in Fiona's voice, she grasped her sister's hand, nearly knocking her wine glass over, and gasped as Fiona caught it. Mari's surprise turned into a laugh, "A moment nearly ruined, and soon enough. Any longer we'd be two undignified mildly tanked-up women, sobbing like fools. I don't know about you, but I'm ready for bed." They took everything inside, but they left the dishes for morning. Mari slept well, but Fiona slept on and off, hearing Haley's warning about Connor's voice.

Sonny's surgery was three weeks away and he was anxious for it to be over. Waiting was nerve wracking, his mind going over and over how it could turn out fine, or not turn out fine. The days he felt hopeless were excruciatingly long. He wasn't in terrible pain though, so at least that was something he could appreciate. And Mari had started making lists for his party. No doubt, he was looking forward to his big bash, and that made a great difference in how he faced the world. This had to be the party of all parties, he would think, but his attitude shifted almost daily, one being optimistic while the other wasn't. The worst thing, of course, was the possibility that he may die. Those thoughts haunted him, and he did his best to shelter his family. During those low moments, he berated himself because he knew that he had to undergo surgery in the best frame of mind possible. The party was important because, no matter what was wrong in the world, at parties, people's faces glowed, and they smiled, inanely sometimes, because of the drinks they consumed, the silly stories they shared, and everybody's bad jokes were hilarious. "I need people around," he'd said to Mari.

Pretty soon, the lists for food and games were finished but she wondered aloud why she had so much trouble with the guest list. It was scant. She left out the neighbours and co-workers, partly due to the fact that they weren't especially close to the neighbours, and she couldn't invite all his co-workers. Their living room and dining room were only so big. To herself, she denied that she didn't want to invite them. But, there was a lack of complete trust in them, mainly regarding George.

"Here's the party list," she said as she set it on the kitchen table. He picked it up to survey it, finding it scant, but he knew why. Bravely, he felt a surge and he added their neighbors, and included all of his co-workers.

His illness had blind-sided him, but he could handle it all, the treatments, the feeling lethargic and queasy afterwards, all of it a complete drain on his whole system. What really ate away at him, was seeing what all of this was doing to Mari and their kids. He wanted to show them that no matter what life deals you, live it with as much positive energy you have in you. He remembered words he'd read: *It's not the days you remember. It's the moments.* He was becoming philosophical, like his wife, 'he smiled.' That's where his strength lay now. He was making moments. He handed the revised list to Mari, "Now there's a party list." She took it from him, looked it over…and smiled her best smile.

"You're inviting George and Hao? We barely know them, and you know how responsive to overtures they've been."

"I know, but why not try. I'm really inviting Hao. He comes with the package." She loved Sonny without reservation, but she couldn't help but acknowledge, silently of course, that he had not always been that charitable.

"I don't just love you, I like you. I'll call everybody."

"I have my outfit all planned out. I bought this t-shirt. It's perfect. Come here." She followed him to the bedroom, where he shook it from a hanger, and held it up in front of him. She read: Dance while you still can.

"That's the spirit. But, you'd better brush up on that weird thing you do, that you absurdly call dancing. And, you'd better start soon. I refuse to be embarrassed by you."

"What? This?" He bent and locked his elbows, jabbing his arms and legs around to his made up acapella. She laughed hard, holding her arms up, like she was captioning something, "We could call it The Funky Scarecrow."

"Hey, never mind, K-Fed can't dance like this." They dissolved on the bed, acting goofy, laughing their heads off. Mari suddenly jumped up and ran for the bathroom before she peed herself. Sonny felt joyful, something that he had not felt since his diagnosis.

CHAPTER 15

THE UNPREDICTABLE PREDICTABILITY LOVE AND DEATH

Fiona experienced some better days as the weeks turned into months, yet she still experienced times where she felt something could shatter her thin calm. She'd been broken into, something she would never forget. Further to that, nothing new had been reported about the murder in weeks. Top it off with the other things that were going on like Sonny's illness and April's rough journey toward sobriety, well, it cruelly toyed with her. Especially the break in. That memory almost constantly occupied her, and she would erupt with crying spells and anger, directed toward the nameless, faceless man who had destroyed her feelings of safety. It was almost ghostly, the not knowing who had done it. Feelings of defeat would coil within her, because she sensed that the murder may never be solved.

Then, one this bitterly acrid night, she felt a strong urge to challenge the shadowy obscurity of the ground beside her house, and suddenly she found herself outside, desperately needing to be free. Fighting for a lungful of air, she felt for the knife in the back pocket of her jeans. Its steely sensation against her palm helped screw up the deep and resolute part of her that kept her exhausted and her soul, shattered.

Please, I'm so tired.

Without thinking about it, she charged the sheath of darkness that were the trees. Those remote, unremitting giants! Surrounded by darkness, she stood there wildly panicked, her eyes darting all around her. Looking toward the sky, she saw slits of light cast from the moon through the bending branches, and she followed them. But that is all she saw in those slits, all of a sudden gone black, and she began darting this way and that, completely enveloped by the forest. She was lost. Then she heard crunching. It crackled in her brain. Was it a bunny, a raccoon, or had she run directly toward the fiend who had killed that girl? In her sudden irrationality she had left the front door open and Hercules had bounded out behind her. Responding to the crackling and crunching sounds, he raced into the black forest, barking furiously. The crunching sounds retreated quickly, the dog in barreling pursuit. She grabbed Pal, who by now, was by her side. Fiona fought to hold his collar and he barked and pulled her several feet before she could hold him. She heard Hercules shriek in pain! Panting heavily and pitifully howling in pain, he came back with blood dripping from an open wound on the top of his nose. She tried to soothe him while Pal, now free from her grasp, futilely chased off into the direction from where Hercules had just re-emerged. A vehicle that sounded like a truck drove off in the far distance. Pal returned to her side and gratefully she followed them back to the house, managing to lock Pal in. Quickly, she bundled Hercules for the trip to the vet. Swiping at her eyes that ran in rivulets, she stared straight ahead and murmured to him. It was heart-wrenching, listening to him whine and heave, and with each painful groan, her gut twisted. She'd caused this. She pounded her thigh and felt waves of desolation flow through her. She stopped the car and coaxed the dog in, and after explaining what happened, the veterinarian called the police, not touching the dog.

"Something of importance may be provided by something here," the slim young male vet said, as he ran his hand through his blondish hair. He pat Fiona's shoulder.

The officers, one of which was the female one who'd been on the scene at her place when she'd been broken into, put gloves on and checked Hercules over. Together they gathered hair matted with blood and found thread in his teeth. Her face lit up, "This is good evidence. The thread must be from part of the clothing he wore, probably his pants."

"At least this madness, or whatever it was that come over me, has turned into something good."

"And so? It's not worth endangering your life over. "

Ashamed of her carelessness, Fiona cast her eyes down and said, "I don't intend to ever do anything like that again," as she pet Hercules, who licked at her hands.

When April got home, Fiona was there and she shared what had happened.

"Are you crazy Fiona? And if you're not, you're bi-polar-or something. They just haven't diagnosed you yet." Fiona started to cry. April patted her arm, her anger spent. She walked away and lovingly put Hercules to bed on his well-used, matted blue blanket. Coming back to Fiona, she offered her a half sleeping pill and told her they would talk about it in the morning. Fiona accepted the sleeping pill, an immensely tight hug, and fell into bed. Over coffee that morning, Fiona tried to explain to April how crazy she'd been feeling about everything, the feelings of isolation and fear that something bad would happen again, and that in those frantic, panic-filled moments, she'd recklessly challenged it all. She told April how frightened and angry she was about bringing their baby into such an unsafe world. While April could understand that, she could not accept Fiona's blind expression of it, and she expressed her feelings in no uncertain terms. Then, attempting to reassure her, she went on, "Things WILL return to normal. We'll enjoy our home, we'll walk through the woods. Things will be right again." A spark of hope returned to Fiona's eyes. Still, her heart was heavy, and the next week held very little cheer too. She had reverted to doing the things she did when depression fell over her. Things like aimlessly wandering around the house, straightening everything in the cupboards, and crying hopelessly. During those moments, life seemed transient, easily ended, too often violently. April continuously pleaded with her to see her counselor and do whatever she needed to do to bring herself out of her deepening abyss...again.

In a way, something positive happened as a result of Fiona's reckless charge into the woods. She told April how the truck sounded; a thunderous sound. Days later, she informed the police further with as much information that she could remember about it. She said that he gunned the engine in short bursts, then gave a final thrust to his getaway. Also, his exhaust had a different sound from other trucks she'd heard. She did her best to describe it, her words indicating that the muffler sounded like it was "wearing out." And for weeks, that noise bounced off the surrounding undergrowth, the deciduous trees and the pines around their house. She did her best to smother those sounds, but it continued to resonate in her head. During a period of two weeks after that, she spent her time working, taking care of the house and the dogs, but the rest of the time she stayed in bed, worrying, reading and sleeping.

Life went on, day in, day out. On one of those days Sonny packed for the hospital.

"Mari, where did you put those new pajamas I bought?" he asked as he walked toward the kitchen. He bumped into Mari as she was approaching him, "Whoa Sonny, have you been jittery. Try to relax." She walked to the closet and fished the pajamas out of the bag on the top shelf.

"Wouldn't you be Mari, if it was you going under the knife?"

"Sorry, I'd be scared as hell. But, it'll go well. Here you go, 'she said as she handed the pajamas to him.'

He pulled everything out and began re-packing. She knew that if she tried to help he'd be annoyed, so she left him alone. Ten minutes later he stood in the kitchen doorway, informing her that he'd be ready in a few minutes. She got her jacket.

Bags in hand, jacket on, he reappeared, "I'm ready." Mari put her cup in the sink, eyeing him.

"You might want to wear shoes."

Saying nothing, he put his bags down, turned on his heel and went to get his shoes. Minutes later they were on their way. It was a blur for him upon entering admittance. They checked him in and Mari accompanied him to his room. It had been newly painted a soft blue and he had a view of the darker blanket of sky from his window. Nice. He breathed deeply and unpacked. Mari helped him settle in and she said that she and Haley would be back in the morning pre-surgery. They kissed, Mari whispering words of assurance. Reluctantly she left.

Sonny settled down in his new pajamas, the cute nurses stepping in and out performing their administrations. He liked their company. Finally left alone, he opened the novel he'd brought, but he couldn't read.

He placed the novel in his lap and waited for the surgeon to make an appearance. When he did, he gently shook Sonny's arm to wake him and introduced himself.

"Good morning, I'm Doctor Blake and I'll be performing the surgery." He was tall, well built, and his smile and manner was easy. Sonny felt very comfortable with him. He outlined the procedure and encouraged him to relax. Sonny attentively followed his every word. Dr. Blake told him it would be very early in the morning when the attendant would roll the gurney in, load him up, and he would be wheeled to the operating room. He'd be put under, and the next thing he knew he'd be awake, with the nurses taking care of him. He shook Sonny's hand and exited as quickly as he came in. At the door he stopped, turned and said, "Sonny, you're going to do great. Get a good night's sleep. The nurses are prepping you early." Sonny sank into the bed and was asleep before he knew it. The next thing he knew was that he was being prepped while Mari, Haley, and Vince, stood in the hall. They kissed him and followed the gurney to the waiting room next to the operating room. He came to in recovery, unaware of how much time had passed. He couldn't breathe or talk. The nurses bustled about and he panicked trying to get their attention. It was damned scary. Minutes later, they assured him that his experience was common when coming off aesthesia, and that soon he would be brought back to his room.

"Was the surgery a success?"

The nurse patted his hand, "The doctor will speak to you shortly... just rest."

In the meantime Mari and Haley reveled in the good news that Sonny's surgery had been completely successful. Sitting and holding hands as they listened, they'd jumped up and hugged each other, both crying with relief, then laughing with relief, while the doctor waited so he could finish his report about how well things went. All the cancerous tissue had been removed. They went for a celebratory lunch, talking about the fact that they could have lost him. What if he hadn't pulled through the surgery? What if they weren't able to get all the cancer because it had spread? Once they got that out of their systems they reminded each other how well things had gone. After a relaxed chat, Haley left and Mari found herself in Sonny's room, coffee in hand. She sat and watched her husband sleep. And hour later, he awakened and weakly called Mari's name, she having dozed off, her cold coffee sitting in her lap. Putting the cup aside, she went to him and kissed him, "How are you?"

"I feel like shit. It hurts just to breathe, let alone talk." Mari told him as much as she knew about his surgery and Sonny was elated by the positivity of her words. Then the surgeon came in and quickly assured them both that there was every indication that he would get well. Both happy, Mari went home and Sonny dozed. He went home a few days later, a bit weak and clutching the prescription for pain medication. He was on his way. He just had to regain lost ground. Again, he thought of how the recent months had been for him. While he had tried hard to digest that the news about his cancer, a lightning bolt to his very core, he learned so much. He'd needed to be self-centered during all of it, but now that it was over, this whole experience had opened doors. More and more, he found himself going back to the time he was a child, then a teenager, and finally he reviewed his life as a husband and father. He knew that too much of Sonny stood in the way, and as a man now with a good family, he needed to acknowledge that he'd been a real pain in the ass. He'd been egocentric for most of his life. He'd needed constant stroking, constant attention, and he was sulky if he didn't get it. Certainly, his wife, sick about how things were going, helped him to see that it couldn't always be about him. With her unflinching strength and generosity, they were on their way to having something better.

Just last week, he'd told her that he'd been reading from the book "What Dying People Want/Practical Wisdom for the End of Life," a book that Mari had purchased and had left lying around. He told her, "Guess what I found? That book you read from almost daily when I became ill. At first, the title scared me. Then, when I started to read it, it occurred to me that it was more a book about living, than it was about dying. It teaches you how important is to open up to the people who are important in your life, while you still can. Guess what else I found? A soul. It just needs tweaking," 'he grinned that boyish grin of his.' He further revealed that when he got to the section called "Life Review" he couldn't stop the flow of thoughts and he apologized for being smug and vain, and unable to really listen. Humbled, he thought of how he'd rebuked her when she needed acknowledgement and attention. That had been his failure as a husband. Mari held his hand and smiled that flash smile of hers. She thanked him. In that moment, Sonny had an epiphany. This is where he belonged. With her. With Haley and Vince. He couldn't describe the achingly strong feelings of love he had for them.

Feeling the chill in the air, April held her big, round belly, and looked to the sky. Earlier in the afternoon, it had looked like a clear blue flat sheet with white clouds. That suddenly changed when the wind picked up and it looked rumpled, waving around in drifts of blue and white. Her new AA buddy's name was Cassie, and she'd also become a good friend. They played in the dried out, brownish leaves that constantly swirled and re-landed, pushed by the increasingly stronger, blustery wind. They were supposed to be cleaning the yard, not having this much fun. Since coming home from rehab April was happy and glowing, and Cassie had certainly helped with that. They related well, they could talk unabashedly, completely uncensored, certainly because they shared a problem, but also because they were so alike; fun-loving, raucous, and a little crazy. The window was open, and Fiona heard April joke, "Cassie, we can be crazy and party-and remember what happened."

She laughed softly, hearing this before she dropped the curtain, and walked away. Certainly, it was hilarious watching April do anything now with her protruding stomach, and that too had also been why she was laughing and enjoying their energy. Yet, deep down, she envied them, because she couldn't join in their uninhibited playfulness. It was like she would be intruding on their friendship, their battle, their exclusive club, whatever it was they shared. Sometimes she felt so alone in her thoughts. Nobody would understand how she was feeling, desperately confined to thinking about the night that she could have met with horror at the hands of a killer. But, determined to be positive, she thought about Mari and Sonny's party that was taking place this afternoon. Oh, to have fun again, to let go of any inhibitions she had, unlike April, who never had any. Her mind slipped back to when Warren and she had stopped having fun a few years into their marriage. There had been a time when they could laugh, had smoked a little dope, had danced in their living room, and made crazy love till they were sweaty and panting. It seared her memory. Then her thoughts flickered to how difficult he got, how reactive he was, how unkind he was.

But, she was changing. Her heart was softer. Sometimes she could actually feel the transformation. It's almost like her heart warmed up and swelled. She had Mari to thank for that. Mari, who never let her get away with anything untoward. Sure, Mari understood how she felt, and acknowledged those things all the time, but she was tough with her. That was who she was. Now it was time to be there for Mari. And for Sonny. She would put her best slim pencil skirt on, her shimmering white top, her black pumps, and she would enjoy herself. April would, she knew. She'd shopped for something flirty and sassy, and she had sashayed in it for Fiona, even though she complained about being cumbersome and un-sexy. Fiona had watched her, smiling her approval of the little yellow and blue-flowered dress, but she wanted to have that tummy growing on her. Jealous moments like that reared up sometimes, and she couldn't help but feel so empty. Empty of the fetus that she once had growing inside her. April's pregnancy was a grim reminder of that. Especially when April laughed and touched her swelled belly, or when she pushed on the bumps that moved under her breasts, "I'm just afraid the baby's leg will get stuck under one of my breasts. That could be a tad uncomfortable," she'd laugh. The experiences April talked about were things she would never experience. But, she was going to mother this baby soon. Their gift of a little human was coming.

Would the crime be solved by then? She couldn't help the feeling that their happiness would be intruded upon, tainted somehow, if he wasn't captured. Their baby couldn't come into a world where such bad things happened, and worse, where it could happen again if the killer wasn't caught. But, she was careful to contain negative thoughts. She could not let April or their baby be affected by her disquiet.

As time wore on, she had to admit that some things were improving in that work was going well, she was religiously taking her medication, regularly attended counseling sessions and she kept up her involvement in group therapy. It helped to be around people with similar problems and sadness, and she was buoyed by them because they worked so hard to communicate their distress, as well as listen to others who were distraught. Life hadn't been tough on her only.

However, something had happened at the last group session that had made her giggle. She was attracted to someone in the group. Not that he knew it. He didn't know anything but his anguish. When it was his turn to speak in group she watched how his whole body was involved in getting things out. Donny was handsome, with dimples on each side of his mouth, and he had strong, compact, smooth hands that he held tightly fisted together whenever he conveyed the things that drove him to hopelessness. It had made her uncomfortable at first because he expressed his anger in gulping sobs, his face contorted. She found herself very afraid for him, and of him. After a session like that it would take forever for every muscle in her body to relax. She would wonder if he'd get better and would they ever connect? Sometimes, she'd think how April would say that you should approach love, sex, cooking and eating with reckless abandon: "Just go for it." April would feign annoyance too, "Ever wonder why men can have sex with lots of women and it's acceptable, but if women do it with fifteen to twenty men, she's a tramp." Fiona would giggle, and would give her playful shit whenever she flipped off, "Sleeping around is a great way to meet people."

Anyway, on the particular day in group that she'd nearly dissolved into laughter, it was specifically in remembrance of April's funny, naughty quips. She'd had to stifle a bubbling up of giggles, both hands covering her mouth. Because, at the very moment that Donny was expressing deep feelings about the wife he loved and lost, the poor woman next to her began having a meltdown. Excuse me, she thought, but it was hilarious. Still, she would die of embarrassment if she bust up laughing now!! It was an indecorum and a quirky thing that Fiona owned, this laughing at the wrong times, and that day she had almost lost control of herself. Fiona washed the few dishes in the sink, smiling as she remembered.

Finished, and with hands dried, Fiona went to the door, "Hey you two, cut it out. We have to get ready for the party." April called to her friend who was at the edge of the trees with Pal and Hercules, "Hey Cassie, would you like to join us for Sonny's party. I know Mari won't mind an extra guest." She turned to Fiona, "Would she?"

"Of course not. Join us Cassie," she called out to her.

"Are you sure?" Patting her legs to get the leaves and dust off, April looked up, "We're sure."

"Okay, I'll go home, clean up, pick something up to drink, and I'll be there. Thanks guys."

It seemed that everyone filed in all at once, calling hellos, putting their drinks in the fridge, in available coolers on the back porch, then they milled in the living room, spilling in and out. Connor made his way to Sonny who was clearly enjoying himself.

"So Sonny, how have you been feeling?"

"I couldn't be better now. We've been planning this shindig for some time, and it feels good having everyone under the same roof, just to have fun."

That's great. Something smells good. What's cooking?"

"Lots of stuff. I know Mari threw a great chili together and the kids brought dips and things. April prepared something too. Cooking is really not her best thing. Can't wait to see what surprise she brings. And, she's bringing a friend." Just then the phone rang. Sonny picked it up, "Hi April, I was just talking about you. Where are you?"

"Oh okay, well, get your friend and get over here." Sonny set the phone down and turned to Connor.

"Her friend was going to drive over herself, but her car has a flat. April's swinging over to pick her up." He beamed.

"It'll be nice to see your sister-in-law again. I see her and Fiona pull in here sometimes. Mari and her sisters share similar qualities. You're so lucky to have all these attractive women in your life." He smiled, but it didn't seem real.

"Yeah, they're great. Hey, you seem a little up-tight. Something the matter?" Connor was trying hard to relax the muscles of his cheeks, but the blood in his temples pounded. He touched his forehead, "Oh, just work issues that are getting to me."

"Well, this is a party. Work will keep. Relax bud."

Sonny walked away and he felt a little queasy after that conversation: *I get the impression that he's envious, doesn't like me, something, well...who cares?*

He shook it off and went to look for Mari to tell her that April and her friend were going to be late: "Cassie had a flat, so April has to swing over and pick her up. She said to tell you she'd be here soon."

"Oh good. I was wondering what was taking her. You feeling okay hon?"

"Are you kidding? I feel great. Might just be one of somebody's little appetizers." He patted his stomach and kissed her lightly.

"Gonna play cards with the kids."

As Sonny left the kitchen, Fiona walked in and told Mari that she was going to have to leave the party a little earlier than April. Someone's called in sick and I've been called to work the morning shift. Mari voiced her concern about her going home alone that late at night.

"It'll be okay. April will have to take Cassie home, but she won't be too long getting home after me."

"Fiona, I'll drive you home. Then April can drive you to work and bring you back tomorrow to pick up your car."

"Can't. April has plans very early, not to mention her meeting. I need my car. It's too complicated otherwise."

"I guess it'll be alright, but call me as soon as you get home."

"I will."

She left the kitchen, practically tripping over Connor who was standing outside the kitchen door, a drink to his lips. Fiona almost collided with him and he looked into her eyes, "Oh sorry," politely excusing himself.

She darted away, "It's okay."

She thought about the horrible evening before. Late in the evening, he'd entered the house from the back door off the kitchen and her heart had raced, because even though he didn't say anything, she felt his agitation, palpably. It was in his stance, the penetrating way he looked at her, then how he stood still as if he was calculating his next move. This alternated back and forth for what seemed like a life time. It was scary. Rigidly, she'd stood in the living room, and suddenly, he turned and headed for the shower. Relieved, she stilled her shaking hands.

Wondering how she could continue to be vigilant without arousing his suspicions, she waited for what was next. Immediately after his shower, he emerged wearing fresh clothing, and he had something in his hand. She wasn't sure but it looked like an item of clothing. He walked toward the back door with it, and she heard him open and close it. Clutching her arms in front of her, she quickly got up and peeked around the living room wall that led to the kitchen door. She was just in time to see him drop it into the trash can. She scurried to the couch, sat down, switched the channels on the television, and waited. A few seconds later he was back in and he barked at her to get him a beer, without even glancing at her. She hated him so much that moment it made her stomach churn. He took every opportunity to remind her that it was her job to wait on him. Doing what she was told, she walked into the kitchen and got it for him. With a perceptible shaking of his hand he took it from her and he headed for another part of the house. Nothing was said.

While flipping through the stations again, she tried to find something she could watch. She had to make an attempt at normalcy so that he wouldn't detect anything untoward on her part. Her plan was to retrieve the item that evening because tomorrow morning was garbage day. She could not risk the chance that it would be taken away. Around eleven o'clock he went to bed. She walked into the computer room and picked up the gardening book while she waited for him to fall asleep. Ever since she was a little girl, she found that looking at or drawing flowers held her concentration and shielded her from thinking about the colorless, unhappy rooms that made up the house she grew up in. Where the yard hold didn't show little hedges, flowers, swing sets, and wagons. Her home had never been child friendly, and her parents were less than friendly with anyone. Nor were they loving with them, especially her father. He could be really strange sometimes, jabbering away about nothing, or talking garbage about how his wife annoyed him because she was "so stupid and useless." Looking through the book would help her wait and she walked back into the living room with it. She leafed through it, but not for long. She felt paralyzed and her hands were clammy.

After a while she walked to the entrance of the bedroom. Certain that he was asleep she got the bag from the closet, moved silently to the back door, and slowly opened it. She stepped out and her hands shook on the door knob as she gently closed it, her hands shaking because of the sheer, numbing fear that he would come running into the kitchen, having heard something. The wind came up as she tiptoed quickly to the garbage can. Rummaging around, careful not to bump the metal cover on anything, her hand touched something soft that was the colour of the thing he'd held. It was a pair of pants. She pulled it out and made her way quickly into the dimly lit kitchen. She heard him get up. In a split second she opened the cupboard door under the sink and stuffed the item in. He entered the kitchen and peered at her, "What the fuck is goin' on? I'm tryin' to sleep here and you're wandering around like some stupid, skittish cat. Settle." His hand shot out and he pushed her.

"Sorry. I got a book from the library and I felt like a little tea."

"You were outside. I heard the door close. What were ya doin'?"

"I got the newspaper out of the car that I bought today. I forgot to bring it in." Today's paper was sitting on the coffee table, the thought entering her mind that he could have already seen it there. He stared at her, then his eyes shifted to the kitchen window, looking out at the dark sky, toward the alley. Finally, saying nothing, he walked away. She let her breath ooze out, gripping the kitchen counter to steady herself. She put the kettle on, got her tea ready and took it into the living room, shakily holding it with both hands. Setting the hot tea on the coffee table, she waited about ten minutes of so, before walking to the edge of the hall. She listened and heard him snoring. Hurrying into the kitchen, she pulled the pants out from under the sink, and saw that one of the legs was ripped near the hem. She folded them and placed them in a plastic bag, then hid it on the top shelf of the front hall closet. She thought: *It does not mean much. He'd ripped his pants and he threw them out.* Still, she would not ignore it. She had to take them to the police as soon as possible. No more stuffing things inside her, ignoring things that could be important. She finally admitted to herself that she suspected him of being the murderer! With those thoughts she felt icy tingles go up her legs and arms and she clasped her arms tightly together. Through her adult life she'd cavorted with a madman and she had to do what she thought was right. It despondently lived in her, and it crept into her thoughts daily-that he may be the man who'd killed Kristel.

For days, she walked past that closet door and thought about the bag, knowing what she had to do. She had to make a move soon before her resolve diminished or worse, she negligently lost her resolve to do the right thing. After a lot of self-reproach, she reached for it and clutched it tightly to her, wild with unanswered questions: *Why was he so agitated that day? Where did he rip his pants? Why did he throw them out? Stop pretending you don't know.*

He'd been treated so cruelly by his father and she couldn't stop the thoughts about the craziness that filled their home. What he must have gone through. And, he would say that "dear old Mom" was there in body, but it seemed that nothing touched her. You looked at her, and she was blank. She allowed stuff to happen. He said that if he looked to her for help, she turned away. When he talked about his father, his mouth would twist around the words that painfully dug into him the most, "useless little punk," "scrawny little bastard." Yet, she knew that even if his father was the master of dastardly deeds, there still was no accepting what he could possibly had done. No excuses could be made for who he had become.

She gripped the steering wheel tighter and fought traffic to get to police station as quickly as she could. Confused, ashamed, and dismayed, she thought about how long she had waited to act. If he had committed a gruesome murder, he had to pay.

He sat in the recliner and relived the moments he heard her squeal in pain as he pushed himself into her. Relishing it even further, he remembered how he had hog tied her and slashed at her throat in a sawing motion. Just before her death, she had gripped the leg of the living room table, and he'd watched until her arm stopped jerking. Slugging on his beer and chewing on his nails, he wondered how he was going to do this one. The bitch had secured her windows, added lighting, and her car was always parked really close to her front walk. It was just pure luck that the young one had sacked in that chaise, drunker than a skunk 'he shook his head and snorted on the last of his beer.' But those fucking dogs! No matter when he was there, they couldn't be avoided.

He glanced at his Nosy Rosy sister. She watches me and I'm really getting fuckin' bugged. Heh, she's the least of my worries. Dropping his empty beer on the floor, he watched a game show and fell into a deep, drunken stupor.

CHAPTER 16

THE PARTY IS OVER

Haley's skin crawled whenever she was close to Connor. He seemed transfixed by her in a surly sort of way. She'd always disliked his presence for that very reason, although she didn't encounter him often, so she had found it easy to ignore him. Having him at the party brought him face to face. She furtively watched him and saw that he had creepy eyes for other women there also: *What a sleaze.* She ignored it as best she could. Haley didn't want to ruin anyone's good time, so she kept it to herself. And when she chanced to talk to Fiona, she'd become a little loud, "Is this a good party or what? Whoops, I'm getting loopy. Three shots of Sambuca will do that. That's two too many, 'laughter.'

"You're not driving hon. Rex will take care of you."

"Yeah-hey my Dad is having a good time too. That is so good to see."

"It is, for sure, 'smiling' and well, everyone is. It feels good to just be having fun."

"I can't know how much stress you've been under-and Aunt April too. There's been too much of that in this family. But, you look so good. That dress rocks on you." To which Fiona smiled, "Thank you sweetie" she said and leaned in for a hug.

Rex came up to them and grabbed April's hand. "Sorry to break this up, but this girl has to come with me." He pulled her away.

"Gotta go," she shrugged and told Fiona, who smiled indulgently and watched them disappear into the kitchen. She'd been on her way to talk to Vince and Sally and she found them deep in conversation. Looking back and forth between the two of them, she said, "Hey, excuse me. I have to go soon and we haven't had a chance to talk. You'll have to bring Sally over sometime so we can get to know each other better. It's been way too long Vince. How are you two doing anyway?"

"Great. And yeah, we'll certainly do that, come over and everything."

While they chatted, Connor slipped out the back door, leaned into the side of the house, stopped to light a cigarette and slipped across the street. He walked past his car in the driveway and entered his house through the back door. As he settled on the couch, the phone rang. Checking call display, he saw that it was Sonny."

"Fuck."

"Hi. We lost you. What are you doing home in the dark?"

"I just didn't feel good and I didn't have time to say anything, know what I mean?"

"Gotcha. Hope it wasn't les hors-d'oeuvres," he chuckled.

"No, no. Food's good."

"Well, come back. The party's really picking up. Everybody's here now. And Mari has all the food out."

"Huh. Don't know if I can handle that."

"So try, okay. We've got a game of cards going."

"Great. Talk later." He put the phone down and watched the house, thinking about how it would feel to do Fiona, or April even. He unzipped his pants.

Sonny looked around at everybody as he chomped on his Thai flavored chicken wing; *Whoo, a little spicy.* He got rid of it and looked around. Everybody was talking and laughing. Vince and Haley were poking each other. *Some things never change.* He made it over to the group where the kids were, who were chiding each other about something or other. He heard Vince say, "I plan to dodge that bullet. Sorry, that was a bit flippant, I guess, but you'll have to pursue that career."

"What bullet? What career?" Vince continues, "We're only beginning to talk about marriage, so babies and stuff have to wait"…he tipped his beer in the air, acknowledging Sonny's presence.

"Really! May I ask why?"

"Well, for one thing, we're budding stars in dance 'he reached for

Sally's hand' and we want to enjoy this part of our lives before we get into planning a wedding and stuff-like babies."

"We did expect we'd be grandparents one day, either by you or your sister. I won't mention this to your Mom. It's on you guys to talk to us about what your future plans are at some appropriate time."

Haley piped up, "Yeah Dad, it is. And I was saying that Rex and I have discussed the possibility that we might never be parents."

"Oh! That IS your choice, of course. He cocked his head.

"Listen guys, take it from me, none of us knows what the future will bring. Lots of things can happen. But whatever happens, I'll be around for it all." He hugged Haley.

A bit teary, she answered, "You will Dad. You're home free. I bet you're going to live till your eighty, ninety even." Smiling broadly, so her Dad wouldn't see how emotional she was on the brink of becoming, she shook it off, heading for a second helping of something. Alcohol always made Haley hungry.

Fiona wound up the conversation with Vince and Sally, bid her good-byes, truly happy, but sad too. She didn't want to leave the party early. She forced herself not to dwell on the fact that the assailant was still out there, and she was driving home alone. A sudden charge of panic shot through her because she could not control how much this nameless, faceless man abrasively scratched at her mind. It happened daily that her mind would drop into the dark world of rapists and murderers, and she could only imagine what the killer looked like, where he was, and was he closing in on another victim…possibly her or April.

Quickly, she slid into her car, reached for the seat belt, started it, and glanced over at Connor's house. She thought: *Sneaky creep.* Finding her will, she shut him out of her mind.

Inching out of her parking spot, scrutinizing the darkness, she peered ahead and looked behind her as well to make sure that no one was following her. She sped up and determinedly headed for home.

He pounded the steering wheel with his fist feeling the sweat forming on his right hand and he rubbed it on his pants. Excited, he touched the knife's blade that lay on the seat, and felt it slice his forefinger. He sucked on it and wiped it on his leg, all the while thinking about how he would cut her, do her, then finish her off by repeatedly stabbing her. He yearned for that feeling of satiation. He remembered how coolly detached and pleasurably exhausted he became when he did Kristel. What a high! Something like a hit of crack. The woods that provided such great cover so he could watch the bitches almost whenever he wanted to, would be this one's grave. The earth wasn't really hard yet and it would be easy to dig up. The shovel lay on the floor board behind his seat.

Sonny informed Mari that he was leaving to follow Fiona. He didn't like the idea of her being on that dark county road that led her home. Mari didn't argue. She was so grateful that he was a strong and solid man again, fully able to care for his family again.

"Be careful, hon," she voiced, seeing him off.

Fumbling with his seat belt, securing it across him, Sonny looked for his cell phone that had dropped from his hand. *God-damn it!* Impatiently, he sped up to catch up to her. That truck ahead. His mind rejected the feeling that it could be the killer. Whoever it was, something told Sonny to pull over for a few seconds, so he wouldn't be noticed. He felt for the cell phone again that was tucked in the slit between the seat and the gear shift. Grabbing it and placing it on the seat near him, he set off again, lights off.

On the dark road that led to her home, Connor couldn't believe his eyes and he shouted: "What a fuckin' break! There she is. Bitch, let's go!"

Fiona glanced into her rear view mirror and saw headlights that were quickly approaching. She white-knuckled the steering wheel. The darkness of the road took away its civility. It was downright jarring to be on that road by herself. Her finger found the button to switch the interior lights on, then she rummaged in her purse with tight fingers to find her cell phone. She couldn't feel it, so moving her purse, she found it tucked against her thigh. She grasped it and switched the light off. That truck was gaining quickly as though to pass her, and it was weaving. Her mind processed the alien, yet circulating probability that evil was pursuing her and she dropped the phone. Her wheels hit the stones. She tightened her grip on the steering wheel. *Steady. Steady.* The truck inched closer. Stones flew. Like this wasn't really happening, she kept her cool, slowed down a bit-and waited for his next move. In a minute he was beside her and pushed her closer to the ditch. As he gained on her, he slammed on the breaks in front of her car. She did the same, put the car in reverse and screamed sharply. Would she be able to stay away from the ditch?! She reared back, turning the wheel away from the ditch, terror mounting as she felt the passenger front of the car tilt toward the ditch. Survival the only option, she gunned the engine, kept control of the wheel, and pushed back with all that the car had, finding her in position to be able to complete her u-turn. He backed into her and the sound of metal scraping against her car detonated in her head. Ignoring her fear, she kept her foot pressed to the pedal. Miraculously, in seconds, she was able to make the turn. Quickly, she straightened her car in the other direction, released her breath, picked up speed, stupidly giddy now, a mixture of triumph and absolute fear propelling her.

He was stunned! Astonished, he watched her drive in the other direction. Then, his eyes trapped by the rear view mirror, he saw a vehicle approaching fast, that hadn't been there before! He had to get away. Moments later, he heard sirens. Knowing this road like he did, he knew he was close to a slip in the forest that not too many knew about. It would hide him. Reaching it, he crept the truck in.

Sonny grabbed his cell phone and called the police. He quickly told them what was happening, hung up without waiting for them to respond, and called Fiona's cell. She answered.

"It's me. I'm behind the truck that was following you and I've called the police. Get back to the house. Quick. The police are on their way."

He couldn't believe how steady his voice sounded, his heart pounding, his hands wrapped around the steering wheel, tight, like he wanted to clutch whoever's neck of the man that was pursuing Fiona. He wanted to kill him!

"Oh God Sonny. Just don't get close to him!"

"What? I'm okay. When they catch the son-of-a bitch, I want to be there. The only thing you have to do is get back to the house."

He hung up and called the house.

"Hi Dad. Where are you?"

"Haley. Be ready to meet Fiona at the door. Someone tried to run her off the road. She managed to get away. She'll be there soon. I called the police and I'm still tailing him."

"Did you see who it was?"

"Not sure. Too dark to tell."

"Oh God." Sonny heard the fear in her voice.

"I hear ya'. For right now, take care of Fiona." He dropped the phone.

With thoughts racing around in his head, Sonny slowed to a crawl, turned his lights on, and strained to see an opening in the trees. It was too dark and he bypassed it. He stopped, and suddenly the cops drew up. He got out.

"You alright? Who were you following?"

"Not sure. It might be Connor Smith, our neighbor across the street. He was at my party and left early, said he was sick. Whatever, he's driven in there somewhere, down there, 'he pointed'." The cops exchanged knowing glances.

"You go home. We'll find him."

"I want to be there when you get him."

"We're wasting time." The cop opened his car door. "I'm not arguing with you! Go home! And, if you see him, don't approach him. Call us."

Oblivious to what the cop said, Sonny got into his car and headed back toward home, straining with every nerve in his body. The probability that it was Connor nauseated him, and thoughts of hurting or even killing him built up to the point that it completely consumed him.

When Fiona got back, she saw Mari at the door, and she ran straight to the safety of her sister's arms and released a torrent of tears. Mari led her in to where what had been a party, was a party no longer. The atmosphere had shifted from fun and laughter, to an indistinct and dreamlike quiet. Present in everyone's mind was that what was happening was leading to closure. The nightmare might soon be over. They somberly waited for what was to come.

CHAPTER 17

THE LAST ROAD

Connor moved slowly, shadowed by darkness, eyes blazing, down the man-made bumpy road, desperate to get back home before the cops could get him. *All gone wrong/So fast/Think! Think!* Connor tried to slow his staccato mind, and he rubbed his forehead, trying to rid himself of the headache he felt coming on. He turned his lights off, and weaved swiftly but carefully back, using the route he frequented "to cruise," the road he always used to enter and leave his block without detection from across the street. Tonight it seemed to take forever to get home, but no matter how tense he was, he kept steady so as to not make undue noise. He stopped before exiting the end of the road, looking all around for any sign that a vehicle might be approaching. Slipping his window down, he listened. It was silent, and the skunk he smelled moved about some garbage at the side of the road. Edging out, he drove slowly and turned into his alley, using the running lights to ease into his garage. Looking around he didn't see anything. He opened the truck door and placed one booted foot on the ground, and with not a moment to spare he slid the latch on the gate and quickly walked up the path to his back door. The knife in one hand, keys ready, he let himself in. Keys dropped, he made his way to the living room. Leaving the lights off, he peered out with slit eyes, staying put for a few minutes. He noticed Sonny's shady outline just entering the blind area along the side gate from the street. Like a hunter, he gripped the knife harder, and turned, his eyes riveted toward the back of the house. He crept to the kitchen and stood at the back door and thought: *Sonny could have been on my tail from the start. Didn't notice. I'm slipping. Must've gotten the cops on my tail!! Fuckin' bastard!!*

He refocused, and enjoyed the sudden feeling of the hair rising along his arms and on the back of his legs. The sensation extended to making a lethal connection to the blade he held, the blade that killed that sweet little blonde. Then he played the game of hide and seek with his new prey. His mind hummed.

I overpower, then I kill, I overpower, I kill...

The door was unlocked. He spoke in a measured whisper: "*Hope he tries to come in. I'll slit him open. Listen officer, he threatened me in my home. Had some crazy ideas for some reason. I acted in self-defense.* He laughed inwardly, his mind razor sharp.

Sonny crept along the side of Connor's house, where he heard eerie whispered noises coming from the backyard area. *What is that?* He stood as still as he could, gripped by the ghostly sounds, well aware how perilous this was for him. He couldn't stop though, driven by the force of immense anger and disgust for the man who had killed a young woman, and who could have succeeded in killing Fiona. Sickening hate gnawed at his insides. He pushed himself against the side of the house and muttered through clenched teeth, "Yeah Smith! I'm coming, you demented scum bastard!"

Still at the back door, waiting, tensing, Connor felt possessed by thought tormented, rasping music that played over and over. Enflamed and excited by his homicidal thoughts, he could do nothing but wait for the right moment. He rubbed and scratched at his arms as his brain pounded. He wondered how the kill would feel. He fantasized about the knife breaking through skin and bones around Sonny's neck and heart, his warm blood flooding over his hands. He would savor the grisly sounds of Sonny dying. Hideous to others, insanely musically maniacal to him. He slowed his breathing, waiting.

Sonny wiped his stinging eyes with his sleeve and folded his arms tightly across his chest. Then, protected by the dark, but unprotected by voices that screamed at him, grating and echoing, faster and faster, he pressed on. *Kill the son of a bitch!*

He went to the door and stood. In that mindset, blood throbbed through his veins. And, as murderous thoughts overtook him, he was outside of the usual sphere he occupied. He was not Sonny. He was ready.

Something rolled into his head. Keen, he looked at his hand. It seemed detached and it wouldn't try the knob. He'd crossed the divide in his mind that kept him human. In a stupor, the wind snatching at his hair, he walked to the edge of the landing, dropped off and walked back to the side of the house. The storm was gone. Weakened, he hit the ground holding his churning stomach. Momentarily, everything quieted.

With the knife blade warm in his hand, Connor opened the door and darted out. His step quick and light, he peered down the side of the house. He spotted Sonny. Sitting as he was, he would not be ready for the attack. Knowing that he had the best of him, he charged. In a frenzy, he grabbed Sonny by the hair, lifted his knife and swung down, just as Sonny knocked one of his feet out from under him. The knife that he didn't see coming at his neck, missed its mark, slicing across his right shoulder. Connor hung onto Sonny's hair and Sonny yelped, but with his sudden emergent and desperate writhing, Connor was forced to let go. Heavily, he landed partly on top of Sonny's lap. Dumbfounded by his re-burgeoning strength and swiftness, Sonny pushed him off and climbed on top of him, not knowing that Connor still held the knife. Catching its glint from the light of the front yard lamp post, he pressed harder on Connor's back with his whole weight and inched close to Connor's ear. He ground out, "Messing with me isn't as easy as messing with a woman, IS IT!"

He heard police cars approach, wind down, and brake at the front of Connor's house. The swiftness with how Sonny overpowered him caused waves of panic to flood through Connor. In the frantic reversal that Sonny had on him, he feared that the game might be over. He reared his body up, knocking Sonny off long enough for him to scoot from under. Powerfully, Sonny lifted his weight back on top of Connor but afraid that if the cops didn't get to them soon, he would weaken. Connor could deliver the blow that could kill him. The sound of the cops running up to them, caused Sonny to yell, "He has a knife. He has a knife!" They quickly pulled Sonny off and held Connor down. Officer Robertson held Connor's wrist, careful to not touch the knife under his hand. He knocked his hand against the ground until he released it. They dragged him up.

Sonny gritted the words out, "This is the son of a bitch woman killer. He tailed my sister in law tonight in that truck," 'pointing toward it in the alley.' The truck he re-painted. But, I knew it was him." His voice changed from shrieking to a soft whine as tears started to slip down his face, "I finally knew it." He almost fell to his knees, leaning against the house for support.

Connor spat, "I was at Sonny's party earlier. I left sick and I've been home ever since. I heard something outside and I had a weapon close by, like every other scared fucker around here. I came out and he attacked me!" One cop couldn't resist, "You're holdin' the knife and he attacked you. Good one Smith."

A woman's voice called out from the screened window next door. "I was home all evening, sick. Mr. Smith wasn't here all night. He drove his truck in just minutes ago."

They all looked to the blackened area behind the screen. "That's Hao. Thank you, thank you." Sonny was beside himself with gratitude. An officer called back to her, "I'll be over there later to take a written statement," and then with swiftness Office Robertson advised Connor of his charter rights and quickly handcuffed him, telling him they had enough evidence to charge him with the murder of Kristel Slater.

Connor began to struggle and hurl invectives at Hao, "You stupid, dumb fuckin' Chinese bitch. You'll get yours. And you Sonny, you son of a bitch, I'll get this charge dismissed. You'll be sorry. Sorry, you hear me! I'll destroy you." Wildly, he cursed devils over and over, and wound down with useless, pathetic gabble. Wide-eyed, Sonny listened to Connor's crazy ramblings and couldn't believe how swiftly he made the switch to what was standing before him now. Exhausted, he slumped over. The officers hauled Connor to one of the police cars, secured him inside, and returned to Sonny. They questioned him in brief about the night's events and learned that Cora was at the house.

"Sonny, you'll have to come to the station tomorrow so we can record your statement. And hah, you stubborn fool, coming to his house, 'he touched the slit in Sonny's blood wet jacket,' close one. We were on the way." Sonny's hand went to the slit in the shoulder of his jacket and he realized how close it had been. Blood seeped onto his fingers.

"There was nothing else I could do. Fiona was in danger. I had to nail the bastard. Something took over. I wanted to finish him off, choke the life out of him, but I couldn't do it."

Grasping his shoulder, Officer Robertson said, "He had a weapon. He almost did you. Let's get you home." He steered him across the street.

Passing the police car holding Connor, Sonny shouted, "You're gonna finally get what you deserve, you crazy bastard."

When Connor's head snapped up, Sonny briefly looked into eyes that were pools of cold black fury. Feeling sick, he looked away and kept walking, thinking: *There's no semblance of humanity in him. It's like, a flesh and blood human seemed to be sitting there, but he looked different. He had slipped into an unknown entity. This ugly, blank replica of a human reproduced as Sonny looked on. He didn't recognize him.*

Sonny never wanted to set eyes on this waste of a sub-human ever again.

As he was escorted beyond the car toward his home, Connor followed him through slit lids and thought: *He's like some rock star!* He heard the words, "You're gonna finally get what you deserve." His mind lit like a flare and he twisted in his seat, pulling at the cuffs that held him.

From her watch, Haley called to Mari when she saw two police cars screech to a halt in front of Connor's house. Everyone squeezed and peered from every window space they could find. Vince and Malcolm stepped to the front door and Mari stepped in front of them.

"You are not going out there. Vince, your Dad will be all right. The police are here. We'll know soon enough what happened." The look in her eyes told them that they had better listen. They backed from her and huddled with the others.

Deep inside, Mari never felt so frightened for Sonny, more in these precarious moments than when he was diagnosed with cancer. The not knowing where Sonny was increased her terror about what might have happened. Throbbing jabs grew in her head until she thought she would scream, but she felt that she needed to make sure that calm remained, because it was evident that hysteria was building in everyone. The air was thick with fear, and their voices mixed with the names Sonny and Connor.

Mari held Haley. She felt her heart beating against hers, her tears warming the shoulder of her tee shirt. Rex tried to comfort his wife, patting and rubbing her back. Looking toward Fiona, Mari saw that she was holding herself up using the back of a chair. Mari went to her and grabbed her arm under the elbow. Gently, she walked her to the front of the chair, murmuring comforting words. Fiona sat and grasped Mari's hand. She couldn't say anything. Mari patted her and said, "I'm going to watch for Sonny and the police from the dining room window. I'll be back to check on you." Touching her icy hands, Mari tried to warm them with hers. She felt so sorry for her sister. Fiona looked up into Mari's kind eyes, love and gratefulness deriving from hers.

Mari stood at the dining room window, straining to see what was going on across the street, but the police cars with their lights swirling obstructed what was happening behind them at the side of the house. Within fifteen to twenty minutes, Mari saw the officers approaching the house with Sonny walking between them.

She ran to the door and opened it, with almost everyone converging behind her, except for Cora, who remained seated.

Mari ran to Sonny, grabbing him hard, not expecting to hear him moan and pull away, his voice pained. But, all she could manage was, "Thank God you're safe," her voice breaking to a shriek when she felt the blood coming from his shoulder. He held her until her shivering ceased. The officers waited, and finally Robertson said, "He's not injured badly. He's alright. I'd like to speak to Fiona now."

"She's inside." They stepped aside, allowing him in. He waited while everyone greeted and hugged Sonny, Haley clutching him like she wouldn't let go. Then, Officer Robertson spoke. He announced that Connor had just been charged with the murder of Kristel. Fiona gasped, holding her hands over her face. She heard the words and she became lightheaded and nearly lost consciousness, like she was suspended in time, and not really there. But, reality returned as the officer spoke

. In the midst of this, a low wail filled the room, and everyone turned to look for the source of the ear-splitting, desolate, lonely sound. It was Cora. The sudden silence in the room resounded. Then, just as suddenly, the quiet conflicted with the loudness of Cora's wail. It was disturbing, because the room had felt oddly empty when everyone was concentrating on listening to the officer. Nobody moved. Mari looked around the room spellbound by the wealth of emotion she saw in people's faces, as if she didn't know where the next second would take them. Mari gathered her senses, went to Cora, and sitting next to her, she reached for Cora's hand, and smiled at her.

"It's okay. You're here with us and we'll take care of you."

Cora could only look at Mari in wonderment, because no one crossing her life had ever shown interest for her wellbeing. Officer Robertson couldn't help but smile and he moved in on Cora too, congratulating her for how strong a figure she'd been for helping to tie up the case. Loud enough for everyone to hear, he turned and said, "This brave lady, suspecting that her brother was the killer put herself in grave danger, bringing items to us that amounted to being strong evidence against him. Cora's testimony will be very important. And, the clincher is that we have recently received DNA linking him to Kristel Slater's murder." The bright, shiny faces of everyone there reflected gratitude, and Cora was overwhelmed.

April walked to Fiona and hugged her tight.

"Hear that Fiona, they have lots on him, the most important thing, D.N.A." Fiona nodded and smiled. It was really over.

Mari thought that in this crazy, scary way, Sonny's party had culminated with all good things. Sonny eyes held pain, but they reflected a myriad of other emotions. His power and self-confidence had returned, and it showed in how he stood. He was proud of what he had done, although all who were close to him couldn't be as excited. Certainly, the police felt that Sonny had placed himself in extreme danger, but they also recognized his contribution. Mari recognized the flicker of strength and pride in those eyes. He deserved to own it.

Unexpectedly energized, Fiona clutched everyone by turn, feeling lighter with each turn, happy tears all over her face. Never would she be tormented and fearful again, because Connor would be behind bars.

Mari went to get her journal, ripped the dream page out of it and shredded it. Occurring now was the zenith over fear and strain, and tonight would hold hers and everyone's remembrance of it.

The conversation turned to questions about how Connor had maintained his position in the community as an upright citizen. But tonight he had been exposed as the evil, cruel, narcissistic murderer that he was, and this evolvement would be significant for the people of this town. Profoundly, for the Slater's as well. They too could reclaim peace and security, with the knowledge that Kristel's killer had been apprehended.

Mari felt worn-out, but she was attuned with those around her. With things settling down as they were, she took Sonny to the hospital and they stitched his wound.

The next day the town was informed that an arrest had been made. They published his name. The buzz that rippled across town was disbelief that it was the affable Connor, followed by exhilaration that Sonny had helped to make it happen.

However, months dragged before the trial approached. It was the beating heart of everything in town. It was very frightening for Cora to testify because she had to recede into the dimly lit world of remembered nightmares. Her testimony about their father's attempts to exorcise demons chilled the courtroom. It hurt to dredge all those childhood things up, but she was proud that she had found the strength to join with the police to capture the monster that, incredibly, was her brother. He would receive the stiffest punishment that could be meted out. She was not afraid. And fortunately, with the testimony of professionals who agreed that he did indeed know right from wrong, the court handed down a life sentence, no parole.

No one felt the freedom and the deliverance from fear more than Cora did. As a young woman she knew something was wrong in her house, but nobody in the house spoke to it. Not her mother, not her brother, and not she. In the debris of it all she grew up, peculiarly silent-a habit of secrecy that she learned well. That was safer than doing anything else. And what could she do? She had no tools with which to fight. Her mother, her brother, and she were helpless to do anything to stop the life they were forced to live under his roof. Horribly abusive of his family, her brother bore the brunt of most of it. Her father's crazy religious ideology caused him to attempt to get rid of the demons that festered in Connor.

As a teenager she withdrew more, because she had no defenses against what was happening. The home was filled with fragmented, strange nonsensical pieces of things, and she'd completely withdrawn. It was so scary and irrational.

She could not go to her mother, because, when she did approach her, she ignored her and turned away. It only got worse. When she became a young adult, she heard strange chants emanating off the walls of her home, she felt unknown fear, and knew that her father was mad. Not being able to understand what was going on, she escaped from the home, and the past became a sealed tomb.

Life always catches up, the seals break and events pour from darkness, tumble from the deep insides of you. Her life became a muck-sodden tract that she could not psychologically escape from. As a woman, she felt so small. She couldn't have helped her mother, her brother, certainly not herself, so closing the doors was all she could do. She left the house, a very guilt driven, introverted, lonely young woman. As part of a new beginning, not wanting to continue with "intolerable suffering," she received counselling, and hoped that perhaps one day she could let go of the cold, restraining hand of a miserable, desolate past.

For quite a few years Connor and she went their separate ways, but circumstance brought them together again in that small Canadian town. She'd married, but it hadn't lasted, her husband finding that he could not connect with her. In spite of the counselling she'd received, she never felt worthy, and nothing was resolved. She thought that maybe if she reconnected with her brother, it might help them both. After all, who else but her brother would understand that she too had been the target of the madness that lurked at home. Her father constantly ridiculed her, called her ugly names, the worst being "dirty little whore," and "stupid ugly bitch." Together, they might be able to unravel the perversion that had warped their lives. A frantic and naïve idea on her part.

Connor behaved with her as he did with his wife, which was the way she remembered her father behaving with her mother. He was so screwed up that she could barely have a conversation with him. Still, as weak as she still was, she stayed, and living with him was a game of avoidance. She became tense and withdrawn, a dreadful carry over from when she'd been reared in their awful home. She could not risk angering him and she dealt with things as her mother did. She withdrew and felt hopeless. If it wasn't for the fact that she suspected, with certainty, that Connor was a cold blooded killer, she wouldn't have snapped out of it to become the brave, determined woman she finally became.

At his trial, he heard the overwhelming evidence, smelled the fear of his victims, felt their repugnance and hate, and also felt the revulsion and shock of the onlookers. He glared at Cora, who did not return his stares. The only time she looked his way was when she was on the witness stand. Her bearing was different and he was struck by it. Whacks on his face, over and over. Leaning forward in the witness chair, her forefinger extended and shaking, he couldn't believe what he was hearing. He had taken her in, allowed her to live in a nice home, had shared his table, and now this! How dare she! She talked about the abuse of her and their pet. They knew about his mental forays into darkness, his book on Satanism, and the torn pants that she'd retrieved from the trash. Connor recalled that evening. She'd cleverly snowed him. He looked into the eyes that were so much like his mother's eyes, only the deadness he'd seen in his mother's eyes, changed in his sister to strong, brilliant sparks. He was at her mercy. His own sister betrayed him when she'd contacted the police.

After the trial Cora felt morally renewed and reaffirmed as human being and as a woman, knowing that she had done was the only thing that she could do.

Connor had no remorse whatsoever. His hate only grew and festered in his rotting brain and in his decaying heart. In the end, there was nothing left but skin and bones, and hatred that postured aggressively as the murderous bully he was. It was over for him.

It's incredible that hate shrouded his everyday kind of face because he had worn the mask of normalcy. The mask that embodied a shell and only behaved human. When he was cornered by Sonny and the police, the mask slipped. Sonny came face to face with the stench of a wasted shell. He'd witnessed it when he'd passed the police car that imprisoned Connor. It was scary in that he had hid it so well, and that he could overpower his victims when he decided to. Sonny had decided to vanquish that glance, and to also vanquish his very existence.

With the "good lawyer" he hired, they attempted to use the psychotic defense. They attempted to paint him as deeply disoriented and delusional, hearing the devil's voice. He was crazy and didn't know what he was doing. One of the things that came to light during the testimony of the psychiatric professionals, was the fact that violence was a release for murderers like

Connor. He became calm for a time until it bubbled inside and he needed another outlet, a thrill, a vengeance. Which boded the authorities to investigate him in relation to other murders.

On occasion, he'd looked through the bars-escape on his mind. Those thoughts ended abruptly, replaced by cold liquid fear and raw anger, his jaw moving, like he was trying to chew something that refused to be broken down. The thoughts that he could not escape crept up his spine. Bars would hold him for the rest of his sorry life. Hysteria taunted him that while he had been the hunter, now he was trapped. Tunneling back into the sick part of his mind, he made no movement, checking out, only to become maniacally defiant, without warning.

After the trial, Hanna sent a letter to the newspaper, giving thanks.

Dear Readers:

I'd like to share my feelings about what happened to us as parents and as a couple resulting from what happened to our only daughter, Kristel. A deep chasm grew within each of us, but I was able to fight through it all better than my husband did. He became a broken man, and his fight back to sanity and healing wasn't easy. His slide into a deep depression came on full one day. I was grief stricken once again, because not only had I lost my daughter, I was losing my husband as well. He had to immediately be admitted to psychiatric. He spent almost three weeks there, a complete breakdown crippling him. I spent the first week at his bedside as he lay, almost catatonic, almost mute, his eyes empty. Gradually, during the end of the second week, he improved with the help of anti-depressants and a therapeutic plan of action put into place.

I want to share things about Kristel. As a child she was a bouncy, smiling bundle of energy and love. She wanted to be around people and was always willing to share her part of the world. At the park, she always gravitated toward other children, sharing her wagon that was filled with rag dolls. But, her favourite person was her father. "Daddy," she would say musically, "I love you too much."

One day I'd wandered through the living room to put my camera away and saw something precious. Abe was kneeling on the floor laying down carpet and she was glued to his hip, patiently waiting for him to be done so they could go to the park. The magic in this picture is in her expression. She looked up at me with the sweetest face: It said, "I'm with Daddy, and there's no place else I'd rather be." Click. Needless to say, it's one of my favourites.

Before Abe got well, our heartache poured into each other, as water flows from cup to cup. Finally though, Abe healed and we found wonderful ways to uplift our lives, developing a wanderlust for traveling, socializing with old friends that we'd lost contact with, and we took Kristel wherever we ventured. We learned to co-mingle grief with happy reminiscences of her, until grief gave way to delight and joy remembering her. And we encouraged others to speak about and remember her. That in itself was therapeutic and life enriching.

Finally, thanks to the police. The killer is in a place where he cannot hurt anyone else. That makes it so much easier for us, and although it's not easy to do, again, we haven't wasted time hanging onto debilitating anger and anguish over our precious daughter's death. It would not do to keep ugly emotions inside me where my beautiful daughter lives. Abe has learned to do the same.

I want to thank each and every one of you that deluged us with cards and letters after she was taken. It consoled and supported me so that I could keep on and do what must be done. Thank you Mari for your steadfastness, warmth and assistance when we needed it, and thank you community. It's a place we've learned to love.

One more thing. Life can change in the blink of an eye. Don't fritter away moments. Be happy. See you around town. Hanna Slater

Over time, the pall that had hovered over the town for so long, lifted. There was an idyllic calm once again, and it remained.

When they listened
The wind was the wind
And the leaves were the leaves